I0603761

Hudson
River
Tarry Town

PIRATE LOVER'S CURSE

SLEEPY HOLLOW HUNTER

BOOK THREE

SHERI QUEEN

Wilda Press

PIRATE LOVER'S CURSE

A Sleepy Hollow Hunter Novel

Also in the series:

Bounty Huntress (Sleepy Hollow Hunter Book One)

Brimstone (Sleepy Hollow Hunter Book Two)

Cover Design by SQ Flemming

Editing by Carrie Gessner

Wilda Press

CHAPTER 1

TRAPPED

"No! Not again!" I cried out to Alex as he started slipping away.

"Hurry," he whispered.

I strained to keep him in view, but he continued fading into the darkness from which he'd appeared. I stretched out my hand, hoping to take hold of his arm and pull him to me. My hand groped in the emptiness. It was too late.

The temperature rose back to normal in the bedroom. Our connection was lost. Not even the piece of brimstone that I kept around my neck seemed to help us connect for very long anymore. He remained in the cold Underworld and out of my reach.

Alex's appearance worried me. Gone was his professional business attire of white button-down shirts and slim jeans that set off the beauty of his bronze skin and his extremely fit six-foot body. He now wore a black hooded sweatshirt and dark slacks. I could see the usefulness of the dark clothing when trying to blend into the elements of the Underworld, but I was concerned he picked those items to hide his weight loss. My frustration with not finding a way to bring him home mounted with each failed attempt to be with him.

I tossed aside the sheets tangled about my bare legs and sat on the edge of the four-poster bed. A sliver of moonlight flickered on the floorboards and across my toes. The light blended with my flesh, soaked into it, and teased the lykoi in me as if daring it to run wild in the last glow of the moon. It was the in-between hour when the darkness of night gave way to the rising sun. My inner cat stirred, sensing my agitation.

I gazed around the room that had become my home after Sebastian asked me to move into his house. This place wasn't me, yet I couldn't leave. He'd become overly protective once he'd realized I was the descendent of his true love. But I had my reasons for agreeing to live with him. By staying, I could go through all my great-great-grandmother's journals and learn more about the magic running through my veins.

Whether it was his being an ancient vampire or just his preferences, Sebastian had a great appreciation for the finer things in life, like luxurious accommodations from a long-ago era. It was a far cry from my humble and sparsely decorated apartment. I'd given up my lease after the Headless Horseman attacked us and blew up Mutther's bar, but part of me wished I'd kept it.

I pushed the heavy velvet curtains aside and pressed my head against the cool glass. Tonight was the latest attempt Alex and I had made to be with one another. We'd endured months of separation with fewer and fewer intimate interludes to keep us going until we could be together. We had no idea what was happening to interfere with those moments. My breath fogged the windowpane as I stared out into the bleak forest. I wanted some small comfort to get me through the coming day. What I wouldn't give for a cold beer right about now, but I knew there wouldn't be any in Sebastian's cellar, where he kept a vast collection of rare whiskey and wine.

I strode naked to the chair I'd tossed my clothes on and mumbled my displeasure about the lack of beer. My frustration about whatever was keeping me from crossing the veil of death to be with Alex made me itch with the desire to shift into my lykoi, which was already pushing for release to race through the woods surrounding Sebastian's hidden home.

I paused, wondering what Alex had seen in me. Lykoi cats were not a pretty hybrid, which generally didn't bother me, but I felt a tad homely next to my breathtaking panther boyfriend. Lykoi tended to be scraggly with tufts of hair around the face that brought out the wolf in us. I'd never seen of any lykoi besides me to know how I compared to them. I was different—or as my uncle said—unique.

My human form was adequate, although I'd never win any beauty pageants. I was average. My skin was on the pale side, my height moderate and my dark hair contained a white streak that had been there for as long as I could remember. Thankfully, Alex found me to his liking, and I found him more than desirable. Thinking of him made my pulse race and made the longing to touch him even more urgent. Desperation weighed on me.

I dressed, pondering the amount of crap in my life and my inability to fix any of it. My lykoi pushed harder to take over. I had to get away. "I can't do this anymore!"

"Do what?"

I spun around while pulling my t-shirt over my head and nearly fell. "You can't keep doing that."

Hulda, my very dead great-great-grandmother, stared blankly at me. "I don't know what you mean."

"Popping in whenever it suits you. It's unnerving." I yanked on my pants, slid into my biker boots and snatched up my leather jacket. I decided not to wander the woods in my lykoi state. I would take Miss Kitty out for a spin instead.

Hulda followed me down the stairs and into the kitchen. Her 1776 skirt flowed about her lower body and nearly reached the floor as she hovered a few inches above the wood planking. Her high-necked blouse gave her an air of formality that made me think that she dressed for Sebastian and his old-world ways when she was alive. She was more translucent than I remembered, but her voice was as strong as ever.

"Where are you going?" she asked.

"Out." My grumpiness made her frown. Oh, well. You couldn't please everyone.

Sebastian had left while I was sleeping. As head of the Sleepy Hollow Council, he was under a lot of pressure to deal with the problem of several supernaturals killed during the last week. He'd also been glowering at me a lot lately. I hadn't been much help as a Sleepy Hollow Hunter. My preoccupation with finding a way to bring Alex out of the Underworld was getting on Sebastian's nerves. He, too, wanted Alex to return to the land of the living but keeping others from dying was more pressing. I could see his point. Alex was already in the Underworld, and we didn't need anyone else joining him. I craved a break—and a beer.

"Are you coming?" I said. "I'm going to Mutther's."

"No," Hulda said. "I'll continue my work here."

"Suit yourself." I had no idea what she was doing. Her body was too insubstantial to turn a page in a book without putting a significant amount of energy into it. I'd seen her try when we were toiling over potions that we hoped would stabilize my power long enough for me to work on the spell to open a portal. We hadn't been successful, which added to our recent tension. I had an inkling she was withholding information from me, only I didn't know what it could be.

She could still visit the Underworld but for much shorter periods. She could no longer take me into the Underworld with her. Whatever was messing with my powers seemed to be affecting her as well. That meant Alex had been cut off from being the supplier for Maude, the Underworld's black-market leader. I could imagine his challenges now that I couldn't bring objects to him for Maude.

I put it out of my mind as I opened the garage bay door. Miss Kitty, my faithful Harley 1200, purred when I started her up. Riding her gave me a sense of freedom as I drove down the tree-lined driveway and through the protective barrier that kept Sebastian's home hidden from the rest of Sleepy Hollow.

Dawn crept closer as I rode. Bits of sunlight touched dew-covered trees. The leaves were turning their fall shades of yellows, reds, and oranges. I felt a sense of urgency as we approached the one-year mark of the confrontation with the Headless Horseman that left Alex trapped in the Underworld.

I sped up on the main highway and headed toward Mutther's bar. He'd been slowly rebuilding after the fire. Even he, who usually had my back, couldn't deal with my moodiness. He'd opted to live in his partially finished bar rather than stay at Sebastian's.

His place was north of town, well away from prying human eyes and within Nick's wolf-pack territory.

Somehow Mutther had managed to stay on good terms with the leader, even though he wouldn't join them. They'd become friends, and both were now part of the Sleepy Hollow Hunters.

I sped on, maneuvering the curves in the road. Gravel spew from beneath my tires. My short-cropped hair blew wildly in the wind, which must have made me look like a pissed-off porcupine with its quills standing on end. The long white streak in my bangs slapped against my cheek. I slowed as I approached Mutther's place. A construction crew made up of Nick's pack members slung lumber over their shoulders like they were twigs. The framing was complete, and they'd put up the last of the walls since my previous visit. Some crew members worked on the roof. Others went in and out of the building with wires and pipes to complete the inside details. Mutther had installed plastic sheeting around one area at the rear of the building, which he used as his office and sleeping quarters. I parked Miss Kitty a safe distance away and strode toward them.

"It looks like you'll be able to sleep indoors tonight," I said, grabbing a beer from a cooler Mutther kept for the workers.

He gave me a sideways glance. "No. The answer's no. Don't even think about it."

"No, what? I didn't ask anything."

"It's all over your face. You want to stay at my place and not Sebastian's," he said.

"Only for a short while. You know, just for a change of scenery." I stared up at him with what I hoped was innocent longing in my eyes.

He stared right back at me. "Not happening. Why do you think I put up with living inside a plastic tent? It was to get away from you and your moodiness." He walked past me to the front sidewalk.

My plea fell on deaf ears, but I tried. "Fine. Be that way," I said. I followed, enjoying my beer. A new sign sat propped against the building. "Nice. When did it get delivered?"

"This morning." He smiled as he ran a hand over the sign.

MUTTHER'S BAR would again cast its neon glow on the sidewalk as soon as they completed the exterior. I was not too fond of that glow when I first encountered the original bar. It had made it difficult to access the now-defunct portal to the paranormal hotel where Alex had taken refuge. I had tried to keep from being noticed by Nick and his biker crew, but the sign's light impeded my progress. But I got the job done. I'm not a massive creature in my lykoi state, but I'm fast.

I would never have thought my life would have changed so much from that encounter. Mutther had become one of my closest friends, and Nick was like a fierce teddy bear who always backed me up. Nearly a year had altered so many things, yet Alex remained in a realm of dead people. Mostly dead, I corrected myself. The unnaturals, as Hulda called them, were scary. They were living beings caught between the living and dead worlds, and they would do anything to get back to our side of the veil. But the longer they remained in the Underworld, the less human they became. I supposed Alex was technically one of them, but he was not like them at all. He wouldn't hurt anyone to cross back over. And I wasn't about to leave him there to lose his humanity.

I focused on the sign and the workers bustling around me. The activity was just what I'd hoped to find to fill the void inside me.

CHAPTER 2

STORIES

"Want a quick tour?" Mutther said.

"Why not?" I said. "I have nothing better to do at the moment."

He stepped over the threshold and guided me to the main room. "No luck with Hulda's journals?"

"Nope."

I didn't want to think about it right now. My frustration with not reproducing Hulda's potions was getting to me.

"How about you? Any luck with the recent deaths around here? I overheard some talk about people dying but couldn't find out any details."

He paused and turned to me. "Sebastian hasn't kept you updated?"

"He's been avoiding me."

Mutther snorted. "I can't imagine why."

We continued the tour, passing a woman installing plumbing in one of two bathrooms.

I did a double-take. "Two bathrooms? Anything I should know?"

"No," he said. "It seems I'm no longer a good choice for

a portal to the hotel, but I'm okay with that. It keeps the troublemakers out of here."

"Hey," I said. "I resent that. I'm not a troublemaker."

Mutther roared with laughter. "You, Janda, are pure chaos. A troublemaker has nothing on you."

I kind of liked that idea. I did have a reputation to uphold. And Uncle Damon would agree wholeheartedly with Mutther's assessment. I grinned.

"Thanks," I said.

"For what?"

"For cheering me up."

We climbed the stairs to his apartment.

"Any time," he said.

He opened the door, and we stepped into a much larger space than his old apartment. It had an open floor plan, a gourmet kitchen, marble counters with high-top bar seating, and a gas fireplace in the adjoining sitting area.

"I'm impressed," I said. "But you don't cook."

"I'm working on it. Plus, if I ever want to sell the business, it will increase the value of the place."

I spun to face him. "You're selling?"

He put up his hands. "Whoa. Hold on. I said *if* I sell. I still have obligations here and have no intention of leaving when there's so much weird shit happening."

I relaxed. He wasn't abandoning me. "Good to know."

After peering into his bedroom and the bathroom with the oversized soaking tub, I had to admit this was pretty darn nice. It was modern, whereas Sebastian's house was a throwback to Victorian times. I cocked my head and looked up at him with renewed respect. "You're a never-ending source of surprises. This is a great place. I didn't realize you had such good taste."

The corner of his mouth lifted as he tried not to laugh.

"Why thank you, Miss Gray, for your compliment and professional opinion." He spoke like Sebastian did at times, but unlike Sebastian, he was teasing me. "And I'll ignore the last part," he added.

"You're welcome." I turned on my booted heel and strolled down the hallway, exaggerating the sway of my hips as I went.

It worked. He was laughing his head off behind me.

The living room furniture had been delivered and sat in a heap wrapped in layers of plastic. Mutther wiped dirt from his jeans and rolled up the sleeves of his flannel shirt as far as his biceps would let him. He began moving the pieces into place. I ripped the protective film from the cushions. We worked until each item was unwrapped and a mound of plastic filled one corner of the space. It felt good to do something productive.

He took two beers from his refrigerator, handed one to me, and sat in an oversized modular chair that could also be added to the sofa as an extension. I sank onto the couch and gulped my second beer of the day.

"Does anyone call you by your real name?" I'm not sure why it never occurred to me to ask before.

He pondered my question for a few moments. "Not that I recall. I guess it's just easier than saying Matthias Utther."

"What about Matt? Should I call you that instead?" Then I thought better of it. "Never mind. Mutther suits you."

He chuckled. "See? It just works."

The small talk, or maybe the beer, eased the tension in my shoulders. Either way, I was getting some of my old energy back. I also felt guilty about not holding up my end as a Hunter.

"What's going on? What hasn't Sebastian been telling

me? Or, for that matter, Uncle Damon?" I perched on the edge of the cushion.

Mutther took a big breath, let it out slowly, and rubbed the dark stubble on his chin. "It's not good. There have been three deaths as of last night. All the victims are supernaturals. None perished the same way. The locations are different. The first was a tracker from Nick's pack. He'd been following a lead on a possible hide-out for the Headless Horseman."

"A lead?" This news didn't make me happy. "Why wasn't I told?"

"Don't get on me about it. Nothing came of it. It was one more of the caves on our list of brimstone mines. Sebastian has us checking out every single known site. Since the last portal you jumped through closed, he's been chasing even the slightest of possibilities. So far, they've been dead ends."

"Who was killed?"

Mutther's tone softened. "Ben. He was too inexperienced to be going solo. We should have had someone go with him. We just never thought anything would happen. It was a simple recon mission. Look. Gather information. Don't engage."

"But something did happen," I said.

"Yeah." Mutther put his head in his hands, propped his elbows on his thighs, and stared at his work boots. "He was crushed beneath a boulder."

"That's horrible." It was a miserable way to die. I wish I could blot the image from my mind. "How do you know it wasn't an accident? Maybe it was a landslide."

He looked up at me. "Because he didn't die right away. He left a message scratched in the dirt."

I sucked in a ragged breath. "Oh, God."

"Yeah. It tore Nick up. He's ordered everyone to pair up. No one goes out alone."

"What did Ben write?" I was afraid I knew. The Horseman had eluded us for months. He'd managed to avoid being pulled back to the Underworld by the demon, but we had no clue where he was holing up. There'd been sightings on moonlit nights once in a while, but nothing solid to go on.

"Pirates," Mutther said.

I scrunched my brows in disbelief. "Say that again."

"I kid you not. He wrote pirates. We're as baffled as you."

"Okay. Pirates in Sleepy Hollow. We aren't in a time-warp here, Mutther. What the heck?"

"I'm just telling you what I know," he said, his voice tinged with exasperation. "But that's not all. The next death was just as puzzling."

"Meaning?"

"This is going to sound weird," he said. "But four nights ago, some of the pack was horsing around by the river, letting off some steam. They swore they heard a woman crying on an outcrop of rocks. When they got nearer, it stopped. No woman."

The hammering of shingles being attached to the roof above us fell to the background like drums rhythmically beating out a warning message to anyone who would listen. I was listening. I just didn't understand the message.

I took another swallow of my beer and waited for him to continue.

Mutther took a swig of his beer, too. "A strange apparition moved along the shoreline. They were about to go after it when there was a shout, and something large tumbled over the bridge railing and landed with a huge splash in the river. They looked up at the bridge in time to see several figures drift away from the rail and disappear."

"I don't get it," I said. "Are you saying a gang tossed someone from the bridge? A hit job, maybe? The mafia has been known to do such things. We're close enough to the city, and it's happened before. Take a poor sucker for a scenic ride out of New York City and up the Hudson. Then cement his feet and toss him into the water. Did they ever find Jimmy Hoffa?" I paused for dramatic effect and nodded. "Yeah, you know what I'm getting at."

"This wasn't a hit. Not exactly. Two pack members swam out to where they saw the splash. After a few dives, they found him."

"Him?" I said.

"The town historian. Old Brian."

"Brian? No way! He's a harmless old guy. Well, as harmless as an aging wolf with dementia can be, which is pretty freaking harmless. Who would want to hurt him?" I was stunned. I loved Old Brian.

"It's sad is what it is," he said.

"I didn't get to tag along with my uncle much when I was a kid, but there was one time when he brought me to a pack gathering. He left me with Brian. Mainly, it was to be sure I wouldn't get into trouble, but I could have listened to Brian's stories for hours." I became a bit nostalgic at the memory. "He recounted all sorts of legends and lore. Ships that ran aground after following a siren's song. Ghosts and curses that made you afraid to sleep in the dark. And buried treasure that men fought over and died trying to claim." I sighed. "I'm going to miss him."

"It was pirates they saw," Mutther said.

I blinked, coming back to the present. "What the hell are you saying?"

"I'm saying pirates are killing paranormals."

There was an edge to his voice that made goosebumps rise on my arms. He was serious.

Holy shit!

"You know how that sounds, right?"

"Of course I do," he snapped. "The Council is downplaying it all to keep panic at bay. Scribbles in the dirt that only a few people saw and the writing can't be verified. Drunk pack members out for a good time hear what must be the wind making eerie sounds and think it's a woman. An old man with dementia who wanders off and accidentally falls from the bridge." His voice rose, and his nostrils flared. "But they can't twist what happened last night."

I held my breath in anticipation.

"Old Brian's son Stanley was killed. His throat was cut."

I felt nauseous. This was surreal.

"Were there any witnesses?" I said, barely getting the words out.

"Not that we know of. They did find something, though. Clutched in his hand was a piece of an old map. He must have been trying to keep whoever attacked him from getting it." Mutther swiped a hand over his face, rubbing his forehead. "I'm not supposed to mention this, but the piece had a symbol in the corner where the Compass Rose would be on a map. It was a skull and crossbones."

I stared, wide-eyed at Mutther. "A pirate's map?"

"What do *you* think?" He glanced upward as the hammering overhead grew louder. "I better see what's happening on the roof, and you better get back to Sebastian's before he comes looking for you. That vampire is obsessed with your safety."

"Can't I—"

"No."

I sighed. With Mutther refusing me a sanctuary, I had no choice but to return to Sebastian's. It wasn't like I was going back to prison, although Sebastian's increased security made it like one. I forced myself not to dwell on it.

We went outside, and Mutther gave me a quick hug before heading toward a ladder leading to the roof.

"Catch you later," I said.

"See if you can find anything in those old books about what we discussed," he said then waved me off.

Whether or not he was trying to give me something constructive to do with my time didn't matter. I had an idea that deserved more attention. I hopped on Miss Kitty and pointed her toward Sebastian's.

CHAPTER 3

POTIONS AND CURSES

I found Hulda in the basement. She was circling the table where we'd been working on potions. The potion kettle was simmering on the fire, just as I'd left it when I gave up on my work last evening. She smiled briefly and didn't admonish me for my absence. We picked up where we'd left off. I stirred the liquid and added another log to the fire, which someone had kept burning while I was gone. Sebastian must have returned. I added the remaining ingredient from our most recent recipe trial and stirred vigorously counterclockwise. It bubbled for about twenty seconds before erupting like a mini-volcano.

"Crap! Why me?" I was a mess.

"Try adding a smidge less sulfur tuft." Hulda maneuvered past splatters of thick potion dotting the walls of the makeshift lab as she offered advice.

I wiped gelatinous brown goop from my cheek, only to have it slide from my fingers and drip down into the crevice of my breasts. My black tee became glued to my body where the mess landed, giving me a spotted leopard appearance.

The lykoi cat in me resented the leopard-like resemblance. It was persnickety that way.

I glowered at my long-dead great-great-grandmother. "You're not helping."

She shrugged, not at all bothered by my disrespectful tone, tilted her head toward the ceiling, and tuned me out to focus on the footsteps overhead. The longing on her face for Sebastian, who paced the floors above us, made me feel intrusive, so I left her to her thoughts and returned to my task.

Sebastian had wisely allotted us space to work in his basement, away from anything I might accidentally destroy. We were in an area that had originally been home to a number of enslaved people who cooked the household meals in the oversized fireplace I now used for our experiments. The walls were made of the same stone foundation that the house had originally been built on. I noticed decorative carvings in the heavy beams supporting the floor above and wondered if it was someone's attempt to make the dismal space homier. The earthen floor had an oval braided rug spread out beneath the table, and two wooden stools sat on either side of the fireplace. Thick wood beams supported the floor above us and were positioned so low that people of today who were of average height could give themselves a concussion if they weren't careful to avoid the obstructions. I couldn't imagine sleeping here the way people did in the past. It made me grateful for the upgrades Sebastian had made to the home.

The structure was considered large for the time it had been built circa 1800. When Sebastian had taken the house from its former owner, he'd freed the slaves. I never got the takeover details and wasn't sure I wanted to know. Sebastian's methods could sometimes be bloody. I wasn't one to talk. I had my share of kills, no matter how justified they were in my role as a bounty hunter for the Sleepy Hollow Council. And if no more people had to endure living and working in the space I now occupied, then I had no issues with how it had come about.

Cool drafts made their way through gaps in the stonework, sending a damp chill to settle in my bones. I drew upon the warmth emanating from the hearth to manipulate the energy and fend off the cold, but my concentration tended to falter when I was frustrated, thwarting my efforts to retain the heat. Tiny stabs of frigid air prickled my arms like insects seeking my blood. It was good they weren't actual bugs because they'd have to get in line for a taste of me. I was on more than a few enemy lists.

I ground my teeth, shoved an old wooden spoon into the pot, and stirred the potion with more force than necessary. The brownish liquid slopped from side to side until bubbles rose from the copper kettle in another geyser-like eruption. This time sparks flew out.

"Oh, my!" Hulda squealed and took flight as a cluster of dried herbs hanging from a beam above her caught fire.

I grabbed a dish towel and smacked the embers out of existence before the fire could spread, but not before it scorched my forearm. I cursed at the blister rising red against the white of my skin. Sebastian may not have thought it through when he agreed to my request for a workspace. At my current rate, I was likely to blow up his house or set it on fire.

Sebastian might get a bit crispy if there was a fire, and while I didn't know much about what could kill him, I figured it would take more than my exploding recipe to do him in. He'd be more irate that his belongings, especially his collection of rare wines, would be lost. It was one of the few pleasures he said he could relish as the flavors touched his tongue and reminded him of drinking blood.

I'd once allowed Sebastian to drink from me to save him from a disease coursing through his immortal body. I had no problem understanding the myriad of sensations associated with the whole blood-sucking event. It was akin to sexual release. It was that strong. And if wine gave him even a fraction of that sensation, then I would not be responsible for taking that from him with my carelessness. I also didn't want to become homeless from burning down his house.

As for my great-great-grandmother, well, she was dead. What could fire do to a ghost? It wasn't like the flames would hurt her. Fleeing from the burning herbs seemed to me to be more of a survival reaction retained from when she was alive.

While I swept the debris into a pile, she settled near her leather-bound journal in which, many years ago, she'd written numerous recipes for healing balms, poultices, and medicinal potions. There were detailed drawings of plants and miniature maps that told where to find the required herbs and other natural ingredients as well as their optimal time for harvesting. But within the margins of the pages, in writing so tiny it was barely visible, Hulda had added other notations. These scribblings seemed routine, unimportant unless you knew what you were looking at.

She had developed a system for hiding her magical expertise. Buried within the small journal were instructions for how to enhance what she deemed God-given powers. She'd never intended her knowledge to be used for anything but good, yet there would always be someone who might wish to exploit it and, more importantly, kill her for it. So she'd placed the journal in Sebastian's personal library the night before she died.

Foreboding or simple precaution?

To this day, she wasn't sure why she'd done it. She'd been killed a short time later while she stood valiantly alongside the villagers who'd shunned her. She'd fought to defend the place she called home.

She'd told me all of this in such great detail that it was almost like being with her during her final hours. I'd also read what the history books said about the witch of Sleepy Hollow—my great-great-grandmother. They hadn't been kind to her, yet she died trying to protect them.

I glanced at this remarkable woman whose incorporeal brows knit together in intense concentration as she attempted to flip through the pages of the potions journal she'd written over two hundred years earlier. My heart ached for her lack of substance to complete the action, yet she continued undaunted. She'd used a great deal of energy helping me in and out of the Underworld. So much so that whatever made up her body's non-living state was flickering in and out of view. And here I was, wallowing in self-pity at my inability to conquer a potion. It brought a rush of guilt and shame, making me bow my head over my pot and avoid meeting her gaze. I sucked in a sigh and regretted it instantly when fumes burned my throat and tore at my lungs. I coughed and wheezed until my eyes filled with tears. Hulda paid me no mind. Lucky her, she didn't have to deal with the stench choking me half to death.

"You're close, Janda," she said, peering over at me and offering a wan smile that indicated the opposite of her words.

I pulled the worn book toward me. "That's bullshit, and you know it. What am I going to do? Alex is counting on me." I snapped unnecessarily and instantly felt terrible for taking my worries out on her.

Her lips pursed in disapproval of my swearing, but she said nothing. She moved to hover over my shoulder and peer at the journal.

"He's fine," she said reassuringly. "He's more than fine. He's doing a fantastic job as an underground ferryman."

The idea of him in his Underworld role made me mad. He was an errand boy for Maude, the power player of the Underworld who had helped him survive when I couldn't. I didn't share well, especially when it came to Alex. Even though Maude wasn't a threat to my relationship with him, her control over his life irritated me.

"That's not where he should be! He should be with me in Sleepy Hollow." I tossed the book back on the wooden table strewn with my numerous failed attempts to find a potion or spell that might stabilize my power. It slid toward the edge, almost toppling to the floor. I grabbed for it before it ended up in a mud puddle. The hazard of losing my cool in an earthen basement soaked in the remains of my potion-making forced me to be more careful. More than anything, my pride had taken a hit, and feeling helpless made me reckless.

The time away from Alex had me coming undone. Every day that passed without making progress made the nights even more unbearable. My dreams had taken on a nightmarish quality. Where I used to be able to physically touch him and make love to him in the realm that existed between sleep and wakefulness, I now endured the agony of watching him approach and then fade from me before we could make contact.

It seemed I had more in common with my great-great-grandmother than our ability to enter and exit the Underworld. We both yearned to be with someone we couldn't.

Hulda's long skirt swished gently in a semi-transparent

way as she moved toward the fireplace and a warmth she'd never truly feel again. The light drew the dead in anticipation of moving on to something more, something that promised a release from their inner torment. Hulda didn't want to move on without Sebastian, who was an immortal. So where did that leave her?

Hulda's breath came out in a long sigh. "I wish I could help you with cleaning this."

"Thanks, but I made the mess. I'll be fine." I swept goop into a dustpan and tossed it into my fast-accumulating trash pile. After putting the broom away, I sat on a wooden stool and faced her. "Can I ask you something?"

"Certainly," she said, giving me her full attention.

I'd been pondering my idea on my drive back and wondered how to ask what I was about to ask without offending her. "You lived in quite a turbulent era and have a lot of talent in the magical department," I said.

"I suppose that's true," she said.

"Well," I paused, "have you ever done spells for others who may not have had the best intentions?"

I swear she raised her brows at me, although her form flickered right then, and it was hard to tell for sure.

"Are you asking if I've done black magic?"

I squirmed under her scrutiny. "Um...Maybe."

She drew closer, her essence inches from me. "Never."

"Sorry. Yeah. I didn't think so, but something Mutther said today got me thinking along those lines."

"What exactly did he say about me?"

"Not about you, but about what I might find in the vast collection of books here." I was struggling with words to express the feeling niggling in my gut. I picked up her journal, filled with page after page of what she knew about magic. "You mentioned the power of what's in here and how you didn't want it to fall into the wrong hands. What if it did? What if someone else could read your recipes and the hidden notes? What if they used it in a bad way, like a curse?"

She stepped back. Her head bowed.

"What's wrong?" I said.

"I can't say. Not at the moment, at least. I need more time to be sure."

"Can I help?"

Hulda vanished.

That did not go well, but now I knew she was hiding something—something big.

I returned to the slop I'd created and scanned the recipe in the journal for where I'd gone wrong. *Stir gently counter-clockwise for twenty rotations.* I may have been a touch overzealous in my stirring. I took the contents and emptied them into the trash. I'd have to start anew, but I was beginning to doubt this was the right potion.

Time to browse the journal for other options.

I flipped through the pages, growing weary of the task, and then stopped cold when I spied a tiny notation in the corner of a page.

Thank you, dear sister, for this revelation.

I pulled the book closer. The writing was not Hulda's. I was positive someone else had penned this note. I ran my finger over the text. An herb or two was listed, from what I could tell, but the recipe wasn't exactly a recipe. It was one of the few incantations Hulda had written down and was beyond my ability to decipher. It seemed to be in a type of code far different from anything else I'd come across in her journal. My stomach clenched as I reread the message. Did Hulda have a sister? Did I have a distant aunt in my family tree that Hulda didn't want me to know about?

Heavy footsteps joined Sebastian's above me. At least two people had arrived. Their voices rose in a heated conversation. I strained to hear what was being said. I placed the journal back on the table and started up the narrow steps leading to the floor above me. There were more than a few people who owed me explanations, and I would make sure they paid up. Right now.

CHAPTER 4

PIRATES AND PR

I reached the study to find the space overloaded with testosterone. Sebastian and Nick stood eye-to-eye, muscles tense and teeth clenched. In the latter, Sebastian was the more formidable one. His fangs looked like daggers, which they kind of were. He was tall and slim with angular features. The one dark aspect was his hair that reached his shoulders, which he often pulled back into a ponytail tied with a ribbon. He kept his nearly translucent skin covered in formal suits that never seemed to get creased. His black leather shoes had pointed tips, which gave him the impression of being a man with many angles that could have been chiseled from white marble. He had an aura of eloquent deadliness about him and stood his ground against Nick.

Nick's qualities were more earthy. Like many of his pack, he was broad, brusque, and burly. He let out a low growl, his wolf making it clear he would not be intimidated by a vampire.

Silas Vang, Alex's were-cat clan leader, stood grimly just inside the double doors, his arms crossed in disapproval, not interfering in the debate unfolding. He was not a big man, nor was he young, but with his expertise in martial arts, he was more than capable of dealing death blows in rapid succession. He had been the one who had hired me to bring Alex back from the paranormal hotel last year. I'd won Silas's approval when I'd helped clear Alex's name after he had been accused of murder.

Silas glanced in my direction and nodded as I stood in the open doorway. The other two didn't seem to notice me. I decided to rectify that immediately.

"You two look ridiculous." I strode across the room, pushed my way between Sebastian and Nick, and went to the desk with maps and various pieces of paper with intel on the current crisis. The heavy curtains were drawn as usual. Sebastian kept the space lit with candles and oil lamps. The fireplace gave adequate heat, but the desk was too far from it to help with lighting. I pulled an oil lamp closer and did a quick scan of the map. Several new areas had been crossed off. I lifted it and turned my attention to the others. "If you're done with the petty bullshit, I believe I've been kept in the dark long enough. No pun intended although it is pretty damn dark in here. But if this map is current, then I'd say you're not making much headway in discovering the Headless Horseman's location."

I let the map drop onto the desk and proceeded to sift through the papers.

Sebastian, territorial as ever, took them from me and began organizing them in a fashion that eluded me.

"Are we to assume you're ready to take an interest in our endeavors, Janda?" His tone dripped with conde-scension.

I bristled at his attitude but refused to let him get to me. "I've always had an interest. I've merely approached this differently than you and the rest of the Council." I met each man's gaze with defiant calm, which was rare for me. I was often defiant, but I was hardly ever calm.

"Duly noted," Silas said.

The comment surprised Sebastian and Nick, most likely just realizing Silas was still in the room with them. I did my best to keep from smirking.

Silas came to stand at my side. His support touched me. He was almost as obsessed with retrieving Alex as I was but for different reasons. Alex was Silas's second, and without him, Silas would have to consider other options for who would be his replacement as clan leader upon his retirement.

"Well, Sebastian?" Nick said. "Janda is right. She deserves to know everything, yet you seem intent on keeping certain aspects of this case from her. Why?"

The wine decanter looked relatively low by Sebastian's standards, meaning he'd been partaking in it much more than usual. Some people ate when stressed. Sebastian drank wine. He poured himself a glass without offering any to the rest of us. He took his time with the drink. He held it up, swirled it, sniffed it, and finally sipped it. Then he went to his favorite chair and sat down.

"Very well," Sebastian said. He motioned for me to take a spot on the loveseat. "I will explain what I can. However, there are many things that are still eluding us." He waved his hand to encompass Silas and Nick. "While you have been occupied with finding a way to save Alex, there have been sightings of strange things."

"Not to mention three deaths," Nick said. He took up a spot by the fireplace, standing with his forearm propped against the mantle. "The supernatural community is up in arms with tension so high I'm afraid it won't take much for us to turn on one another."

Silas joined Janda on the loveseat. "Nick is right about this. If we don't get a handle on things soon, then who knows what will happen? We are already starting to argue among the Council."

"Our arguing is not what Janda needs to hear about," Sebastian said. "She needs to understand that outside forces are putting pressure on us and our limited resources."

"What resources are you talking about?" Janda said. "And what outside forces?"

"He means the civilian population is taking notice," Silas said. "The police are pushing the Council to find the perpetrators. We don't know where to start and lack the workforce to deal with it all."

"They aren't the only ones who want the Council to solve these cases immediately," Nick said. "My pack is getting restless. We want justice for Ben. But even if we find the murderers, we cannot destroy them."

"Are you talking about the pirates?" Janda said. "Because I've already found out about them. But my question is—how do ghosts murder people?"

Sebastian and Silas both seemed surprised by my revelation but not Nick. I was willing to bet that he already knew Mutther had told me.

Silas glanced over at Sebastian. "That's what we've been debating, isn't it, Sebastian? How much physical power does a ghost possess?"

I considered Hulda and understood now why Sebastian might be defensive about the subject of ghosts.

"Janda would know better than any of us, which is why

I'm wondering why you haven't mentioned it to her," Nick said.

"Because she has enough to worry about," Sebastian said. "And because she may have a connection we are just beginning to understand."

My mind had been wandering to Hulda's attempts to move physical objects and how much energy it took. I caught the last of what Sebastian said and snapped out of it. "What connection?"

"Hulda," said Silas.

I looked at Sebastian for answers. His lips formed a thin line of displeasure. I waited. Sebastian shifted in his chair. He was stalling.

I stood up. "Okay. I can't take this anymore. I may have been preoccupied with helping Alex, but that doesn't give you the right to keep me at arm's length. It doesn't give you the right to withhold information from me. And it sure doesn't give you the right to decide for me. That goes for all of you! Got that?"

Nick had the good sense to avoid eye contact with me. Silas cleared his throat. Sebastian went to refill his wine glass. He then returned to his seat.

"I told you I'd explain what I could. Now, if you want to be angry with me, that's your choice. I made my decisions, and I am not sorry for it."

"You are something else," I said.

"Yes, I am," he said. "I'm someone who has been trying to keep you alive. I'm also someone who understands the pain you're in."

He had me there. I lost some of my bluster and sat down again. I let out two long breaths.

Nick glanced my way and raised a brow. "As much as I hate to side with the vamp," he said, "he has a point. The

Headless Horseman wants you dead and wants that bit of his mask you took with you to the Underworld. He has motive and means to make you disappear."

"He can't kill me until he gets what he wants. So I have some time to nail his ass first."

Alex's warning rang in my head. *Hurry.* I didn't know how much time I had left to defeat the Horseman.

Sebastian leaned forward in his seat. "You asked how a ghost, or in this case, ghost pirates, could kill someone. We need your link to Hulda to find out. I didn't want to bring her into this, but the others are right. We must discover as much about these ghosts as we possibly can."

"Janda," Silas said, putting his hand gently on my shoulder, "we need you. We don't know how to kill a ghost. And if there's any way to capture them, we still don't know how to contain them. We know there are ways to get aggressive ghosts to move on. We have to deal with their unfinished business and bring them closure."

Nick finally moved away from the fireplace and sat in the chair across from Sebastian. He scooted it closer to the side of the loveseat nearest to Silas. He wasn't going to take any chances with getting into Sebastian's space even though the two had gotten over their spat.

"You can see how the shit keeps piling up around our ears." Nick gestured with his hands as he spoke. "We've had three deaths, which I'm grateful I don't have to rehash with you, and ghosts breaking in and trashing places. The locals are getting anxious. Detective Brent is doing what he can, but it's been tough. His nephew Shawn is a rookie cop trying to fend off the worst publicity. They're over-whelmed by the media searching for an angle on the murders."

"We've had to downplay it," Sebastian said. "That in

itself has caused issues within our groups. We're short-handed and being outsmarted by a bunch of ghosts."

It said a great deal about the direness of our situation for Sebastian to admit they were failing.

"I think I can help with one thing," I said. "You need a PR person to help field the bad publicity. You need Angie."

"Angie?" Sebastian said. "The college kid the Mad Monk abducted?"

"She's perfect for the job. We've chatted a few times since then, and she's rock solid. She's human. She has experience with the shit-storms of the supernatural world, and she can help the rookie cop," I said. "Tell me about this Shawn guy."

"Here's what you should know about the police department," Silas said. "Detective Brent is a shifter with an attitude."

"You can say that again," I said. "He was none too nice with me."

"That's hardly a revelation," Nick said. "You're not the endearing type at first glance. You're kind of annoying."

I shrugged. "Fair enough."

Silas continued. "Brent is set in his ways, but he's a damn good detective. He brought on his nephew, who by the way, is not a shifter, to work on the force. Shawn was top of his class. He knows who lives in Sleepy Hollow and that not everyone is who they seem to be. It makes him an excellent person to aid with covering up the mess the ghosts have made."

"It sounds like Angie would make a good addition to the police force." I turned to Sebastian. "Can you pull some strings to get her a job there?"

"In this instance, I'd say no strings will need to be pulled. Brent can use all the help we can give him. I'll make the call now." Sebastian rose and dug out his rarely used cell phone from his pocket.

I waited until he'd left the room to make his call before I turned to the others for more details about recent events. "Nick," I said. "What about these break-ins? Do we know what these pirates are after?"

"There's not much to tell. The places trashed have been the town hall, the historical society, and the curator's house. We don't know what they've been searching for or if anything was taken."

Silas rose and began pacing slowly, his hand smoothing out the hairs on his short beard. "There's the piece of map that was in Stanley's hand. We've focused on what it is but not where it came from."

"Can we tell how old the map is from that piece?" I was curious to see how far back it dated.

"Yes," Silas said. "That's a good place to start. It looked old. By dating it, we could discover when the pirates were here."

I glanced at the door. Sebastian was still on the phone.

"I'm willing to lay odds that the pirates and that map date to when Hulda was living in Spook Rock," I said. "I also think she knows something about it, but I don't want to say anything to Sebastian until I know for sure."

"What makes you say that?" Nick said.

"Hulda has been evasive with me," I said.

"Do you think she could give us insight on capturing or destroying a ghost?" Silas said.

"The hell with capturing them," Nick said, getting to his feet. "I want them dead!"

"Hush," I said. "Sebastian will hear you. Besides, they're already dead, you idiot."

"Dead. Destroyed. Whatever. I want payment for these

deaths. Someone has to be held accountable. If not the ghosts, then who?" Nick slammed a hand against the mantel. The candles sitting on it almost tipped over.

"Look," I said, "I get you're angry, but try to keep the candles from falling and starting a fire. I'm sick of fires."

Nick gave me a sheepish grin. "Yeah. I guess you would be."

Sebastian came in and saw the candles askew. "I leave you alone for a minute, and you try to burn my house down?"

"You're a bit testy, aren't you? I was simply moving them around. Hardly cause for alarm," Nick said.

I bit my lip to keep from grinning. No way did Sebastian buy such a flimsy excuse.

"Well, don't touch them," Sebastian said.

Nick lifted both hands in the air. "No more touching."

"It's done," Sebastian said. "Silas, I'll need you to stop by the station and fill Brent in on Angie's details. He will require parameters that Angie should follow, including who she should contact for the information that she can pass along to the public. Brent let Shawn know what Angie will be doing for us."

"I can do that," Silas said. "As soon as we're done here."

"Thanks to Janda's solution for public relations, I would say we *are* done." Sebastian picked up his glass of wine and took a sip.

I could tell he was staring at me over the rim of his glass. He didn't let on if he'd heard anything we'd been discussing in his absence.

"We're not quite done," I said. "What connection do I have to all this?"

Sebastian sighed, which of course, since he didn't need to breathe, was more of an old habit. It was a sign of his resignation. I didn't back down. I waited for him to speak. It was a test of my patience.

"As I mentioned earlier," he said, "I don't have all the pertinent information. It is pure conjecture."

"Go on," I said.

"We have two coinciding events. First, we have the Headless Horseman, who is no longer tethered to the days around All Hallows Eve and can venture forth at least when the moon is full. Those are the only times he's been sighted. We know he's interested in you and the mask piece you prevented him from getting. Second, the pirates have been searching for something. We don't know what it is yet. We do know they've been able to search through buildings physically. It would seem they can also kill people. How? Are the two events connected? This is what we've been discussing."

I could see where Sebastian was going with this and what he might want from me.

"Will you talk to Hulda?" Silas said.

Sebastian looked grim. "The connection is this," he said. "You are related to Hulda. The Horseman killed her, but none of us knows if it was just that she was in the wrong place at the wrong time or if the Horseman killed her for another reason. That makes you our only hope of finding out if there's more to Hulda's death than it appears." He slumped back in his chair. "And if there was more, then I have truly let her down when I didn't stand by her side."

The room grew quiet. The flames on the numerous candles flickered, then extinguished. We looked at each other. A slight aroma of gardenias wafted over us.

Hulda.

CHAPTER 5

GHOSTS

I hadn't seen Hulda but knew she had passed through the study while we were planning our next move. I was sure the others detected her but hadn't said anything. We went our different ways and agreed to meet later in the evening. Someone had to inform Brent about his new assistant, Angie, but I begged off that one. I promised the group I'd approach Hulda about ghostly power. Hulda, however, was not making it easy. Her brief show of presence had been followed by silence.

I retreated to the basement laboratory. Everything was as I'd left it earlier, except for one difference. The pages had been flipped in the journal.

"I know you're here," I said.

Nothing.

"I can wait. I'll keep struggling to find a potion to help me—with or without you."

She didn't bite. There was nothing left but to try another potion. I read through the open page and wondered whether she wanted me to do something about this new potion or if she had turned the pages to throw me off from what I'd seen before.

The fire was getting low, and the room temperature had dropped at least five degrees. I tossed a few logs into the fireplace and stoked the flames. I tried to get motivated to work on another recipe but couldn't. I dragged a wooden stool nearer the hearth and sat with the journal, reading through the entries more carefully than before.

Here and there were the usual side notations in what I knew was Hulda's writing. Mostly they pertained to ways to improve specific herbal remedies, which she'd been known for back in her day. Hidden amongst those notes were other ones. Sometimes a single word of agreement appeared, and other times, suggestions to alter the recipe. These were not in Hulda's handwriting. I was convinced it was the same person who had written the "dear sister" note.

"You have a sister. Don't you?" I waited for her to show herself. She didn't. I skimmed the journal for any clues but gave up after an hour. "I could really use your help. Can you tell me how much energy it would take to kill someone?"

A hint of gardenia surfaced and then faded. I'd gotten Hulda's attention, but it wasn't enough to coax her out. I thought about the pirate ghosts and decided if my great-great-grandmother was refusing to answer my questions, then a trip to the historical society archives was in order to check out the scene of the curator's murder. I placed the screen across the front of the fireplace and ensured nothing was near enough for any stray sparks to cause a fire.

"Okay, then. I'm leaving."

I paused, waiting for a response. Hulda had either left or didn't want to be with me. In a few short months, I'd come to rely on my great-great-grandmother's companion-ship and advice. A pang of loneliness stabbed at my heart.

Sebastian left a short time after seeing Silas and Nick off the grounds. I thought he might seek me out first, but he didn't. There was tension between us that hadn't been there before, and I didn't like it. I retrieved my phone from the hall closet, which was the only spot in the entire house where I could charge it, and dashed through the kitchen and out the rear door. The air sizzled with the enhanced protections Sebastian had installed. I was pretty sure Hulda couldn't wield that level of magic as a ghost, which meant he had to have sought help from some other witch.

When I reached the garage, I noticed the magical barrier wasn't the only thing he'd enhanced. I spotted several thermal cameras, similar to ones Alex used in his safe room designs.

Since my arrival, Sebastian had divulged his location to Mutther, Nick, Silas, and now a witch I didn't know about. The new security measures were put in place in case anyone was followed here.

I caught sight of a couple more cameras in the trees near the driveway. They were definitely the work of Alex's company. It made me think about the business Alex had left behind after being trapped in the Underworld. I wondered who was running it for him. I'd have to make a mental note to ask Sebastian about it. For now, I made sure to lock the garage and would be more cautious leaving the property.

I scanned the surrounding trees. Could ghosts get past the layers of protection? It was yet another question I had to ask my great-great-grandmother if she ever hung around long enough.

Miss Kitty's engine purred beneath me as I started her up. I drove off down the driveway at a decent speed then paused before passing through the barrier. I had the sense that someone or something was present but saw nothing.

"Hold down the fort, Grandma. I'll be back soon." I looked over my shoulder at the receding house and floored it onto the main road. The air was crisp. The smell of conifers tickled my nose. My lykoi liked it. I would have to let my animal side stretch its legs soon.

I slowed upon entering the town limits. It wouldn't do to have the police burdened with handing out speeding tickets when their services were required elsewhere. But there were no cops around. None. The town also had fewer pedestrians than usual. People were spooked.

I drove down Grove Street to the historical society. I could smell the river as I parked on the empty street in front of the old brick home of Jacob Odell that housed the historical society archives. I tipped my head back to better view the single tower at the center of the house's roof. The rust-brown shutters could have used a touch-up to address the peeling paint, but otherwise, the place had been reasonably maintained. A few windows had curtains, while others had shades only partly raised.

The remnants of crime scene tape clung to a bush along the steps leading to the front door. This was a family neighborhood, and it made me wonder why no one had reported a disturbance when it had been broken into and the curator murdered. Then again, we were talking about ghosts. Yet I couldn't shake the feeling we were missing something obvious.

A "closed" sign hung on the door. I tested the knob and found it was unlocked, so I pushed it open and went inside.

"Hello," I said.

I stepped over a ribbon of crime tape and peeked into the rooms on either side of the entry. They'd been trashed, with books strewn on the floor. A sweeping noise came from the upper floors, like someone was using a broom. The sound echoed down the stairs.

I got halfway up the staircase when a young woman leaned over the rail on the third level. She was in the upper spire.

"Can I help you?" she said.

She had long black hair pulled back in a ponytail. Wisps of curls had sprung loose to frame her face. She had high cheekbones and full lips. Her lipstick matched the red shirt that was tucked in her jeans at the waist. Her long, slender fingers gripped a broom handle.

"I hope so," I said. "I'm Janda. Do you have a minute?"

She propped the broom against the rail and started toward me. "Sure. I could use a break. I'm Gwenn. I've been asked to help restore order." She looked around her at the chaos of overturned furniture and scattered documents. "If that's even possible."

A Bengal cat stuck its head between the rungs of the upper-level railing and met my gaze. I swear it was assessing me to see if I was a friend or foe.

"Nice cat."

The cat meowed once and then retreated to wherever it had come from, presumably bored by my presence.

"That's Hudson. He says you're one of the good guys," Gwenn said. The gold in her eyes twinkled as she smiled.

We met on the second-floor landing. "You got all that from a single meow?"

She laughed. "That and the fact that he waltzed off to continue his mousing adventure. He had one cornered, but it got away. He won't give up until he catches it."

"I could use a cat like that, but I'd be more likely to catch it myself," I said.

"Shifter. Right?" Gwenn said.

"Lykoi," I said. "You probably never even heard of my kind before."

"You're a cross between cat and wolf. I'm impressed," she said. "You're not very common for this area, but I've heard of a few overseas."

My interest was piqued. "Really? You know what I am? Have you seen others like me?"

"Not personally, no, but I am aware of who and what you are, Janda Gray."

"Hmm. Who spilled the beans?" I hadn't told her my last name.

Her laughter reverberated off the picture-lined walls of the staircase. "Come on. Let's go to the kitchen and grab a coffee. We can chat there." She led the way, still chuckling.

I caught her scent when she went past me. "You're a witch."

"Yes. A witch in Sleepy Hollow. I fit right in, although there seems to be a rather large group of shifters in this area, more than there are witches."

"I don't know many witches, so I couldn't say. But I do know a number of shifters." We reached the kitchen, and I pulled out a chair at the farm-style table and sat down. "I'm pretty sure I encountered some of your handy work at Sebastian's."

Now that I'd been exposed to her, I was positive she had done the additional protection spells. Her scent still clung to the air inside Sebastian's garage.

She pulled two mugs from a cabinet and brought the carafe of rich black coffee to the table, setting a steaming mug in front of me.

"I've known Sebastian for a while. We met at the paranormal hotel a few times. We were supposed to meet about a year ago, but my pass suddenly went blank right when I was at the portal. Weirdest thing. It hadn't ever done that before, and Sebastian was counting on me to help him. I had to get a message passed to him telling him I'd been refused entry. The hotel does what it wants."

"You can say that again," I said. "I'm guessing that's about when I showed up and gave Sebastian some of my blood."

"That sounds about right," she said. "I found out later what had happened, so I suppose I have you to thank for saving my friend's life."

I shrugged. "No thanks necessary. I got ample reward by meeting the man I've come to love, Alexander Holden."

Gwenn glanced down at her mug of coffee. "Yeah, I heard about what happened to him. I'm sorry."

I could see she meant it. "Me, too. That's kind of why I've come. Can you tell me anything about the ghosts that wreaked havoc here?"

She took a sip of her coffee and leaned back in the chair. "Sorry. I only arrived today. Sebastian called me to see if I could clean things up and act as the temporary curator now that Stanley is dead." She leaned in toward me and lowered her voice. "I can tell you one thing, though. This disaster was not caused by ghosts alone."

I put my mug down. "If not the ghosts, then what?"

"Oh, there was ghost activity but not the way you might think. I detected an aura when I first arrived that's faded since then. There was malevolence here. Human malevolence."

"Shit. I knew it." I got up and walked to the kitchen doorway. "Do you mind if I shift and let my lykoi sniff around?"

"Sure. Go ahead. I'll let Hudson know."

My curiosity got the better of me. "You can seriously talk to animals?"

Gwenn laughed. "Only Hudson. He's a special case. I'm not Dr. Doolittle. Trust me. If I could talk to animals, I'd be rolling in money and wouldn't take temp jobs. Hudson and I would be basking in the island sun instead of freezing our asses off in New York."

I liked this woman. "Yeah, sorry. Dumb question. But you *do* talk to Hudson. Yes?"

Gwenn got to her feet. "It's more like he communicates with me. I hear his thoughts as if he's talking in my head. It's not a thing I normally tell people, but I know I can trust you. You're a cat." She put the mugs in the sink and led the way up to the tower.

Hudson met us at the top.

I knelt to stroke his golden-brown fur. "Hey, Hudson," I said. "I'm going to shift and don't want you freaking out."

The Bengal purred and rubbed against my leg. Gwenn nodded for me to proceed. I removed my clothes and stacked them in a neat pile by the stairs. Then I went lykoi.

"Huh," Gwenn said. "You're not as big as the standard wolf. You're more coyote proportioned. But you do have the features of a wolf and a cat, especially around your face, although I thought you'd have a bit more fur on your body."

I hissed at her.

"Oh, sorry. No offense. I think you're pretty cool."

I twitched my tail and walked away, nose in the air. I had a job to do.

CHAPTER 6
A WHIFF OF EVIL

I started my search in the hallway. My approach was methodical. I'd begin with the perimeter and then move inward. It wouldn't take long since the room was empty. Gwenn had already swept debris into a large pile at the back of the hallway, which was a shame. I'd go through that last. I admonished myself for not coming sooner. Hudson sat at the far-left wall and stayed out of my way.

Before long, I'd discovered the location of the murder near the window. The stench of old blood pricked my nose. There'd been a lot of it—a faint residue of fear mixed with the blood. Stanley's last moments had been filled with agony. I shook off the sorrow creeping up my paws and moved to the window. There were no shades or curtains. If what Gwenn suggested was true, there was at least one human attacker. I turned to talk to her, and that's when I saw a slight unevenness in the floor nearest the baseboard that ran beneath the window. Water damage could have caused the buckling, but as I drew closer and got a good whiff, I could see a tiny slip of parchment protruding from a crevice. I'd have to shift back to human to get at it. But I had to complete my investigation first.

I moved methodically across the room from east to west, and then north to south. Nothing else surfaced to give me any indication that a human or ghosts had been here. I hissed in frustration and left the room. The pile of debris Gwenn had collected consisted of more crime scene tape and a broken lantern. I went back to the room and glanced at the ceiling. No lights. Anyone entering at night would have to bring a light source. The lantern must have belonged to the dead guy, but I hoped the hidden scrap of paper would reveal why he was up here after dark.

I returned to the hallway and pawed at the rest of the debris, avoiding shards of glass when I nudged the lantern, which rolled on its side. I froze. There was a brief wisp of a human scent—not from the curator. I turned wide-eyed to Gwenn.

"What? Did you find something?" she said.

I shifted back to my human form. "Yes," I said, snatching up my clothes and dressing as quickly as possible. I tugged on my boots and strode to the pile. I bent down and sniffed again. The scent was faint, but it had a touch of the river to it.

"Can I have this?" I said, picking up the lantern. "I'm not so sure this was Stanley's after all. You had it pegged. There was a live person here. I think this lantern was his, but why it got left behind is unclear. It seems a pretty sloppy thing to do."

"Take whatever you want. I'm throwing it all in the back dumpster anyway." She came to sniff at the lantern. "It's too faint for me to detect. Witches don't have the same keen olfactory gift as shifters. It may be the same person whose aura I glimpsed when I first came up here, but I can't swear to it. There have been quite a few people contaminating the scene. I can't be sure of anything at this point."

"I can," I said. "I know the other smells. I don't know this one. It's not someone from around here, which makes this case even more interesting." I looked around for something to pull up the floorboard. "Do you have a crowbar or hammer I could use?"

"Let me look in the broom closet. I'll be right back." She took off down the stairs.

Hudson meowed, brushed against me, and pattered to the slip of paper wedged in the floor. He meowed again and pawed at the floor.

"Yeah. I saw it. Just waiting on Gwenn to give us something to lift the board." I wasn't sure if Stanley had been trying to unearth it when he was interrupted or if he'd been trying to hide it. It seemed more plausible he had hastily shoved it under the boards, and the one piece had torn in the process. From where I stood at the window, I had a good view of the front of the building. Stanley would have been alerted to anyone coming in from the front. How he'd gotten the board back in place was another matter.

The cat curled next to the spot and purred now that he'd gotten his point across.

I didn't need to be Dr. Doolittle to understand what he was trying to say. "I hear ya, Hudson. We'll figure this out."

Gwenn hurried into the room and handed me a hammer. "It's all I could find. What are you trying to do?"

"Tear up the floor," I said.

Her eyes grew wide as she froze mid-stride. "I don't know about that. I can't be held responsible for more damage to this place. Old Brian didn't keep up with things in his later years, and neither did his son, Stanley, when he took over for as curator. I found several rotten boards. The

Council won't be happy with the repair costs, and I don't want to make them angrier."

"You can blame it on me," I said. "I'm used to it." I bent down to begin loosening the wood. A large indent was on one end, right over the nails securing the flooring. "I think I know how Stanley did it." I got up and placed my heel into the indentation. If I'd been a larger person and had heavier boots on, it could have been possible to smash the board in place.

"He used his foot?" she said.

"Looks that way, which means he was trying to hide it in a hurry." I knelt and started dismantling the hiding place.

Gwenn fidgeted while I took the hammer to the uneven boards, tugging until one finally gave way. I kept at it until I ripped apart three sections. I heard groaning behind me as Gwenn watched my efforts. It had to be done. And three boards would hardly be an issue compared to what I hoped to discover.

"Oh, my!" Gwenn said, peeking over my shoulder. "What's that?"

I tugged the parchment free from its confines and smoothed it out against the floor. "A map."

She squatted next to me. "That looks vintage."

"If I'm right, this may be the reason Old Brian and Stanley were killed. Someone wants this and won't hesitate to kill to get it. Do you own a gun or other type of weapon?"

She pulled back as if the suggestion was offensive. "No. Why would I have a weapon?"

"Protection," I said, rising. "You better get one, although I don't know what good it will do against pirate ghosts. On the other hand, it could cause quite a bit of damage to a living person."

The sunlight didn't brighten the room enough for me to analyze the map. I folded it and stuffed it in my pocket before attempting to replace the floor I'd ripped up. "Sorry. It's not going back to the way it was. You'll have to tell the Council to take it from my pay." I hadn't gotten a paycheck in over a month. You had to work to get paid. Who knew?

She seemed resigned to having to deal with it. "Oh, well. I don't suppose it can get much worse around here. Maybe they won't notice."

That didn't seem likely to me, but hey, we could only hope. "Let's go back to the kitchen where the lighting is better. I want to examine the map more thoroughly."

Hudson had abandoned his spot and led the way down to the kitchen, where he proceeded to tangle himself in Gwenn's legs.

"Fine," she said, reaching for a ceramic bowl and milk from the refrigerator. "Here. Drink up. You're so spoiled."

Hudson purred and lapped contentedly at the milk. I made room on the table to lay out the map. The parchment was a square roughly twelve inches by twelve inches. A section of one corner was missing. I'd bet my next month's salary the map would match the piece found in Stanley's hand. It would also go a long way in the Council's eyes if I handed the map over to them, but I wasn't ready to give it up. Not yet.

"It's old," Gwenn said, fingering the edges of the parchment. "It appears to depict the area before the land was developed." She ran her hand over it and mumbled something about revealing what lies hidden.

The map glowed briefly and gave a sudden burst of golden-white light.

"Ouch!" Gwenn yanked her hand away, rubbing her palm against her leg.

"What just happened?"

The brightness diminished and left the map just as it had appeared a moment ago.

"It's protected," she said, still rubbing her hand. "Someone doesn't want us to see what's invisible to our eyes. Janda, this map carries a curse. You may want to rethink your intention to keep it and hand it over to the Council."

"How did you know I was thinking that?"

"Because if you weren't, you would have already contacted someone on the Council."

Gwenn was smart. Too bad I tend not to take good advice.

"That's not my style. It's staying with me a while longer." I followed the lines of the map that showed the river and the nearby forest surrounding Sleepy Hollow. If I could find just one landmark, I might be able to orient myself. I also needed the missing piece.

"Sebastian was right about you."

I looked up from the map. "I can only imagine what that vamp said about me."

She laughed. "He just said you were tenacious."

"Okay. Not so bad. I expected worse." I sat in my chair and gazed around the room. It was sparsely stocked. A few cans of tuna sat on a shelf. I spotted one can of SPAM. God, who ate that stuff anymore?

Gwenn poured us fresh coffee and returned to staring at the map.

"Where are you staying?" I said.

"Here."

"You're kidding? Here? You know that can of SPAM is probably left over from war ration days. I mean, this is not a well-equipped kitchen. And where do you sleep?"

"There's a cot in a small room adjoining this one. Hudson and I can share it."

The thought of old, dirty sheets made me shudder. This place was awful, even in bachelor's terms.

"Janda, I'll be fine. Really. I've been too busy cleaning upstairs to do much else, but stores are nearby. I'll make a run shortly."

I gave up. "Suit yourself." I picked up a pen from the counter and wrote my number on the only thing available. I handed her the napkin. "Call me if you change your mind."

"Thanks." She tucked the napkin in the pocket of her jeans.

"Before I leave, could you teach me that spell you just did?"

Her brows creased, and she leaned forward in her chair to check me out in greater detail. "I thought you were a shifter, not a witch."

"Yes and no. My parents were both shifters. My great-great-grandmother was a witch. I don't know that any witch power trickled down to me, but I'd like to try. I have her journal with various spells and potions. I've just touched on the potions part, but I think I should learn to do a spell or two. If you'd teach me, I'd be happy to repay you somehow." I didn't mention that I sucked at potions. I wasn't sure spells were my thing either, but I wouldn't know until I'd tried a few.

"We should work up to that one, but I'll give you some pointers. We can start now if you'd like."

"Why not the one you tried on the map? I have to find out what it's hiding." My fingers tingled with anticipation. I had to know why this map was so important.

"Look," Gwenn said. "It got me good, and I know my stuff. You don't have any experience with spells. Worse, this seems more like a curse. Whoever cast that spell wanted to hurt anyone who tried to force the map to reveal its secret. They are not playing around. You could be seriously injured."

"Okay. Maybe jumping into the deep end isn't the best idea, but what can you teach me for defense against ghosts?"

She shook her head and grabbed another refill of the dark roast coffee. I marveled at her consumption. If I drank one more cup, I'd be wide awake well into the morning hours. I had enough issues sleeping without being hopped up on caffeine.

"Sorry. I don't think there is a good spell as a defense against ghosts." She frowned. "This is what I don't get about all the pirate ghost sightings and the murders they're supposed to have committed. Ghosts, even malevolent ones, have difficulty focusing their energy long enough to do basic hauntings. For the most part, ghosts are relatively harmless. That's not to say people haven't died because of what a ghost may have done, like pushing a small object that landed on someone or caused the person to change course to avoid the object and then getting hurt in the process. But that's all energy intensive."

"You're debunking the ghost murder theory?" I couldn't say I was surprised by her reluctance to go along with what the Council had surmised. I had my doubts about it as well.

"Think about it for a minute. Do you believe a few ghosts—we don't know how many at this point—could push a giant boulder off the edge of a hillside onto someone to crush them? We're talking vast amounts of energy to accomplish such a feat. Why did they even need to kill someone in the first place? What was this kid Ben doing that was a threat to them? Then we have Old Brian getting tossed over the side of a bridge. Really? They were able to lift him up and over the rail?" She stood, mimicking the effort it took to lift someone and shove them off a bridge. "Not to mention poor Stanley getting his throat cut and bleeding out upstairs. These murders were all in different locations. All were different ways in which the people were killed. All of them would have required a great deal of energy and physical exertion to accomplish. We're not talking ghosts pushing around small objects here. It doesn't make sense." She plunked back in her chair and swigged her coffee, then looked down at the empty cup in surprise. "I think I may be a little over-caffeinated. Time to switch to water. Do you want one?" She reached into the refrigerator and pulled out two bottles.

"I'm good," I said.

She sat the extra one on the counter and stooped to pet Hudson. He'd been avidly watching her wild gesticulations during her analysis of the murders. He meowed and jumped onto the table. I scooped the map up before he could damage it.

"He won't bother it," she said. "Hudson just wants a good look at it. He's curious."

"You don't say?" My tone was skeptical, but Hudson stared innocently up at me with his golden eyes and twitched his tail. I wasn't convinced his sharp claws wouldn't rip the parchment but spread it out on the table anyway. Darned if that cat didn't take his time sniffing it and gently pawing at the corner where the missing piece had been torn off. "What's he doing?"

"Investigating." She said it like he did this kind of thing all the time.

"And what is he telling you?"

"Nothing we didn't already know." She picked the cat

up, placed him on her lap, and stroked him. "He smells evil intent. It's cursed."

"Which leaves us where?" I said. "We have more questions than answers." At some point, this had turned into us and not me. Gwenn was easy to bounce theories off of and did bring up more than a few legitimate points, ones I'd already been contemplating. We weren't dealing with a simple matter of ghosts.

Gwenn's eyes twinkled with delight. "I'm glad you asked. We go ghost hunting."

"You seem a little too eager," I said, giving her a narrow-eyed stare. "You should probably leave this to me."

"I can help. I won't get in your way. I promise," she said.

I sighed. This was not how I expected the day to turn out. I came for information about the murder and ended up with a partner. Mutther had always been the one to help me, but he was busy with his bar and had duties the Council gave him. Nick and Silas were off dealing with the PR nightmare and hoping to get Angie updated on her new role at the police station. And Sebastian was up to his fangs with keeping the various groups from breaking free from the Council and causing all sorts of discord in the supernatural community.

"I have a feeling I'm going to regret this," I said. Hudson leaped off Gwenn's lap and padded across the table to nuzzle me. "What have I gotten myself into?"

CHAPTER 7

HULDA'S SISTER

I tucked the map into my jacket pocket, grabbed the lantern, and left Gwenn to do her shopping. After meeting with Sebastian and the others tonight, Gwenn and I would lay out our strategy over a cup of coffee at the bagel shop near the historical society. *She* would have coffee. *I* was going for authentic New York bagels. Sebastian didn't consider bagels real food, and his pantry was getting low. Besides, the bagel shop had excellent internet, as well as electric outlets where people who lived in the current century could charge their cell phones. Sebastian claimed books held the knowledge we required. Give me Google any day.

In the meantime, Gwenn promised to see what she could unearth from the rubble that might help me with Hulda. For my part, I'd focus on gleaning more information about the lantern's owner. I pinned my hopes on one of the others being able to help with the scent on it.

I'd done a quick pass through the other rooms, but it was useless. Until Gwenn restored order, I couldn't search the archives for anything. Whatever might exist regarding

Hulda's early days and her family members may or may not be located under all the mess. Nothing had stood out during my search that would show the area around Sleepy Hollow from a few hundred years ago that we didn't already know. We might spot something unusual if we could compare the map we'd found to an original of the town. The closest thing to an original town map was Sebastian's map that focused on the mining and natural caves. Still, it was a place to start.

My frustration mounted with each obstacle. I was going around in ever-widening circles and getting further from my goal.

Gwenn insisted there was no spell for a witch-in-training, as she labeled me, that would help ward off anything from the spirit realm that might do me harm. That meant no defensive spells any time soon, if I even had enough witch in me to do one in the first place. She assured me there were other options, like particular charms that could be created to help. Unfortunately, I didn't have the time to wait for one to be made, and Gwenn didn't have all the ingredients to make one. I mentioned my little laboratory in Sebastian's basement, which might have the required materials for her to make a charm. She was delighted by the prospect of going to Sebastian's. Since it wasn't my house, I'd have to run it by Sebastian first, even though Gwenn had been the one who boosted the protection spells at his place. I wondered how Hulda felt about another witch entering her domain. Maybe that would force her to show herself.

It rained as I drove Miss Kitty out of the Village of Tarrytown and to the wooded areas around Sleepy Hollow. It wasn't a blinding rain, just an annoying shower. Cold water trickled down the back of my neck, making its way to my ass and adding to my disgruntlement. Thankfully, the map was safe in the inner pocket of my jacket, and the lantern was tucked inside a small satchel attached to my bike. My thoughts kept returning to Hulda and the Spook Rock area where my great-great-grandmother's home had once stood. I changed course and went for it. Hell, I couldn't get much wetter, so why not?

As I pulled off the highway into Rockefeller State Park Preserve, the rain slowed to a drizzle. I followed a narrow road that was more path than road in some spots and hit a pothole, one of many the area was known for since budget cuts hammered the town's fiscal resources. Muddy water splashed against my legs.

Ugh.

So, maybe I *could* get wetter.

I kept riding, eager to get to the large boulder that had a history of spiritual happenings. This wasn't an area I frequented but finding my way to Spook Rock was pretty simple—follow the signs. Tourists love signs. That was one budget item that the town board made sure to approve. Bring in the tourist money and keep the coffers filled to some extent. The park had over 1,200 acres that abutted the Sleepy Hollow Cemetery and Old Dutch Church, where Hulda's remains had been laid to rest. It also connected to the Old Croton Aqueduct Park, which I made a mental note to visit soon.

The dark clouds overhead leant the woods a gloomy atmosphere that fit my mood. The humungous boulder loomed before me. I parked Miss Kitty next to Spook Rock and surveyed the surroundings. The rain kept sightseers and hikers away, granting me the privacy I sought. I slid past the boulder and headed down the slope. Moss-covered chestnut trees emitted a pungent, earthy aroma. I walked along the path known as Witches' Spring Trail, found stepping stones that crossed the natural spring, and approached the remains of the stone wall that once bordered Hulda's home. Saplings and brush covered the spot where the structure had existed. Sprigs of lemon verbena and sage had sprouted between small rocks but would soon give way to late fall frosts. I sat on the crumbling wall, ignoring how wet my butt was getting and absorbed the calmness around me.

"It's a pleasant place, isn't it?"

I nearly jumped out of my skin. "Hulda! What the hell? I swear you get a kick out of messing with me."

She laughed, and when she did, the drizzle glistened as it filtered through her image. My great-great-grandmother was a striking woman with dark hair, rich mocha-colored eyes, and a dazzling smile. Her laughter continued, and I stood in awe as the rain shifted its path in direct response to her laughter, first being drawn closer to her and then being pushed away on her exhalations. I had no idea a ghost could breathe or imitate actual breathing. What she was doing was more of an echo of what breathing would have been like if she were a living entity.

"I'm so sorry," she said, her amusement fading and allowing the rain to find its natural path through her ghostly form.

"Are you done?" I said.

She shrugged. "You must allow an old ghost her little pleasures. I have so few anymore." She seemed more resigned than sad as she spoke.

"Like I have a choice," I said.

She ignored my comment. "You should harvest the herbs before the frost gets to them." She glided over to the stones protecting the tiny plants. She reached down and tugged on one but couldn't entirely uproot it.

I hopped off the wall and joined her. "I've watched you," I said, pulling up some plants and storing them in my outer coat pocket. "You can touch things of substance and even influence their movement, but you can't do much more than that. Is that true?"

She glanced up from her efforts and gave me a sad smile. "Yes. It takes great focus and energy to do anything substantial. If I could do more, I'd be with Sebastian more fully than wisps of perfume or knocking over a book." She let out a tiny sigh, and the drizzle swirled in front of her like a tiny water spout. "I believe we can readily communicate because we have a shared ancestry. We're linked. It's harder to converse with people with whom I have no genetic link and who may not be as sensitive to the energy I cast."

"Plus, Sebastian is a vampire, a walking dead guy. I'd think that would complicate matters," I said.

I didn't like seeing her so sad. I reached out and touched Hulda's arm. I could feel some of my energy meshing with hers in an instant. The next thing I knew, she had freed the small plant from the earth and seemed pleased with herself. I bolted upright and took a step away from her.

"What just happened?"

"I borrowed some of your energy to pluck the herb from the ground." She gave me a sheepish grin. "I hope you don't mind."

"Mind? Hell. I wish you'd explained earlier that you could borrow someone's energy."

"Why?" She slid past me and returned to the stone wall.

"You seriously didn't just ask me that." I shoved the last plant into my pocket. I didn't feel any different after being siphoned. Confusion momentarily put my brain on pause as I paced before her while letting the implications sink in.

"Janda, dear, are you mad at me?" Her voice faltered. "It

was not my intention to make you upset. Please forgive me."

I waved my hand at her and kept pacing. "Not mad. Thinking."

"Oh," she said, folding her hands in her lap.

I spun around to face her. "Okay. Earlier I asked you if ghosts could kill someone. You avoided my question. Gwenn doesn't see how ghosts could have done the things the Council thinks they've done. You just borrowed my energy to pluck an herb. Why couldn't these pirate ghosts do something similar? Maybe they could get enough energy to pull off these murders."

Hulda's image flickered for a moment. She looked down at her hands. "Yes. It is possible." She met my gaze. "It's not an easy task and would require a great deal of energy. I truly do not know how these horrific events happened. You must understand that there is more at play here than you realize."

"Then why won't you tell me? Does this have anything to do with the sister you haven't told me about? My great-great-great aunt, which is far too many greats for me to keep saying." I struggled to keep my voice even and not scare her away.

She tipped her head back to view the darkening sky. "You need to leave," she said.

"Not until you answer me."

"Janda, you must leave at once. It's getting late. The protection spells can't reach out here."

Her voice grew hard, and she glared at me as I'd never seen her do before. I was seeing a different side of my great-great-grandmother. This was the protector side, the one she portrayed in the battle to defend her home during the war.

"Okay," I said. "I'll go if you promise to answer my questions when I get back to Sebastian's."

We were in a stare-down, one I had to win. I put my hands on my hips and didn't budge.

"You are far too much like me for your own good," she said. "Agreed. Now go!" She vanished.

I hurried up the hill to my bike, basking in my victory and doing a little fist-pumping triumphant dance near Spook Hill. If I had a football, I'd have spiked it. I'd won.

Gloating wasn't a good attribute. It tended to bite you in the ass. The uneven ground was pocked with jutting roots and rocks. I slipped, and a thorn from a wild raspberry bush pierced through my jeans to prick my thigh. I brushed past it to reach Miss Kitty. I started her up and froze in horror as six pirate ghosts emerged from nothing and formed a blockade across the trail.

"Shit!"

I revved the engine, but they didn't move. I turned on my headlight, and the beam lit the path behind them. They had no substance. I floored Miss Kitty and drove right through them. I chanced a peek behind me and prayed I wouldn't kill myself by wiping out in one of the potholes. The pirates had turned to watch me go but had not tried to stop me.

Why didn't they attack? I was glad they hadn't, but it took me off-guard. Murderous pirate ghosts had just appeared in front of me but didn't hurt me. Adrenaline raged through my body, causing my lykoi to push for release. I held it in check. I was safe. No need to panic. No need to fight.

Yet.

CHAPTER 8

REVELATIONS

I sped along the highway, glancing over my shoulder periodically. The pirates never reappeared. I wasn't about to stop and see if they would ambush me. I tore through the barrier and up the driveway to Sebastian's house. I debated where to park Miss Kitty. I'd feel better having easy access to her. We hadn't tested the barrier against ghosts, and it wasn't something I wanted to do tonight. Leaving her close to the rear door might be prudent.

Two other cars and a motorcycle were parked by the garage. It seemed the gang was all here. I inhaled and exhaled several times, willing my heart rate to slow down to its normal range. I grabbed the doorknob to the rear entrance, but as I started to turn the knob, the door was yanked open.

"What happened? Are you okay?" Sebastian pulled me inside and slammed the door behind us. He turned me around, inspecting me.

"Back off! I'm fine." I pulled free of his grasp and

straightened my jacket, which had been twisted in the process of being turned like a damn spinning top.

"What's going on?" Uncle Damon said.

"That's what I'm trying to find out, Uncle." I moved away from Sebastian, who continued to give me the evil eye. He clearly didn't believe that I wasn't hurt. "Look. No blood. No bruises. All is good in the land of Janda."

"Cute," Uncle Damon said. "I've heard that line too often from you to know something happened, so start explaining."

I'd forgotten who I was dealing with here. My uncle had heard all my lines and knew when I was full of crap. The commotion brought the others to see what the ruckus was all about.

"Hey, Nick," I said.

He raised one brow and crossed his arms. No help there. I turned to Silas. His lips formed a thin line, and he shook his head.

"Great welcome, guys." I pushed past them, only to find Mutther in the hall leading to the foyer.

"What have you done now?" he said.

"Oh, for the love of Pete! Fine! There are six pirate ghosts. They paid me a visit out by Spook Rock. Damn near shit my pants seeing them pop out of nowhere."

Uncle Damon's eyes grew dark, very dark. His nostrils flared. He was trying his best to keep it together, but I wasn't betting on how long it would be before he erupted.

"I need a drink," he said. He went straight for Sebastian's study and the bottle of whiskey sitting on a sideboard.

Uncle Damon downed the shot in one breath. I used my meekest and most soothing tone once he finished. "It wasn't so bad. I was more surprised than anything else.

And, hey, now we know how many pirate ghosts we're dealing with."

"Sit," he said. He pointed to a chair by the fireplace.

The fact that he treated me like I was an errant child again ticked me off, but I was more than willing to take a spot close to the warming flames. My clothes were soggy, and the chill started to make me shiver. I let the fire dry my backside by angling myself in the chair. The position also allowed me to see my interrogators' movements. I pasted a smile on my face and watched Uncle Damon down another round of whiskey. Silas stood with his arms crossed at the door, Sebastian poured a large glass of wine, and Mutther shook his head at Nick. Those two were communicating in some wolfy way that excluded me. We were in a standoff of who would fold and start talking. The incident had rattled me more than I would ever admit to them, so I uncharacteristically kept my mouth shut.

Sebastian caved. He could not deal with silence. He also probably wanted everyone out of his house pronto.

"What, pray tell, were you doing at Spook Rock?" His voice was low because yelling was unnecessary around a bunch of supernaturals with exceptional hearing.

My smile didn't waver when I responded, which was kudos for me since I wanted more than anything to tell them to back off. I squared my shoulders. "Hulda has been avoiding me. I went to the ruins of her home to see if she would show up."

Sebastian froze with his drink to his lips, then put the wineglass back on his desk and came to sit opposite me. "Did you see her?"

A pang of guilt crept over me for not being more considerate of his feelings. "Yes," I said. "We had an interesting conversation, and she promised she'd reveal more to me soon. She rushed me out of there, saying it was getting late. The protection spells only apply to your house and not to me personally. Honestly, she was a bit pushy."

He seemed to have forgotten he was in the middle of giving me the third degree. He leaned his head back against his chair, deep in thought.

No one interrupted. Sebastian was having a moment.

"Did she seem well?" he eventually said.

"Um. I suppose that depends on your definition." This was awkward. I was talking to a dead-man-walking, aka a vampire, who wanted to know if his deceased and very ghostly girlfriend was doing well. "She gave me a fright and thought it was funny. Popping in on me unawares is a real treat in her otherwise mundane existence. I'd say that qualifies for doing well."

Sebastian roared with laughter. The rest of us just stared at him. He had to be the most animated he'd been in ages. It also gave me a glimpse into the man he had been when he was with my great-great-grandmother. They must have been quite the pair.

Uncle Damon took over the grilling process now that Sebastian had veered in a different direction with the questioning.

"Back to the matter at hand," he said. "What about the ghosts? What happened? In detail."

"Well, I was busy doing a victory dance near Spook Rock."

I hazarded a glance in his direction. He frowned. I might have been better off omitting that tidbit of information.

I hurried to justify my actions. "You know I like to celebrate my wins, and I had just won a staring contest with Hulda. I refused to leave unless she gave her word to tell me about her sister."

"Sister?" Mutther said. "She has a sister?"

"Exactly my point," I said. "I found a notation in one of Hulda's journals that implied she had a sister. That's when she started avoiding me, so I couldn't push her about having a secret sister. I could have all sorts of cousins out there somewhere, but Hulda won't answer my basic questions. I think I have a right to know this kind of stuff. Don't you?" I realized I was rambling and had gone off-topic, but I couldn't help that I tended to talk fast when I was excited about something.

"Slow down," Uncle Damon said. "First things first. We can get back to your family tree in a moment. What about the ghosts?" He balled his fists at his side.

That was not a good sign. I'd seen this mannerism enough to know I'd pushed Uncle Damon's exasperation button.

"You're right. Sorry. Well, there were six of them. I had just finished relishing my small victory and hopped onto my bike when *BAM!* There they were! Pirate ghosts from the Revolutionary War era. They formed a blockade across the road. They stood there, not saying a word or advancing on me. It was weird."

Sebastian had regained his composure and was back to inquisitor status. "How well-formed were they? Their bodies, I mean."

"Funny you should ask. When I turned on my headlight, the beam went right through them. I could see the road behind them quite clearly. They didn't seem menacing at all. I couldn't imagine them being able to kill anyone. I didn't want to stay there to find out, so that's when I figured I'd be able to drive into them to get to the other side." I glanced at Nick, who snickered. I cut him off. "I'll spare you," I said. "Why did Janda cross the road and through the pirates? To get to the other side. Haha. Joke over." I shook my head, then stopped. It hit me. "Nick! That's it! To get to the other side!"

Nick opened his mouth and then shut it.

"Don't you see?" I said. "The pirates want to get to the other side!"

I shot out of my chair and jabbed Nick in the chest. "You're a genius."

"Of course I am," he said, puffing out his chest.

Mutther snorted.

My mind was racing, fitting a few more pieces of the puzzle together, or so I hoped. I strode back and forth across the room. "What if the ghosts only want to find rest? What if they can't?"

"What about the murders?" Mutther said. "All evidence points to them as the culprits. How is killing someone going to give them eternal rest? Sorry, Janda. I don't buy your theory."

I held up my hand. "That's all true. Maybe."

I stopped wearing a path on the floor and stopped in front of them. Their expressions didn't indicate they were on board with my belief. I strode to the desk and pulled out the map I'd found, laying it next to Sebastian's map. The others came to see what I was doing. I pressed as many wrinkles out as possible so there would be no significant distortions in the map.

"I struck out with getting information from Hulda earlier this morning, so I paid a visit to the crime scene to do some sleuthing." I glanced up at Sebastian. "By the way, good choice with Gwenn. I like her and Hudson."

"Who's Hudson?" Sebastian said.

"Who's Gwenn?" Silas said. As the shortest person in the room, he had to squeeze next to me to view the map.

"Gwenn is who Sebastian got to help put things right at the historical society. Hudson is her cat." I left out the part where Hudson could talk telepathically with Gwenn. She'd told me in confidence, and I wasn't the type to betray those trusts.

"You're just going to keep us in suspense?" Uncle Damon said.

He was being sarcastic. It was his jab at me to stop getting side-tracked and get to the point.

I cleared my throat. "Gwenn and I are certain the ghosts weren't the only ones at the historical society. Someone very alive was there. And, if I'm right, Stanley was protecting this map. We found it hidden beneath the floor where he'd been killed."

I shuffled some papers around the desk, which irritated Sebastian.

"How often must I remind you that this is *my* desk and, therefore, what is on it is also mine? What are you searching for?"

I rotated my map for him to see and pointed to the missing section.

Sebastian sucked in his breath. Then he started shuffling the papers on his desk.

"So when you do it, it's okay? But when I do it, it's not?"

"Precisely," he said.

"Okay," I said. "I get it. I'll wait until you find the missing piece, which I'm sure will fit my map perfectly."

We all backed away from the desk to give Sebastian space to do his search. He grumbled under his breath, which of course, was pretty lame. We all knew what he was saying. *Always disturbing my stuff. Ever since she got here. No privacy whatsoever.*

"I can hear you over here, you know," I said.

"I meant for you to hear," he griped.

I nodded. "Okay, then. Let me know how you really feel. I can move out, you know."

"Don't be daft," Sebastian said. "Tonight just proved that you are not safe outside this house."

Now he'd gotten me mad. My lykoi was rising fast. Uncle Damon took two steps out of my immediate space.

"Janda." He used his soothing tone. "He has a point. The ghosts have an interest in you. Until this is resolved, you should not go out alone."

I bristled, barely keeping my lykoi in check. "I'll go where I want to go. If that means I go alone, so be it."

Silas, always the diplomat, cut in. "I'm confident Janda can take care of herself. However, I think it would be a good idea for everyone to have someone to watch their backs when we go out. Pirates appearing out of thin air wherever they please is something that doesn't bode well for any of us."

I relented. "Fine."

The others grunted their agreement, except for Sebastian, who held up the missing map piece.

"Finally," he said. "We are making progress."

We joined him around the desk that now revealed the completed pirate map.

"Well," I said. "Let's not get too enthusiastic. There's a curse on the map."

"What?" Every one of them shouted it simultaneously.

I held my hands over my ears. Men.

CHAPTER 9
HIDDEN LAYERS

"Why does anything pertaining to you have to come with extra baggage?" Uncle Damon said. His dominant pack power surged, affecting the others nearby and making them restless.

The air crackled with his energy. I held my ground. His words stung, but he'd never hear me say it. I'd had lots of practice over the years keeping my hurt from showing, but at this moment, I lashed out with a barb of my own.

"I'm just lucky that way. Kind of like you." I tapped the desk with my fingertips, knowing he hated it and narrowed my eyes at him.

He sure as hell had his own baggage when it came to relationships and pack bonds, especially when it came to anything with my mother.

"If the two of you are done poking at one another, I'd like to move on to the pertinent issue of the cursed map," Sebastian said. He stood a good foot away from his desk and peered down at the map as if it might explode.

Everyone had a hands-off approach to the map after I'd blurted out that it was cursed.

"It won't curse you just by touching it," I said. "At least, not from what Gwenn or I could tell. It has a hidden layer that will attack you if you try to force it out in the open."

"That's just great," Mutther said. "I suppose you found out firsthand?"

"Not me. Gwenn did. I was the innocent bystander."

"Right. How innocent?" Nick said. He moved to Mutther's side and viewed the map from farther away. Neither of them was taking any chances.

Not that I blamed them. They had suffered from being too near me in the past. Mutther was still rebuilding his bar.

"I'm ignoring that," I said. "Gwenn had a hunch the map was hiding something. Call it her witchy intuition." The fact that she had a very clever talking cat gave her intuition a giant boost. The guys didn't need to hear about that part. "She tried a spell to get it to divulge its secrets, and the thing fought back. It sent a surge of energy lashing out at her like a snake bite."

Silas put his hand over the map, gently smoothing the parchment's surface in a slow caress. Then it zapped him. "Ow. Damn thing."

I bit back a laugh. Nick, Mutther, and Uncle Damon also laughed, breaking the tension.

"Well done, Silas. You've proven Janda correct. The thing is cursed or at least protected," Sebastian said. "Now, what do we do with it?"

No one knew.

I offered my two cents. "I had hoped to compare it to area maps from that era to see if anything stood out. Unfortunately, the historical society archives are in disarray, making it difficult to locate anything that might help us. We have the map of the mines that belongs to Sebastian, but that's it unless Gwenn discovers something during her cleanup efforts."

Now that everyone knew not to try anything with the map, we all hunkered down to scrutinize its details.

"What exactly are we looking for?" Nick said. "They look like the same map, except Sebastian's has more about the mines and caves."

"Yes," Mutther said. "But look at how the Hudson River is depicted on the pirate map. I'm assuming we agree it *is* a pirate map. Correct?"

We all nodded our agreement.

"I don't see how the river helps us," I said.

"There are more coves on the pirate one than Sebastian's." Mutther waved his hand over the areas he meant.

"Oh. You're right." I was beginning to understand more about the map's significance. "Wouldn't a pirate have to know safe places to come ashore? They would have been hunted by the local authorities and would be steering clear of the major ports, right?"

"They'd still have to land close enough to towns so they could gather necessary supplies," Nick said. "Besides, anyone out to sea for a long time would also have personal needs, if you get my drift."

I got his drift. I wished I hadn't, but you can't take those things back. Once you hear them, it's a done deal. Now I had the vision of horny pirates stuck in my head. I closed my eyes and shook my head to dislodge the thoughts. I opened my eyes and glared at Nick. "Please. Let's not go there, okay?"

He held up his hands. "It's just a fact of nature, Janda."

I held my palm out toward him. "Nope. Not going there. Enough said."

Mutther spared me any more of Nick's comments by jabbing the map. "Here. If I—"

Pop!

"Shit! That got my attention," Mutther said, pulling his hand back and shaking it.

"I don't think it likes you," I said.

He gave me a deadpan stare. My lips twitched as I did my best to hide my amusement.

"I suggest we keep ourselves under control while touching this map," Sebastian said. "It appears to respond to strong emotions, not in a good way, as we have seen."

Silas had been quiet, stroking his thin beard and peering closely at the map. He straightened and looked at each of us. "Sebastian is correct. It does respond to emotions. It also responds to spells forcing our desires upon it. But what if we asked it?"

"Asked it what?" I said.

Silas's hand paused mid-stroke. "What it's hiding, of course."

Nick's jaw dropped. "You're kidding. What, we go up and nicely ask the map to pretty please, with a cherry on top, tell us what it's hiding?" His voice rose a few decibels. "You're a nutcase!" He walked over to the fireplace, mumbling about being part of a group of idiots and saying what we needed was action like in the good old days. He stood with his back to us, staring at the fire, his fist clenched against the mantel.

A part of me agreed with him. My skin literally itched for action. The problem was that we could not agree on what to do next. Dissension was escalating among the supernatural community.

"Hold on," Mutther said. "I was trying to make a point before that thing zapped me. We need to think like a pirate.

If I was trying to stay out of sight but still be close to where I could access supplies, I'd pick one of these inlets just north of Sleepy Hollow. Far enough away, but close enough to what I wanted."

"Where would that be today?" I said. "Near one of the preserves?"

"Possibly," Sebastian said, "but it could be nearer to Sing Sing and the old quarry."

"We could check those areas out and see if there's anything pirates might be interested in," I said. "Although, I'm game to let Silas test his theory."

"Ask away," Nick said. He stopped brooding and strode over to the desk. "I think I'd like to see how this turns out. Go ahead, Silas. Ask."

"Very well," Silas said. "I will."

While Silas placed his hands on either side of the map, keeping clear from touching it, the rest of us backed up several paces.

"Map," Silas said, staring down at the parchment. "With due respect, I ask you for guidance in revealing what you can that might help us."

We waited. The mantel clock ticked away, and we waited. Nothing.

"Oh! Did you see that?" I said. "It sort of flickered."

We drew closer. It had indeed emitted a flicker of light. Then it went back to its usual annoying self.

Mutther slapped Silas on the back. "Good try."

Silas abandoned his effort. "At least it didn't attack me."

"Maybe you need to be a pirate to get answers," I said.

"Humph," Nick said. "This isn't getting us anywhere. A search isn't likely to do much, either. In case you haven't noticed, we don't know what we're looking for. That piece of pirate paper is useless. This isn't a fairytale where X marks the spot of some long-lost treasure. It's a freaking joke. I need to protect my pack, not go hunting for a needle in a haystack."

I went to the window and looked out at the woods, sticking my hands in my jacket pocket and fingering the plants that still had to be prepped for drying in the basement lab. Night had settled over the landscape. It would be time to meet Gwenn soon, and I had to figure out how to do it without the constraints of the newly implemented buddy system.

The reflection of the desk lamp against the window caught my attention.

Double crap!

With all the fuss when I arrived, I had forgotten to bring in the lamp Gwenn had let me keep. I spun around. "Wait. I have something that might give us a new lead. I'll be right back." I rushed out the door, down the hallway, and into the kitchen. Mutther was right behind me.

"Where do you think you're going?" he said, grabbing my shoulder and spinning me to face him. "You heard Sebastian. No one goes anywhere by themselves."

I tugged free from his grip. "I'm not going anywhere! I left something in my bike satchel."

"I'll go with you."

"Whatever. It's parked by the kitchen door, but sure, come along."

We went through the door, and Miss Kitty was still there. I gave Mutther one of my smug grins, and he gave me one of his eye-rolling looks of disgust.

Mud had splattered the leather satchel, but I wiped it off and undid the buckles of the flap. I gasped. "No!" I turned to Mutther. "It's gone!"

"What's gone?"

"Damn it!" I groaned and kicked the dirt with my boot. "Now I know why the pirate ghosts didn't attack me. Shit, Almighty! The bastards stole the lamp."

Mutther scanned the perimeter. "Let's go inside."

"If you're out there and can hear me, you assholes, I'm coming for you!" I shouted—probably at nothing, but it helped me feel better anyway.

I shuffled behind Mutther back to where the others had gathered in the hall.

"What now?" Uncle Damon said. "Which assholes are you going after? I take it they stole something from you."

"You heard that, huh?" I slipped past him and went to one of the chairs by the fireplace.

"Kind of hard not to," Nick said. "Hey, if you want some help kicking ass, I'm your guy. Anything is better than sitting here."

"Thanks, Nick. If I knew where to go to kick their ghost asses, I'd totally be down with you joining me."

Sebastian poured himself a glass of wine and sat in the chair across from me. He took several sips, allowing me time to calm down.

"Ready?" he said.

"Yeah, okay," I said, disappointment coloring my tone. "When I was at the historical society poking around, I found a lamp. Gwenn had assumed it was Stanley's. So did I until I got a whiff of it. There was a human scent I didn't recognize. Gwenn and I think the ghosts have a human accomplice. I was bringing the lamp here to see if anyone else could identify the scent. Sorry. I screwed up. I left it in my bike satchel while at Spook Rock."

"And the ghosts took it," Sebastian said.

I nodded. "They sure did, the bastards."

"We can conjecture the reason they did not try to attack

or pursue you is that they had been successful in their mission," Sebastian said.

"Which would also indicate they were there on orders," Silas added. "Excellent, Janda."

"Excellent, how?" I wasn't tracking their thought process. I was too pissed to get my brain to do anything besides think of ways to make the ghosts pay.

Sebastian met my gaze. "What Silas is saying is that Gwenn is correct. The ghosts are not acting on their own. You had a lamp that could implicate the human behind this, so it had to be retrieved. That was their mission, not attacking you, just getting the lamp. Which also makes me wonder what they did with it. How could a ghost transport it? Or did they hide it for someone else to grab later?"

"Then we go back to Spook Rock and poke around," Mutther said. "It could still be there."

Sebastian shook his head. "No. They'd have to get it out fast or risk us going back for it. Still, it might be good to scour the area. We might discover a trail the human left behind."

"I'll send some of my clan to comb the area," Silas said. He went out to the hall to call it in to his people.

"If they'd already gotten the lamp, then why stick around? And why not attack me anyway? Why show themselves at all?" My mind churned with possibilities. One stood out. "My light."

Energy and hope lifted my spirits.

"Yes," Sebastian said. "You could be onto something."

"Then fill the rest of us in," Nick said, scowling.

"When Hulda and I went to the Underworld, she told me the dead would be attracted to the light of my aura, my energy field. They'd try to latch on to catch a ride out of there. We always had to be careful to keep a low profile. The pirates wanted a glimpse of my light. They want out of wherever they are and think I might be their ride." This changed a lot of my perception of the ghosts and the killings. Gwenn and I had to talk through this. "It seems to me we're at a point where there are several avenues to explore. The map isn't giving up its secrets. Until we can coax the knowledge from it, we have to do this the old-fashioned way."

"Break into teams," Silas said, entering the room after finishing his call. "I've already sent word to have Spook Rock searched. The rest of us could look at the places on the map that might be good spots for a pirate to hang out. We go there to sift through the scents, see if anything unusual pops up."

Sebastian started pacing. With all the pacing we'd done today, he'd have to look for a new area rug to put on the hardwood floor. "Janda," he said, "what do you recall about the scent on the lamp?"

"Not much." I racked my brain, trying to replay the scene in my head. "It was an antique kerosene lamp. Possibly from the historical society. Or he could have brought it with him. I'm not sure. It had a brass base and top with a long metal handle. I didn't place the scent of the person, only that whoever it was had been near the river. It smelled like the Hudson River water." I shook my head. "Sorry. That's all I remember."

"Hold on," Mutther said. "Didn't you say the glass was broken on it?"

"Yeah. So?"

"The shards could have fingerprints," he said. "Our man, Detective Brent, could run the prints if there are any."

"Wouldn't he have already lifted prints?" I said.

"Not if, like the rest of us, he assumed it was Stanley's," Mutther said.

"Gwenn was sweeping everything up to put in the dumpster. I can call her to tell her we're on our way and not to toss them in the trash." I pulled my cell from my pocket, shook off a bit of dirt from one of the plants, and dialed the number she'd given me. It rang several times before she picked up.

"Janda! Help! I think they're here." She lowered her voice. "This isn't just ghosts. I saw a guy when I looked out the upstairs window. I'm working on some protection spells, but it may be too late. I think they're in the house. I've boxed myself into a rather unfortunate corner, literally."

The others heard her over my phone and flew into action. Uncle Damon was on his phone barking orders and making it hard to hear Gwenn.

"Hold on, Gwenn," I said. "We're coming."

Nick had raced out. I heard his motorcycle peeling out of the driveway. Silas was back on his phone, and Sebastian had vanished.

"My boys are near there," Uncle Damon said. "They're on their way, but we'd better hurry to give them backup."

I ran out to Miss Kitty. I worried how a single witch could defend herself against six pirate ghosts and at least one murderous human. Mutther had the bike Sebastian had given him and was already revving it while Uncle Damon and Silas got into their cars and sped off.

I nodded to Mutther as I hopped on Miss Kitty, and he took the lead. I caught a glimpse of my great-great-grand-mother right before we tore through the protective barrier. She made a swirling motion with her hands and let loose a ball of light that landed on my shoulder and spread over my entire body like armor. I didn't realize she could even cast a spell as a ghost and dreaded the thought of what it had cost her to do it.

I heard her like a whisper in the wind but caught every word.

Put on the armor of God so that you can make your stand against the devil's schemes.

If Hulda was quoting the Bible, then we were in big trouble.

CHAPTER 10
LOSSES

Smoke billowed through Sleepy Hollow's night sky, hovering over the town and threatening to choke us as we approached Grove Street. I coughed but kept going. Firetrucks ran hoses from the hydrant and the pumper truck to douse the flames shooting from the roof of the historical society.

"Gwenn!" I raced up the front steps only to have Mutther drag me back.

"You can't go in there."

"Here! We're up here!" Gwenn shouted, waving her hand out the small window in the upper tower. "We're trapped!"

Mutther wrenched me away from the porch. "Stay put, Janda!" He ran past the firefighters setting up the hoses and bounded into the burning building.

The hook and ladder couldn't get close enough to reach the upper window where Gwenn was trapped. I ran to the back of the house and stopped short at what I saw. Uncle Damon was fending off a ghost that was lobbing fireballs at him. Several other ghosts did the same to anyone attempting to go near them.

"What the hell?"

I pulled a knife from the special casing in my boot and aimed for the ghost attacking Uncle Damon. The blade soared past my uncle and briefly lodged in the fireball the apparition held in his hands. The ball reshaped itself, and the knife dropped to the ground. The ghost turned toward me, making a loud screeching noise worse than running fingernails over slate. It reverberated through my body. I pushed the sensation aside and rushed forward. The pirate ghost released the fireball to the dirt, creating a tiny crater, then shrank back and disappeared. It left behind a puff of vapor that split apart and faded into the shadows. I wasn't sure if the pirate had dropped back to recover for another surge. I took no chances and moved cautiously forward. The apparition didn't strike. I had no clue where it had gone.

Several trees had caught fire during the fighting, but the battle had ceased. Burning debris littered the lawn. The smell of burnt flesh filled the air. I scanned the area for possible attacks. None came.

One-by-one, the remaining ghosts stretched their arms in my direction, letting out a plaintive wail that sent shivers down my spine, and then they evaporated.

And there he was, silhouetted against the burning branches of a large oak tree—the Headless Horseman.

He paused to glare at me, hatred sizzling in his flaming skull. The fiery balls that made up his eyes flared within dark sockets. He was flame and fury, light and dark. He sat upon his charcoal black horse that pranced in place, spewing fire from its nostrils. With a pull on the reins, the Horseman sped into the trees leading to the Old Croton

Aqueduct trail, pausing long enough to reach down and hoist a man up from the ground and carry him off. Three wolves broke off from the aftermath of the melee and gave chase. They wouldn't catch him, but I understood why they tried anyway.

I didn't get a good look at the man before he was whisked away, but he seemed average in stature, and his age was neither old nor young. There didn't appear to be anything remarkable about him except for one thing. He held a sword, which he passed to the Horseman. I prayed I was wrong but was sure I was right. The Headless Horseman was once again in possession of his powerful sword.

All around me, men and women, pack and clan members, lay strewn across the back lawn, where they cradled their scorched limbs and let out occasional moans. Some were badly hurt but would survive. A few had shifted back from their animal form. I wondered what the neighbors thought of it all. Public relations would have their hands full.

I sprinted to the rear entrance, only to be stopped short once more by Mutther. His face was smudged with soot, his pant legs singed, but his forearms caught my attention, as well as his shirt that rippled unevenly across his chest. I might not have picked up on the differences if I hadn't seen him earlier. I'd swear he'd shifted, or partially at any rate, but it wasn't a shift I recognized. His skin had a green-gray tint, and the texture appeared coarse. When he pelted down the back steps, those features disappeared.

He had Gwenn with him. She was wheezing and gasping for air while hugging Hudson. The cat was wrapped in a wet towel and didn't seem happy about it, but she kept a firm grip on him. Mutther steered her to a safe place away from all the commotion. Behind him came my cousin Gabe, carrying his brother, Jake.

"No!" Uncle Damon rushed forward to meet them. They placed Jake carefully on the ground. Two paramedics began administering CPR. I recognized them as members of Nick's pack. They were relentless in their efforts to revive Jake, but he was gone.

Uncle Damon slumped beside his dead son. Gabe gathered them both in a tight hug. The others gave the grieving men space and went off to tend to the wounded.

I stood there, barely hearing my name being called. My chest ached. I couldn't move.

"Come," Sebastian said.

He wrapped his arm around me and led me away. The hum of activity was a massive blur. I vaguely registered Gwen being treated by a young woman who tried to get her to release Hudson but failed. Mutther started toward me, but Sebastian waved him off.

"Bring Gwenn back to my house when she's ready," he said, not waiting for Mutther to respond.

I stumbled twice, but Sebastian kept me from falling. We wove through the crowd filling the street. Uncle Damon's pack members filed past us to form a protective ring around their leader. Nick's pack held the gawkers at bay, and members from Silas's clan stood guard around the perimeter. I could have told them the threat had left, but I couldn't find the words.

Sebastian didn't have his car there, so we borrowed one from a woman in overalls who was part of Silas's clan. She was the mechanic who maintained Sebastian's small collection of vehicles. Some part of me wondered how Sebastian had arrived without a car, but the thought slipped away into the numbness overtaking me. I was loaded into the mini-van, and only after I was buckled did I think of Miss Kitty. "Wait. My bike."

Sebastian took the key from me and handed it off to the woman whose mini-van we had commandeered. She took the key and presumably went to find Miss Kitty. It took some maneuvering, but he managed to steer the van onto Neparan Road and away from the scene of destruction.

I leaned back in the seat and shut my eyes. God, I so wanted Alex with me. The Horseman had ruined our lives and didn't seem likely to stop until he got what he wanted. His mask, though, was out of my reach, just as Alex was.

The drive back to Sebastian's was uneventful. I didn't even recall arriving. I was in the high-back chair beside the fireplace with a patchwork quilt wrapped around me. Sebastian had left and soon returned with the key to Miss Kitty. I held it in my palm and fingered it mindlessly before stuffing it in my back pocket. My jacket was lying on the loveseat. Maybe I'd taken it off, or maybe Sebastian had done it. The tiny plants I'd been carrying around all day had fallen onto the velvet cushions. Sebastian tried to get me to drink some wine, but I couldn't take a sip.

I glanced at him as he hovered over me, tucking the quilt around my shivering body. "When will it end?" I whispered.

He touched my cheek. "When we finish him for good."

"But he has his sword again."

"It doesn't matter." He went for his usual stress reliever of a glass of wine, bringing it slowly to his lips and closing his eyes.

I absently fingered the quilt, gazing at the blocks of fabric held together by a multitude of nearly invisible stitches. I wondered who had given it to Sebastian. The person who had made it was long dead.

He had suffered many losses in his lifetime, both as a human and a vampire, yet he kept going. He continued to find purpose in his existence, despite losing the love of his life. I couldn't fathom how he did it. How did you go on when those you love kept dying?

"You just do," he said.

I jerked my head around to face him. "Oh, sorry. I didn't realize I'd spoken out loud."

"I'm not surprised. Tonight's losses have you reliving what happened to you and Alex. Trust me when I say you will survive this ordeal."

I pulled my knees up to my chest and gazed into the fire. "How can you be so sure? How can any of us know what lies ahead?" I turned toward him. "I don't think I want to keep on trying. I'm so tired. All I want is to be with Alex."

Sebastian grabbed me by the shoulders and met my gaze with piercing coldness.

"You will *never* give up," he said. "I won't let you!"

The fierceness of his tone gave me a jolt. I held back the moisture gathering at the rim of my eyelids that threatened to break free.

He knelt in front of me, staring directly into my eyes. He was drawing on the bond that linked us.

"This isn't just about you," he said, "and you'd best remember that. You need a break. I get it. Who doesn't? But we are in this together. That's how I know you'll pull through." He rose and stoked the fire. "For now, rest. Gwenn will be here soon, so I must prepare her a room."

He left me to ponder what he'd said. It was true. This wasn't just about me. Too many had died or been hurt. I just didn't know what I could do.

I smelled her before I saw her. That light-perfumed scent of gardenias drifted in my direction. My great-great-grandmother settled on the loveseat next to my coat and pushed the tiny plants into a little pile. The effort of moving the plants seemed to drain her. The outer edges of her body blurred momentarily.

"We need to hang those up so they can dry properly."

"Hi, Grandma." My voice was low and soft. I barely looked at her, although I noticed her movements seemed slower and more deliberate than usual.

She leaned toward me and gently patted my arm. "It's time we had our chat."

My shoulders slumped. "I can't. Not right now."

"I understand what you're feeling. You're exhausted, mentally and physically. You think the Headless Horseman has won. You can't imagine life without Alex. And you're tired of fighting."

"Pretty much. So what do I do next when I don't have any energy for a damn thing?"

"You take the fight to him."

I sighed. "I know you've been listening to what the Council's been saying, so you must know we're out of our depths here. For every question we get answered, we have ten more. He's always a step ahead of us. He's well hidden. He's picking us off and creating dissension. How the hell do we take the fight to him? Not to mention he can't be killed."

She shook her head. "He's afraid of you. He's afraid for a good reason. You can destroy him."

"How?"

Hulda tilted her head, listening. "Blast. We must talk, Janda." She faded into nothing but whispered to me as she went. "I love you, Granddaughter."

"I love you too, Grandma."

The kitchen door slammed, and footsteps pounded down the hall. I didn't bother to move. I expected Mutther to bring Gwenn. I didn't expect my uncle, who stood for a moment in the doorway, his chest heaving.

"There you are," Uncle Damon said, crossing the room and pulling me into an enormous hug. "I couldn't feel your bond. You scared the shit out of me!" He stroked my hair, while still holding me. "I can't lose you, too."

I extricated myself enough to hug him back. "I have a pack bond?" I'd never had any sense of connection with his pack members.

"You have a special bond with me," he said, finally releasing me and sitting smack dab on the plants Hulda had carefully pushed into a pile. "I keep your bond separate from the pack. I learned early on not to lump you in with the others. You're unique and, frankly, scary."

"I'm scary?"

"You sure as hell are," he said. "You saved our hides tonight. Those ghosts took one look at you and your glowing armor and ran. I wish we hadn't lost Jake." He bent his head over his knees, his shoulders sagged, and his breaths came out in uneven gasps.

"I don't know what you're talking about that I saved you all, but you shouldn't be here. You need to be with Gabe and take care of the arrangements for Jake's burial. I'll be fine, and I'll come to the funeral. I need to be with our family." I grabbed his hand and squeezed. "Whatever you need from me, just say the word."

He kissed the top of my head then reached for my hand and gave it a quick squeeze.

"I need you to be safe, but more importantly, I need you to stand your ground and fight. We all need you." He hugged me and left to face the painful task of saying goodbye to his youngest son.

I pondered what he'd said. The pack that had kept me

at arm's length all during my childhood needed me. I couldn't wrap my head around the concept. I'd been wrong about my uncle's feelings for me back then, and we'd found our way to a better place to communicate those feelings. Beyond that, I remained someone who wasn't fully bonded with the pack. They had come to accept me once Asher, my childhood nemesis, had been exposed and his plans thwarted. Alex fought and killed him. It was no great loss to either the pack or our community. In the aftermath of the drama surrounding Alex, I'd also gained a modicum of respect from Silas and his clan after revealing that his nephew, Leon, had plans to overthrow him. Leon remained in the supernatural prison hidden in the depths of Sleepy Hollow. I'd been to the prison, which was a nasty place to end up.

Despite those victories, we had a long way to go in our fight against the Headless Horseman. My uncle was right about one thing.

It was time to fight back.

CHAPTER 11

SECRETS

It was well past midnight. The numbness in my body had settled into a gnawing ache in my chest. My brain was still a bit foggy, and I found myself questioning some of what had happened, like Mutther's skin transformation. I shook off the notion of Mutther shifting in some weird way. I had to be present for my uncle. I'd offered to go with him to help with the funeral arrangements, but he was adamant I remain at Sebastian's. Mutther wasn't back with Gwenn yet, and Sebastian wandered around upstairs, preparing a guest room for her. I unwound the quilt that had tangled around my legs and went in search of Hulda.

Our basement lab was cold. The fire had all but gone out. I placed the wilted plants on the table and loaded more wood on top of the old, stoking it until the sparks attached themselves to the logs and the glow of the embers grew into a low flame. The logs ignited in earnest after a few moments, and heat spread out into the room.

"Are you here?" I called to Hulda while bundling the

plants and hanging them on pegs embedded in the overhead beams.

"Yes," she said.

The beautiful, strong Hulda, the witch of Sleepy Hollow, stood before me in a less refined form than usual. Her edges seemed blurred and wavy.

"What's happening to you?"

She shrugged. "I overdid it, I suppose. No need to fuss. I'll be fine."

I raised my brows. "This is not okay." I waved my hand in her general direction. "What did you do?"

"Don't be cross. I'll explain. I've been trying to tell you, but we keep getting interrupted."

"Then you better speak fast. Mutther will be bringing Gwenn here any moment."

"She's a good witch," Hulda said. "You could learn a great deal from her, especially if I'm not around anymore."

"Stop right there." I examined her more closely. Nothing had changed during the last few minutes. She didn't seem likely to disappear, but she had me worried. "Why wouldn't you be around anymore?"

"Sit," she said, pointing to the stool. "I've expended a lot of energy to do some investigating. First"—she held up a hand—"don't interrupt me, or we may not get to the heart of the matter, and I desperately need you to understand what is taking place around you."

I made a zipping motion with my fingers across my lips and waited.

"I hazarded a visit to the Underworld."

I jumped off the stool. "You went without me?"

Hulda frowned. "Didn't I say not to interrupt me?"

"That was before you told me you went to the Underworld."

She sighed, and tiny wisps of fog circled in front of her before becoming one with the rest of the air in the room. "I didn't have the energy to take you with me. It was difficult enough on my own, but I had to discover why it's been so hard to open the portal to go there."

"And?" I returned to my seat but sat on the edge.

"It has to do with my sister."

"So you *do* have a sister!"

Hulda stared at me intently. "Yes. I have a sister. She's also a witch and a huge problem right now."

I bit my lip to keep from blurting out more questions that would only slow us down and let her continue.

"The remarks in the journal are hers. She and I used to work together on herbal remedies and such. She's a gifted witch. But she fell for the wrong man and was betrayed. No one wrongs my sister and gets away with it, so she cursed him and his crew so they would never find peace."

"Let me guess, the pirates. She cursed the pirates who killed my cousin and burned the historical society."

She shook her head. "The murderer is using them. But, Janda, they are trapped here. They can only crossover if they have the coins to pay the Ferryman. And I am not speaking of Alex, our underground ferryman. I'm talking about the one who sets you on your path out of the Underworld. What's worse is the Headless Horseman has somehow found a way to control them and the one doing the killings."

"Oh, shit," I said.

"Yes. You see the problem?"

"I see a lot of problems, like how is the Horseman controlling them, and how do we break the curse? For that matter, what kind of curse is it? Not to mention, who is this mysterious killer?"

Hulda glided back and forth across the room several times, which was her version of pacing. It was hard to watch because each time she turned, her form blurred and she left part of it behind in an incorporeal trail.

"The human is someone your Council can focus on while we deal with the greater problem. My sister is the inadvertent catalyst who started this debacle. We have to get her to undo the curse on the pirates. Once that happens, the pirates will gain their payment for passage through the Underworld. That brings me to the next thing. We could use this to get Alex out."

My breath caught. "We can get him out? Tell me what to do."

"Patience. We can't jump into this without careful planning. We risk losing everything if we let our feelings control our actions." She had stopped pacing and stood still, waiting for her astral body to come together.

"Okay. Fine. Where do we start?"

"We talk to my sister."

I stood. "I'm ready. Where is she? Just don't tell me she's in the Underworld."

"Thankfully, she is not. She tends to hang around the riverbank where she keeps an eye on the pirates."

"How come I never knew that? Shouldn't the Council already have that information?"

She shrugged. "For the most part, she keeps to herself and doesn't draw attention."

"Why do I feel there's more to this than you're telling me?"

"You aren't wrong. Things are complicated between my sister and me. She blames me for the betrayal. Consequently, she has made it so that I am also part of this curse, which also affects you."

"No!" The pieces were falling into place and not in a good way. "She's why I can't reach Alex?"

Hulda nodded.

"I'll kill her."

"She's already dead. But I do understand your feelings. I'm not happy with her either."

"Not happy? That doesn't begin to cover it." I clenched my fists and took several long breaths to clear the rage surging through me. "She's a woman scorned. Of course she would want those responsible to suffer. I get it, but what is different now? We've been able to travel between the worlds before but not now. Why? How do we fix it?"

"As I understand it, the curse has been rather dormant. That allowed us to travel unimpeded until recently. Someone is actively searching for the coins. That activity has caused the curse to surge in strength." Hulda paused. "I'm rather impressed with my sister, actually. It's quite an accomplishment to weave a reactive spell like this one. It also means I can't teach you how to undo it. We will have to first get her to listen to us, and then we must convince her it's time for her to let go of the hurt and anger so the curse will break."

"I'm all for getting her to remove the curse, but how will that help us get Alex out?"

"Once the curse is lifted, you and I will be able to travel between the realms so long as there aren't any other obstacles."

"But neither of us can bring him with us when we return. How does he get out?"

"You can take objects through, but bringing people out is different. You may or may not be able to do it safely. But he can come out on his own if a tunnel is created that he could use. It is tricky. The pirates want to go into the portal.

If Alex can travel in the other direction, then he stands a chance of escaping."

My mind reeled with what Hulda was saying. I latched on to the part where Alex had a way home.

"Janda," Hulda said, "did you hear me?"

I blinked. "Sorry. Just trying to absorb it all."

"I said that our opportunity would be gone forever if we can't rescue Alex before midnight on October 31. After that, there will be nothing we can do. Alex will never return."

"That's in three days!" My stomach clenched. Bile rose in my throat. If I had a paper bag handy, I would have stuck my face in it. I was on the verge of hyperventilating.

Hulda paused to glance up at the ceiling. "We have company. I need time to prepare to face my sister. I'm useless in this state. If I meet her now, we won't succeed. We will go tomorrow night.

She began to fade away.

"Wait," I said. "You still haven't told me what happened to drain you so badly."

"It turns out that I was able to get into the Underworld, but the return trip was not easy. I met with Maude to discuss that we may need the mask piece she's been keeping for us. I hope that's not the case, but we must be prepared to deal with the Headless Horseman. The mask could be used as bait."

"Did you see Alex?"

"Sorry. I didn't see him."

I gave her a slight nod.

Hulda reached out to me, her palm cupping my cheek. She sent some energy through the contact that gave me comfort and warmth.

"I wish I could have seen him," she said. "I left word for him so he'd know what we're doing on this side. He was busy taking a group through the underground escape route. He's had a rough time keeping the passageways clear."

I still didn't understand all of what Alex did or who he helped. On the one hand, he was an assistant to the official Ferryman—the one who gathered souls for passage across the river dividing the Underworld and the Hereafter. The Ferryman took those souls who could pay him over to the other side. Those who couldn't pay were stuck in the Underworld town until they either came up with proper payment or atoned for whatever held them back on their journey.

But Alex's side hustle was acting as an underground ferryman—the guide for souls who couldn't pay the true Ferryman. Alex's job was dangerous. I dreaded the thought of him getting caught aiding souls who wanted to circumvent the official channels. The underground ferryman job was part of Maude's secretive services.

In a way, Alex had a similar purpose in the Underworld as he did here, where he ran a safe room and security business. For all his hard edges, he wanted to help people. He would sacrifice himself to give aid to those less fortunate. I was proud of him for it but also frustrated. By agreeing to be a ferryman and moving people through the Underworld, he had bound himself so that he couldn't use those routes for himself. We had to find a way to get him out before time ran out.

The thud of feet treading through the hall above us grew louder. Muffled voices filtered down through the old wooden planks.

"Go," Hulda said. "I'll see you after the next sunset. You should rest before we go looking for my sister. Both of us must be in top form. She is not to be trifled with. You can find me along the riverbank near the aqueduct trail. Be careful. The Horseman is angry and getting desperate. There's no saying what he will do if he finds you."

The door at the top of the stairs cracked open.

"Janda," Sebastian said. "Can you join us?"

My link to Sebastian made it difficult to hide my presence, not that I was trying to do that, but my emotions were running high at the moment, which acted like a beacon for him to find me. "Be right there," I said.

Hulda looked longingly up to where Sebastian waited. She stepped forward as if to go to him but held back then gave me a brief nod before disappearing.

I placed the screen across the fireplace and made my way up the narrow wooden steps to the first floor.

Sebastian narrowed his eyes at me. "What's wrong?" he said. "Your heart rate is up."

"Nothing I can't deal with on my own, thanks."

His fangs protruded.

"Right. Like that's going to scare me." I chuckled as he stomped away from me. He could be overbearing, but he meant well. He knew I was hiding something and was itching to get me to share it with him. If he had any clue what Hulda and I were about to attempt, he would never leave my side. I'd give him enough information to keep him busy while I slipped away tomorrow to do some ghost hunting.

CHAPTER 12
A GATHERING STORM

The grumbling ceased as soon as I entered the study, which also served as Sebastian's temporary war room for the Council. Silas, Mutther, Nick, and my cousin Gabe argued around the desk. Gwenn sat on the outer edge of the verbal storm with Hudson on her lap.

"Hey," she said, filling the lull. "Are you okay?"

"I should be asking you that."

"I got caught by surprise. It was stupid of me. I'm a better witch than this. I'm so mad at myself but promise I won't make the same mistake again. At the time, I was more worried about Hudson." She stroked the Bengal feline digging its claws into her leg in a kneading motion. "Thanks to your cousins and Mutther, we made it out okay."

"I'm glad," I said.

I went to Gabe, who wrapped me in a tight hug. I'm not the hugging type, but since Alex came along, I'd opened up more to the warm and fuzzy emotions invoked by hugs. Alex taught me about family and that I didn't have to go it alone. Both Gabe and I needed the comfort of family.

I buried my face in his shoulder. "I'm sorry I wasn't there for you."

The words caught in my throat. I felt his tear fall onto my forehead but didn't bother to brush it away. His pain echoed my own.

"Not your fault," he said, releasing a long, shuddering breath and giving me another hug.

I stepped back from him and met his gaze. "We're going to get the bastard."

"That's what we were discussing before you came in," Mutther said. "We seem to be at an impasse. There's no progress on the Horseman's whereabouts, and we don't know how to fight ghosts."

"The historical society suffered a great deal of fire and smoke damage," Silas said. "Any evidence that remained has surely been destroyed."

I glanced over at Gwenn, my mind back on the topic of discussion and away from the ache in my heart. "Were you able to salvage the glass shards?"

"Oh, yes. A few, anyway. I don't know if it will help or not." She held out a small bundle wrapped in cloth tucked by her side.

I took it and unfolded the fabric to reveal two fragments of glass. I raised it to my nose, inhaling several times. "It's there, but it's incredibly faint. It's him, the human who's working with the Horseman."

I passed the bundle to Nick, who sniffed and passed it on to Mutther. One after the other, they examined the glass. Each shook their head.

"Damn. I was hoping one of you would recognize the scent." I slumped onto the loveseat. Hudson leaped from Gwenn's lap to mine. I pet him until he started digging into my leg. "Sorry, bud. I'm not a human pincushion." I passed him back to Gwenn.

Sebastian held the bundle of glass, examining it under the light of his desk lamp. "I've already put in a call to Detective Brent. He's sending Shawn over to talk with us about our next step." He took the seldom-used phone from his pocket and started texting. "I'm messaging him about the glass before Shawn leaves. Maybe they can pull a print from it. The residents of Sleepy Hollow had quite a scare and wanted an explanation. It's giving us a PR nightmare."

"I'd like an explanation, too," I said. "That was some crazy crap going down, and I think it was a setup. The attackers were after my cousins, and the fire was a diversion."

Gabe's head snapped up. "We were the targets and not Gwenn?"

"It's possible," I said. "You had the sword."

"What?" Mutther said. "I thought that was under lock and key."

Gabe flushed. "It was until we got orders to move it. Jake didn't want to mess with it. I told him he worried too much. He was right. It's my fault he's dead."

I knew better than to try to tell him otherwise. He had made up his mind and would bear the burden of guilt for a very long time, even though it wasn't true.

"Who gave the order?" I said. "Maybe we have a traitor in our midst."

Gwenn had a sullen expression as she faced everyone. "It's my fault. I suggested we move all items with an element of supernatural power to a secure storage vault. It was evident after the first attack at the historical society that valuable relics had to be protected."

"No one is to blame," Sebastian said. "All of you are being too hard on yourselves. The Council agreed with Gwenn. Besides, Damon wasn't comfortable hanging on to the sword any longer. We were well aware that wherever the sword ended up would be a target for the Horseman, but we didn't anticipate it would be so soon. We'd been working on a secure vault for some time now."

"It's true," Silas said. "We knew this kind of thing might happen. We've been procuring too many magical artifacts. A vault was the best solution."

"Gwenn was going to add some spells for protection, along with our other lines of defense," Sebastian said. "Unfortunately, I feel Janda is correct. We must have someone who sympathizes with the Horseman and knew the sword was being transported."

"But why hit us at the historical society?" Gabe said. "Stopping there wasn't planned."

"I'd bet money you were followed," Nick said. "Although that wouldn't give the arsonist much time to get the fire started before you were in the area, so hell, I don't know."

"Or the fire was started first because they knew my cousins would be going by there and would stop to help." My mind raced through several possibilities, including Gwenn being the culprit. I quickly discarded that theory. "Someone close to us who knew that the Council was moving artifacts might be responsible," I said, thinking out loud.

"Maybe it wasn't someone close to us," Gabe said. "It was common knowledge the vault was being constructed near the prison. After the safe was completed, we started bringing items in regularly. We only had a few more security measures to add, such as Gwenn's spells, but it was already secure. Once an item goes into it, no one is getting it out very easily."

"It wasn't common knowledge for me," I said. "Did the rest of you know?" I glared at each of them in turn. "That's just great. I'm the last to know. Fine. Is there anything else I don't know but should?"

My temper was getting the better of me, which was sending the fight signal to my lykoi. I did my best to ease off the whole heading-into-battle emotion since the others were beginning to look on edge with my outburst and were probably keeping their inner animals in check. I felt guilty about it, but that didn't mean I wasn't still pissed off with them.

Sebastian's phone buzzed. "Shawn is here. I'll be right back."

He went off to escort the officer through the protective barrier.

"Does he have to do that for everyone who comes here?" I said.

I knew he had to lead Mutther and me the first time. All I needed was to be able to see the house. The barrier recognized my DNA link to Hulda and let me glide right through. It was harder for Mutther, but he was able to get here on his own now. It made me wonder if spells had some kind of artificial intelligence encoded in them. Until now, I hadn't thought about how the others could find the house and get through its protections.

Silas answered me. "It's necessary, at least for the first time a person visits. Afterward, Sebastian only has to be nearby for us to get through. Initially, he gave us vague directions on where to go and met us to enable our passage to the house. It was all rather strange traveling as if we were pushing fog out of our way—an extremely dense fog. It kept surrounding us as we moved, making us lose our bearings. I could imagine being lost in it forever." He shivered. "Frankly, I'm amazed he's even allowing us to come here at all. He's never liked disclosing where he lives. He's very protective of you, Janda. That's why we've met here instead of at the Sleepy Hollow Hunter headquarters. He feels better with the extra layers of security he has here."

"But I come and go all the time. Sebastian can't keep protective spells around me every minute of the day." The room got overly quiet right then, and I finally caught on. "Are you kidding me?" My voice rose along with my temper. "He's been having me followed!"

The feeling of someone being nearby as I left the house suddenly made sense. I ground my teeth.

"Not all the time, or we might have caught the lantern thief when you were out at Spook Rock. We still kick ourselves for that slip," Gabe said. "Don't be hard on us. You have to know you're the one with the bull's-eye on your back. It makes sense to keep close tabs on your whereabouts. In case you haven't noticed, where you go, trouble is close behind. We follow you, and you lead us to the bad guys."

"You're saying I'm the bait? I don't know what makes me angrier, not being told I'm the bait or that you're following me."

The only thing that saved their hides was Officer Shawn, who stepped into the room with Angie, our new public relations person.

Angie ran up and hugged me. "Isn't it exciting? I'm working with you now. I can't believe it."

She beamed, and her radiant energy snuffed out my terrible mood in an instant.

She'd cut her hair into a short, professional-style bob and wore dark pants, a white button-down shirt, and a black blazer. She was smart enough to avoid wearing heels and wore black leather loafers instead. She learned that you never knew when you might have to run from something evil. She'd survived the attack from the Mad Monk some months earlier. I also thought she'd be the one to run *after* an attacker, heels or not. She was tough and a fighter. We'd kept in touch since Mutther and I rescued her and her sister, and I wanted to do what I could to make life easier for her.

"Yeah, it's great," I said.

I was truly happy for her. She was perfect for the job. She was a recent college grad about fifteen years younger than me, who was grateful for the money her new position would bring to her family.

"I'm not so sure you got the best end of the bargain with all that's going on, but I suppose that's why the Council hired you," I said. "I hope you have some ideas for us."

"As a matter of fact," Shawn said, "we were going over a few of them on the way here. Angie is pretty good at spinning tales based on fact that are believable enough to satisfy the people of Sleepy Hollow."

The look he gave Angie left no doubt she had an admirer. He was a rookie cop on his first big assignment. His uniform was crisp, his shoes polished, and his gun handy at his side.

I coughed to regain his attention. "Let's hear it."

Shawn went to sit near Gwenn, and Angie stood poised by the fireplace with her full attention on Gwenn. The rest of us stood around the trio. If Sebastian kept holding meetings here, he would have to invest in better seating arrangements. There weren't enough seats for everyone. I considered asking him about hauling in the dining room table and chairs. It wasn't like he ate much, so why have a dining room? But he insisted on formalities and would most likely scoff at my suggestion, so I didn't bother asking.

Shawn seemed to be doing his best to be professional under the scrutiny of a room full of Council members. "First, we have to hear the details of what happened," he said, withdrawing a small black notebook from his inner jacket pocket. "I have my notes from Detective Brent, but I'm sorry, I have to hear the story from you."

He glanced over at Gabe. "I know this will be difficult for you. If you want to leave the room, but all means, I understand. On the other hand, it would be helpful if you could assist Gwenn with her narrative. That way, I won't have to interview you separately."

He pulled out a pen to take notes and began flipping the pages to a new section. "Once we have the facts, Angie will be better able to do her job. Then we can turn to dusting the glass Detective Brent mentioned and running any prints through the database." He tucked a black case against the chair leg and waited for Gwenn.

Angie nodded to Gwenn encouragingly. "Anything at all that you can tell us would be helpful."

Sebastian gave Gwenn a glass of water. She took a sip and settled into her chair, drawing Hudson closer into her lap. He lifted his head, and I swear he talked to her. She glanced at me and grinned. Yup. He'd sent her a telepathic message. I hoped he'd told her not to mention that the two of us intended to meet to discuss a strategy for chasing the pirate ghosts. It would be difficult enough to elude my protective shadows without them being clued into our intentions. I hadn't had a chance to discuss it with Hulda, but I was confident she would be good with Gwenn tagging along with me when we met by the river. This meeting was about the witches in my family and a distant aunt I didn't know existed. There was no way I'd let any of the others ruin it by following me.

CHAPTER 13
GWENN'S STORY

I looked around the room at the others, sensing the heightened level of tension and frustration. You could feel it in the air, crackling invisibly like electricity seeking a spot to strike. The study wasn't a small room by any means. Its large double doors opened onto walls of books, and an enormous oak library table sat on one side of the room for Sebastian to use as his desk. The tooled leather writing surface of the desk had been used by him for well over a hundred years. The ornate carvings around the edges included a Green Man mask that fit Sebastian's mystique. The lavishly carved fireplace took up a significant portion of the wall opposite the floor-length windows covered in heavy forest green velvet. The marble mantle held numerous candles in brass holders. The only other furniture pieces were the loveseat and two wingback chairs that had also been upholstered in rich velvet.

Yet at this moment, all those details were dwarfed by the handful of supernatural people occupying the space, making it seem cramped. Each of them had the ability to kill in seconds flat. Jake had been just as lethal. Why, then, had he died? I was keen to hear what happened inside the historical society building when the ghosts attacked.

I leaned against a wooden column that partitioned the bookshelves, staying back from the interview so as not to distract anyone.

Gwenn began retelling the events. "Like I said to the others, I was stupid. The ghosts caught me off-guard. I was preoccupied in the upper tower with scrubbing the floor. I got up to stretch and caught sight of a man walking toward the front door."

"Couldn't you have used a cleaning spell? Why do the manual labor?" Shawn said.

He didn't break eye contact with Gwenn when he spoke. I wondered why he sounded accusatory. I almost forgot about not being distracting and was about to ask what he was suggesting when Gwenn straightened and gave him a steely glare.

"I doubt you would understand this, Officer Shawn, but not every witch will use magic for menial tasks. The use of magic always has a price, so why cast a spell when you could simply do the chore yourself?" She wasn't rude, but her tone let it be known she didn't like the line of questioning.

She stroked Hudson, who purred loudly at Gwenn and then turned his narrowed gaze on Shawn. The cat obviously disapproved of Shawn's tactics, just as I did.

"Forgive the question," Shawn said. "All avenues must be explored." He stared down at Hudson and cleared his throat. "So, let me recap. You were cleaning. You stood and noticed someone approaching from the front. Is that correct?"

"Yes," Gwenn said. "He didn't seem like a threat. I was

going to meet him at the door to tell him we were closed, but a sound from within the building made me pause."

"What sound was that?" Shawn said.

Gwenn shifted Hudson, who wasn't giving up his cozy spot on her lap. "I'm not sure what it was exactly. There was a slight popping, like a large bubble bursting. All I know is it wasn't a sound that you'd expect in an old house. Creaks. Groans. Those would be normal. This was not normal."

Sebastian crossed the room to stand behind Shawn. "It's possible you heard the sound air makes when a spirit appears. I would venture to say it was our pirate ghosts entering the premises."

"Really?" I said, unable to keep myself from interrupting. "I don't hear that with Hulda."

"Hulda is one ghost," Sebastian said. "We are talking about six."

This gave me a different perspective on what we were dealing with and didn't make me happy. Hulda had created a portal to enter and exit the Underworld using her special ability. Otherwise, she had to maintain proximity to the general area where she'd lived while human. Were the ghosts doing something similar to a portal to get around Sleepy Hollow, or had they lived in this area at one point in time?

"Damn the ghosts. They didn't kill my brother. A human killed him!" Gabe growled, and his inner wolf surfaced. "We didn't see any ghosts cuntil after we got inside and started up the stairs. They came at us as a group as we made our way to Gwenn. We were almost on the upper landing when things went bad. You could see them blending together and pushing their way toward us. It was freaky. Like they were acting collectively with a single purpose. Then this guy appeared from behind us. He had to have already been up there, and we were too preoccupied to notice. He stabbed Jake and ripped the sword away from him. I hate that sword! We couldn't leave it in the car, which made Jake the one they went after, not me. I'm the oldest. The sword was my task, not his!"

Gabe clenched his fists against his thighs. "I was busy forcing the ghosts back away from the stairs so Jake could reach Gwenn. The next thing I knew, Jake collapsed, and the guy rammed into me and went down the steps, sword in hand. The ghosts parted to let him pass, then formed a protective wall behind him as they escaped. It's my fault they got away with the sword, but I had to help my brother."

His shoulders slumped as he lowered his voice. "But I couldn't save him. He's gone."

"You did the right thing," Mutther said. "I saw them go out the rear of the building but didn't chase them. I didn't realize you were there. I had to go to Gwenn. That's when I found you holding onto Jake, and Gwenn was shouting from the other room. Someone had barricaded her inside by shoving a broom through the old door handle. I tore it off and pulled her out."

He turned to give Gwenn a weak smile before continuing. There was a message in the look he gave her.

"Gabe picked up Jake. I had Gwenn and her cat. By this time, the front of the building was engulfed in smoke and flames. We raced to the back entrance to get out."

Sebastian laid his hand briefly on Gabe's shoulder. "We're all sorry for what happened to Jake. Mutther is right, Gabe. You did what had to be done."

Sebastian returned to his desk and shuffled through the papers until he found the cursed map. "This group—the ghosts, the man, the Horseman, and whoever else may be involved—has an advantage over us. They know where we are and how we operate. We must find whatever they are after before they do. The Horseman wants Janda, but she isn't the only target. It's as if they are searching for something or someone. I'm convinced this map is the key."

"Too bad none of us can make heads or tails of the blasted thing," Silas said. "So, we do what? Double our efforts, keep doing what we've been doing, and hope for a decent lead?"

"Yes," Sebastian said, still analyzing the map and speaking without looking up. "We know more now than before, so do we change anything with our strategy? Thanks to Gabe, we know the ghosts must band together to be effective. And there's a male human in league with the Horseman in some fashion or another. Then there's the Horseman who works below our radar, staying off-grid until he strikes." He placed a fist on the table next to the map, clenching hard enough that the blue of his veins rose to the surface of his pale skin. He scowled before abandoning the map and giving everyone his attention.

"That about sums it up, but I don't see how knowing any of this alters our plans," Silas said.

"We're going in circles with these theories," Mutther said. "Every time we meet, it's the same story, and we aren't any closer to figuring it out. I say we look for the simple approach rather than some theory that has us chasing ghosts. It could be as straightforward as someone hiding from us. Someone who's very good at it."

"And that takes us right back to square one," Gabe said. "Where could anyone hide that we wouldn't think to look?"

"The river!" I said. "I've been getting whiffs of the Hudson in areas where I don't usually smell it so strongly, like in the woods when the ghosts appeared. And the lantern was one item I'm certain had a lingering aroma of river water. Has anyone checked to see if a ship or boat of some kind has been hanging around longer than usual?"

"There goes the simple approach. We're back to the ghost pirates," Nick said. "How are they randomly appearing around Sleepy Hollow? We can't track them or know when they will show up. You'd think the human would be easier to track than the ghosts, yet we know nothing about him. He could be under the control of the Horseman or in cahoots with him and the pirates, but either way, he's dangerous. I agree with Janda. If it was me, I'd want to remain out of range. What better place to hide than on the water?"

"The Headless Horseman on a boat?" Gabe said, sounding skeptical.

"Or just the human on the river without the Horseman," I said. "And possibly the pirate ghosts as well." I was having trouble pulling it all into a cohesive story that made any sense.

Now more than ever, I had to meet Hulda's sister. I gave Gwenn a knowing look. She gave me a slight nod and looked down at Hudson, pretending to be preoccupied with petting him.

"This is all very interesting but not useful for my purposes," Angie said. To her credit, she hadn't offered any insight into the theories we kept tossing out. She did the job of listening and tweezing the facts from the snippets of our stories to use in her own fashion. "I have enough to release a statement about a historical reenactment gone awry where special effects, aka the ghosts, which we won't mention, caused a small fire that spread too quickly to contain." She seemed pleased with the story she'd concocted and began typing on her phone. "I'll have this approved by Detective Brent and released to the public pronto." She straightened, stretching her back. "My job is done, but if you need me for anything, let me know. I'll also dig through some of my Uncle's papers to see if he left anything lying around about the vault project before he was killed that may have landed in the wrong hands. He never discussed it with us, but I'll go through everything at his place again."

"That's very useful," Sebastian said. "Thank you."

"Are we ready to leave?" Angie hovered near Shawn, waiting for him to wrap things up.

"Almost." Shawn removed his dusting kit from his black case and set to work lifting any prints from the glass. "Not much here. A partial. A smudged print. There's not a lot to go with, but I'll run it through the database to see if we get any hits." He carefully packed the glass into his case and stood, adjusting his uniform to its pristine, non-wrinkled condition. "Gentlemen. Ladies." He nodded to us and followed Sebastian and Angie out of the room.

"We should head out as well," Mutther said, giving me a long side glance. "We can start tracking the waterway traffic to see if anything unusual pops up." He turned to Nick. "Do you think you and some of the others could do a thorough search of the shoreline?"

Nick shook his head. "Silas, Damon, and I have divided our people into groups to go through the forest and quarry near Sing Sing. We won't have the manpower to swing back down the shoreline until late morning."

Mutther sighed. "Then that's what we will have to do." He gave me a piercing stare. "You stay here."

"Where else would I be?" I said as innocently as I could.

There was a collective grunt from the men in the room

as they headed out. I was truly offended. Sort of. Damn, they knew me too well. Gwenn stifled a snicker. I grabbed a book from the stand near the loveseat and laid back against the pillows.

"Go have fun without me," I said, calling after them.

Mutther was the only one left. "It's a girls' night. A bit of pampering with pedicures and wine and a good book." I waved the novel at Mutther, who had crossed his arms over his chest as if he would plant his lumberjack physique in the middle of the room for the rest of the night. "You're just jealous about the pedicures, aren't you? Stay. You can get one too."

He rolled his eyes in disgust and strode after the others.

Gwenn and I burst into laughter.

"Okay, spill it," Gwenn said, sitting at the edge of her seat with Hudson still nestled in her lap.

I tipped my head to one side, listening. Once I heard Mutther's motorcycle leave, I raised my brows and grinned. "Now that they've all left, I can explain." I glanced at the mantel clock. It was now four in the morning. No wonder Angie had urged Shawn to leave. "It's late. I'm sure you could use some sleep, but if you're up for a bit of ghost hunting after the next sunset, I could use your help."

"Sure." She never hesitated. "I'm in. Where are we going?"

Hudson perked his ears.

"Smart cat," I said. "He knows when something is up."

Gwenn laughed and gave Hudson a generous scratching behind his ears.

"So, no pedicure?" she said.

I took off my boots and socks. "Oh, we can still do a pedicure. It'll help keep up appearances. I'm not the primping sort, but sacrifices must be made for the greater good."

"I think we are going to get along great," she said, removing her shoes. She was barefoot beneath her jeans.

"No socks?"

She shrugged. I prefer the feel of the earth as much as possible. I draw energy from nature. It's faster to toss aside my shoes and touch the ground's energy when I don't wear socks."

"Huh. Maybe I should try that. Socks are such a pain when shifting." I wiggled my toes. "Let's go to the kitchen, and I'll fill you in while I get our foot soaks ready."

I dug around in the kitchen cabinets until I came across a roasting pan and a very large pot. I held the pot up. "Will this work?"

"Looks good to me," she said. Gwenn was sorting through the spices in the pantry and pulling out a few items we could add to our spa time.

"Oh, I know. We can use a few of Hulda's herbs. I'll grab some chamomile and lavender while you start filling the containers with water."

I was enjoying my time with Gwenn and realized I'd never had someone to do a girls' night with before. This was new territory for me, and I liked it.

CHAPTER 14

GIRL'S NIGHT

I hurried to the basement and halted halfway down the stairs. Hulda was sitting at the table reading from her journal and flipping the pages. Her brows were knit, and her shell-shaped lips were pursed in concentration. Her fingers fumbled as she struggled to turn each page. The most disconcerting part was seeing her form fade in and out. Whatever Hulda had been doing was draining her.

"Hey," I said, announcing my presence. I went down the last two steps and waited until she saw me.

She looked up and smiled. "Sorry, dear. I didn't hear you come down. Is everything alright?"

"That's what I'm wondering. Your substance isn't looking too good. What exactly have you been doing that has you so depleted?"

The edges of her lips turned down slightly. "I've told you. I've expended energy that normally would keep me more visible to you."

"Yeah. You also said it would pass and that you needed

some rest. This," I waved my hand at the journal, "isn't resting. I can help you. Tell me what I can do."

"That's sweet but not necessary. You should be upstairs with Gwenn enjoying some long overdue pampering."

"That can wait. I'm here for you. You're my family."

A gentle glow emanated from her. "Thank you for that. Truly." She glanced back at the journal. "I'm going over the notations my sister wrote to see if there is anything that might help us when we meet her, but I'm not coming up with anything."

"You haven't told me your sister's name."

"Agatha," she said, sighing.

"Would you mind if Gwenn went with me to meet her?"

"I suppose that would be acceptable. You could use someone like Gwenn to help you if things don't go well."

Whatever she thought might go wrong couldn't be as bad as what had already happened. At least, I hoped that was the case.

"Thanks," I said. "I'll let her know when I go back upstairs. I came for some herbs." I picked some from the drying pegs and placed them in a small wooden bowl that I kept on the table. I attempted to keep things casual as I worked. "So about your sister. Is there anything we should watch out for at this rendezvous?" She had me a little nervous now, and I wouldn't go into this thing unprepared. I had zero experience with ghost witches other than Hulda and was unsure whether they could still perform spells in their spirit form.

On the other hand, my great-great-grandmother had done something with the whole Biblical trick she did to me. Although, from what I could tell, it only made me glow like a shiny light bulb. How much of that was Hulda's doing I had yet to understand.

"There's little to tell. She is the epitome of a scorned lover. Agatha is my younger sister by two years. We traveled to the colonies together. It was difficult to leave our home and start over in a strange land. Agatha had it worse than me. She hated the villagers here for shunning us and treating us like we were a blight on their tiny town. I hated it, too, except I learned to get around it. She didn't. Bitterness grew in her until she met a man."

"The one who betrayed her?" I put the last of the herbs I wanted in the bowl and sat on a stool to hear what she had to say.

"Sadly, yes. Things were wonderful for a time. She was a different person. He was a sailor, or as we later discovered, a pirate. She'd wait by the river whenever he was expected and weave baskets we would sell at the market. Everyone assumed she was there to make baskets. They didn't know her true reason for spending hours on end sitting on an outcropping of rocks. She would help his ship get safely through any turbulent water—and sometimes past barricades. Agatha didn't care for soldiers. Why would she? The militia here could be quite cruel to people like us."

"People like us? As in, witches?"

"Yes," she said, clenching the journal with surprising strength.

Her energy surged, causing her shape to pulse erratically. I held my breath until she calmed down.

A dark glint shone in Hulda's eyes, her gaze hardening with suppressed feelings. "Supernaturals have stayed hidden for a reason. Humans hunt us. They hate what is different. They hate feeling vulnerable."

"I can relate."

Her voice softened. "I'm sorry. I forget you haven't had

an easy upbringing, despite being loved by your uncle and cousins."

I didn't want to go down that road—not with the loss of Jake. "When did things fall apart for Agatha and her sailor?"

She shook her head. "I'm not certain. It began with small things, like him asking her to keep him hidden from the militia. She was happy to oblige. But he started asking her to help hide loot. He refused to say where it had come from. She went along with it until he asked her to protect a treasure for his captain and crew mates. By then, it was evident she was dealing with pirates. He pressured her, and she reluctantly agreed. Then he began avoiding her."

"He sounds like a real winner," I said.

"My thoughts as well. Unfortunately, my sister did not like what I had to say about him. I mentioned he could be seeing another woman. She laughed. So, I did what any sister would do. I followed him and discovered he was meeting with a woman from the village. When I told Agatha, she became enraged. She lashed out at *me*! Like it was my fault."

"Whoa," I said. "That's hurtful."

"Quite, but I didn't retaliate. She was my sister and in pain. But my dear sister wasn't satisfied with saying mean things to me. She tore through my belongings, destroying things and writing that note you found in my journal."

"I don't understand. The note was about a spell and not about you revealing the truth about her pirate boyfriend."

Hulda gave a caustic laugh. "It was all about her cad of a lover. She tweaked my spell. His mistress became ill and died. The pirate told Agatha she was a whore."

"Oh, that is so wrong! The bastard." I couldn't help feeling bad for Agatha even though I didn't agree with what she did to the other woman. If Alex was cheating on me, I wasn't so sure I wouldn't tear someone apart. Except it would probably be Alex I ripped into. My insecurities with him being out of my reach had me aligning myself more with Agatha than I cared to admit.

"I'm certain he regretted his rash move," she said, "especially when she cursed him, the treasure, and his entire crew."

"I can see her point in this and suspect he deserved to be punished."

"There's punishment, and there's cruelty. Agatha created a dark spell that cursed her pirate lover, his shipmates, and anyone who had done her wrong, including me."

"What? She cursed you?"

"Inadvertently, I believe. But, yes, she did curse me to eternal unrest. I can remain here but without Sebastian seeing me the way you can see me. I cannot pass on completely unless she frees me from the curse."

"I had no idea. I'm sorry. Maybe we can get her to release you from the curse."

"Don't get your hopes up. She became quite vindictive after her lover's treachery. I don't mind being here forever with Sebastian. He's immortal. I got lucky in that regard, but it would be wonderful if he could see me."

"Have you spoken to her? Or can't ghosts visit with each other like in the Underworld?" I knew for a fact spirits there co-existed and passed the time with one another.

"I tried to see her, but she left whenever I came near. It's sad to lose a loved one like this. We used to be so close." Her voice trailed off, and her shoulders shook in silent grief, unable to shed the tears caused by the pain of her anguished heart. She gathered herself and did her best to appear composed.

"What makes you think she won't disappear when we try to meet with her?" I had my doubts about Agatha. If she was as bitter as I suspected, there would be little chance of getting her to cooperate with us and divulge any information she might have about her pirate ghost ex-lover.

"This time, I'll have you with me, and she will be very interested in discovering more about your talents as a shifter with witch powers. Even filled with hatred, she always loved my child. I don't think she will do anything to hurt you. I hope that your presence will bring her back from the darkness that consumed her. You are her kin and a witch."

"Well, we have yet to discover if I actually have witch powers in me. I haven't made a decent potion or cast a simple spell."

Hulda rose and glided over to me. "You would be surprised what you can do when you least expect it. Take heart. Believe in yourself as I believe in you."

"I have to ask. Did you cast a protective spell on me that made me light up?"

Her eyes brightened with a golden glimmer. "I merely reminded your inner witch what you have inside you. No more, no less."

"Right. But did you cast a spell? Can ghosts do magic?"

She gave me a slight smile and waved me off. "Go. Have your girl time and get some rest. We will meet at the river."

It seemed like this was as much as she was going to share with me. Frustration bubbled within me, and I actually let out an involuntary hiss. She laughed.

"Fine," I said and stomped up the stairs.

I found Gwenn busy in the kitchen with our makeshift

foot baths all set up, two glasses of white wine, and a board of sliced meats and cheeses.

"You look like Hudson does when he's not getting his way," she said.

"Oh, it's just Hulda annoying me with her vagueness and refusing to directly answer my questions."

Then I kicked myself for forgetting who I was talking to here. I had another witch available to me. I put the bowl of herbs onto the table, and she began rubbing some of them together in her palms and letting them float on the top of our foot baths.

I plunked myself into one of the wooden chairs and stuck my feet in the pot of warm herbal water. "Gwenn, can I pick your brain about witch stuff?"

She placed her toes into her pan of water and sighed as she submerged her feet, closing her eyes and exhaling a long breath. She opened her eyes when Hudson hopped onto her lap. She gently removed him and set him on the floor. "Sorry, bud. This is my relaxation time." She pointed to a soft blanket and a bowl of milk. "That's your spot."

I laughed.

"He sometimes has trouble with boundaries. But, as to your question, ask away. I'll tell you what I can."

"Supposedly, I'm part witch," I said.

She nodded her head and waited.

"My question—or one of many—but I'll start with this one—is how did you know you were a witch?"

She leaned back in her chair and wiggled her toes in the water. "What do your feet feel like right at this moment?"

"My feet?" Maybe asking Gwenn hadn't been a great idea after all, but she seemed serious about it and sat quietly while I puzzled out what she was asking me. "Okay. Well, they feel wet."

"And?"

"And warm." I struggled to find the response she was seeking. I swished my feet a bit to allow the herbs to swirl around my ankles while I concentrating on the sensation.

"What else?" she prodded.

I sighed, shut my eyes, and tried to tune out distracting noises like the cat purring and the distant mantle clock chiming. There was a mild tingling in my toes. The longer I focused on that feeling, the stronger it grew. It flowed through the soles of my feet and up the sides of my ankles before morphing into a warmth that spread slowly through my body.

I gasped and opened my eyes.

Gwenn chuckled. "That's how I knew."

"Because your feet tingled? That's how you knew you were a witch? Seriously?"

"I was maybe five or six years old and had jumped into a local swimming hole one summer day. My entire body started to tingle. It sure got my attention. I jumped out of the water and ran all the way home to tell my mother there must be a water demon where we go swimming. My mother laughed so hard! I can still see her with tears streaming down her face and holding her belly." Gwenn laughed at the memory. "That's when I discovered I was a witch. My body intuitively knew how to draw energy from my surroundings. The hard part was learning to control it."

I stared at my submerged feet. "So I *am* a witch." I glanced up at Gwenn and frowned. "Then how come I'm a total failure when Hulda tries to teach me simple spells? I can't be much of a witch if I can't brew potions or cast spells."

"There are many types of witches in the world. Hulda was more of a healer. It's natural that she would excel at potions and medicinal spells. You, I dare say, are more of an action type. I heard how your body glowed and the ghosts gave up fighting. That's your power surfacing."

"But what kind of power is being a human light bulb?"

"I don't know what made you glow. Your magic will reveal itself in time. Then you can begin to hone your skills. Until then, I'm afraid there's little you can do to force it."

I grabbed a towel and dried my feet so Sebastian wouldn't have a seizure about tracking water through his house. Lack of sleep made my eyes burn, but I had one more thing to ask. "What do you know about retaining your power after you die?"

Gwenn's brows rose. "You mean like Hulda and her sister?"

I nodded.

"When my mother passed, her spirit came to me as a comfort to ease the pain of my loss. She didn't do anything that would indicate she could still perform magic, but even in death, her love wrapped me in warmth. Is that witch magic or a mother's love? She didn't linger as a ghost, so I may never know. To me, it didn't matter. But I see where you may wonder if it is possible. I'm sorry to say, I don't know."

Gwenn splashed water up her calves and rubbed the herbs clinging to her legs off. "This was refreshing. Thanks." She dried off, wrapped her shoes in the damp towel, and set them aside while we cleaned up.

Hudson raised his head, then gave a long stretch before easing himself off his cozy spot and ambling over to Gwenn. She picked him up and grabbed the towel. We held our shoes and walked barefoot upstairs, pausing in the hallway. She and Hudson had a guest room at the end of the hall closest to the bathroom. Mine was at the opposite end, which I now realized was closest to Sebastian's quarters. Not that he used them much, but on occasion, I noticed him coming out of his room in the morning when I wandered down to fix my breakfast.

"Did Sebastian get everything ready for you?" I said. "If not, let me know."

"He was wonderful. He even put together a litter box for Hudson. He also gave me an assortment of clothes. He thought of every detail and was quite the gentleman."

"That sounds like Sebastian."

Daylight slipped beneath the long draperies covering the hall window.

"I imagine the search party will be making their way down the river bank by now," Gwenn said.

"As long as they aren't there when we meet Hulda, we'll be fine. We'll follow the aqueduct trail and stay out of sight as much as possible." I'd been thinking about how to get out unnoticed. "Sebastian doesn't keep a large store of food around. We'll grab some shut-eye and spend the day in the lab, then we'll go for an early dinner. All normal. The guys will be satisfied that we are keeping out of trouble, and we will tell them we're going to the historical society to sift through the remains. We then use the trail behind the building to get to the river."

"I like it," Gwenn said.

Hudson leaped from her arms to scamper over to me and twine himself around my legs.

"I think he approves," I said, reaching down to pet the top of his head.

"He says you're a clever cat."

"Um, thanks?" I said.

She tapped her leg, and he trotted back to her. "He likes your lykoi side. Then again, I believe he is biased when it comes to felines of any type." She chuckled and opened her bedroom door. "Hudson and I love a good mystery and can't wait to meet your family."

"That makes three of us."

Once they'd gone, I turned and walked to my room. Fatigue settled over me as I shut my door and threw myself fully dressed across my bed.

"Alex, I miss you," I whispered, drifting off to sleep.

CHAPTER 15

ALEX

"I'd love it if you'd take it off," he said. "I'll give you a hand."

His lips brushed my ear while his hands gripped my hips and drew my buttocks against his hardness. I rolled onto my back, keeping my eyes closed so as not to break the illusion of Alex removing my clothes. I helped by undoing my jeans and sliding them down my legs. I didn't have panties on. He ran his finger along the contour of my body until he reached my shirt. He took it off and unfastened my bra, letting it fall to the floor. Still, I kept my eyes closed. It was so real. I didn't want it to stop.

"I missed you, too," he murmured.

He pressed gentle kisses along the curve of my left breast and worked his way to my nipple. I let out a whimper of delight.

"Let me pleasure you," he said.

He drew my nipple into his mouth and placed his fingers into the wetness between my legs, probing. I bit into my lip to stifle a groan.

"God, I want you more than you can imagine," he said, his voice deep with desire.

The weight of his naked body against mine made me open my eyes. Alex was here. I'd been deep in a dream state that had opened the pathway between us. I dared not speak for fear he would disappear and leave me again, but a word slipped out as my brain finally registered that this was real.

"How?" I said.

He twined his fingers with mine and lifted our joined hands. I was glowing. He kissed my fingers, one at a time, then worked his way down my body. I held my breath until he teased my body to the brink of release. I arched into him, wanting him with every fiber of my body and soul. Alex was mine. My mate.

"Stay with me," he said. "Focus on us."

"You're all I think about," I said.

I didn't understand his plea. I was his totally. We were together. The heat between us rose to a feverish high. But my body betrayed me at the height of release. I lost control of the energy that kept the link open. My eyes grew wide, and my pulse thrummed unevenly. I stared into his dark eyes and knew I was losing him.

"I'm sorry."

He gave me a quick kiss on the tip of my nose. "Don't be. I'm not." His voice grew distant as if he was speaking down a long tunnel. "You can do this, Janda. Find the way. I love you."

Alex was gone.

I pulled the pillow from my bed and threw it across the room. I would have screamed, but I didn't want to scare Gwenn down the hall. I strode naked to the window and pulled back the drapes. I blinked at the brightness. My room overlooked the front of the house, and from my vantage point, I could see Mutther's motorcycle parked in the driveway. I sighed. Getting past my protection detail might be more difficult than I'd anticipated.

I glanced at the small bedside clock. Four o'clock in the afternoon. Crap. The day was almost done, but I had enough time to stick with our plan.

I snatched up some clean clothes and headed to the bathroom. Laughter drifted upstairs. Gwenn and Mutther were in the kitchen and apparently were hitting it off. Gwenn might be the perfect distraction for getting Mutther off my trail. I drew water into the deep tub and sank into it. I thanked God Sebastian had allowed the installation of a gas water heater. It was pure bliss to have hot water. I started plotting how to best use Mutther's attraction to Gwenn when Hudson meowed out in the hall. I glanced over the edge of the tub to see his paw poking underneath the door.

"Okay. I get the hint. I'm coming."

I dragged myself out of the water and only realized after I got out that a slight tingle was coursing through me. My witch magic seemed to be kicking in.

"Too late," I mumbled to myself. Where was it when I wanted Alex to stay with me earlier?

After getting dressed, I headed to the kitchen with Hudson tagging behind me.

"Janda," Mutther said, taking a bite of cheese. "You look like crap for someone who slept all day."

"Love you, too," I said. I poured myself a cup of coffee from the pot sitting on the stove. No cappuccino machines in this house, but the java hit the spot. I grabbed the chunk of cheese Mutther had in his hand and popped it into my mouth. "How long have you been here?"

"I found him sitting outside about two hours ago and

felt sorry for him. I could almost hear his stomach grumbling with hunger." Gwenn chuckled as Hudson rubbed against Mutther's leg. "As you can see, he passed Hudson's approval test."

Mutther shrugged. "What can I say? It's my animal charm."

I shook my head. "Sure it is. And I'm the Queen of England."

He smirked as he tossed down two more pieces of cheese. "Your Highness." He stood and did a mock bow. "I'll be outside."

"Don't waste your time hanging around. Gwenn and I have plans to go into town for an early dinner and then spend a few hours rummaging through the debris from the fire. We won't require your services, thanks."

"Perfect," he said. "We can all stop at my bar on the way. It's looking great. I've been telling Gwenn all about it."

I glanced over at Gwenn.

"I'd love it," she said.

I think she actually meant it. I gave up trying to dissuade Mutther. "Okay. I'm ready to go whenever you two are ready."

Mutther started for the back door and paused. "I'll take a quick look around and be right back. Then we can leave."

"Overprotective at all?" I said.

He seemed nonplussed. "Not at all. You'll know when I'm overprotective."

I couldn't imagine that scenario, so I said nothing.

Gwenn washed the few dishes and stacked them on a dish drain to dry. "Hudson let me know you had a visitor."

I looked around the kitchen for the furry little spy, but he'd wandered off. "He's a handy informant. Did he tell you it was Alex?"

She nodded. "Hudson does manage to keep his nose to the ground to bring me bits of news. I'm sorry things are hard for you with Alex trapped in the Underworld. I can only guess how painful it is for you both."

"I've spent months working with Hulda on potions and spells that might help with reaching him. Nothing worked. It was my witch magic that brought him to me today. But you were right about learning to control it. I couldn't. When my emotions surged, I lost the link." I took a deep breath and exhaled slowly. "He was sucked back to the Underworld."

"This is good news," she said.

I glared at her. "Not from where I stand."

Gwenn had finished the dishes and was leaning against the sink. "All you need is to harness the energy and bend it to suit you. At that point, you will intentionally be able to open the link to Alex."

Hope swelled within me. "Can you teach me?"

"I'd be happy to try, but it's not something that happens quickly."

"How long will it take?"

"I don't know. Weeks, months, years. It's impossible to predict."

"I don't have years, Gwenn. I have days before he's out of my reach forever."

"Oh," she said, sinking into a chair.

"Yeah. Oh." I sat opposite her. "Time isn't my friend. That's why it's so important to get Agatha to reverse the curse. And that's why you need to keep Mutther busy while we're at his bar. I'll go out the back and ride in the direction of Sleepy Hollow Forest for a while before circling back to town. I'll wait for you behind the historical society. Do you think you could get there to meet me?"

"I'll manage," she said, a glint of mischief in her eyes.

I narrowed my eyes at her. "You love this conspiratorial stuff, don't you?"

"Sorry. I can't help it. I have a passion for solving mysteries, especially ones surrounding magic. That's one reason I became a curator of magical artifacts. There's always a story behind them that fascinates me." She grew serious and put her hand out to hold mine. "I know what this means to you. I'll do my part to make sure Mutther doesn't ruin it." She gave my hand a squeeze. "We witches must stick together."

"Thanks." I scarfed down a few more bites of cheese and offered her some before I put the rest away. I'd been looking forward to eating in town, which wouldn't be happening now that Mutter was glued to our sides.

"Enjoy the cheese. I'm afraid our dinner plans are canceled. And unless Mutther has picked up some more tips from his attempt at learning to cook, we may be eating salads tonight."

"It'll be fine," she said, "but I'm worried about Hudson. I don't want to leave him here alone. Do you think Mutther would mind if I bring him?"

"Just do it. He won't tell you no. He likes you."

She blushed.

As if on cue, Hudson came back into the room. He had a piece of parchment in his mouth.

"Hudson!" Gwenn hurried to take it from him.

He sat back and stared up at her.

"What's he saying?" I was intrigued by their communications with one another. Then I saw what he'd been carrying. "It's the cursed map."

"Yes," Gwenn said. "Apparently, we're supposed to take this with us."

I glanced at Gwenn and then at Hudson as I put on my leather riding jacket. "If he says it comes with us, then it does."

Gwenn folded the map and had just handed it to me as Mutther opened the back door. I hurriedly crammed the map into my jacket pocket.

"We're good," he said. "I'm glad Sebastian made it so the barrier no longer sees me as a threat, or it would have taken a lot longer to inspect the area." He tapped the side of his head with his hand. "I still get a buzzing sound and can't run at full speed, but at least it's not like swimming in molasses anymore."

"Glad to hear it." I shoved the map deeper into my pocket. "By the way, you'll have to borrow a car from Sebastian's collection. Hudson is coming with us, and I don't think he'd appreciate being stuffed in a satchel on Miss Kitty."

To his credit, Mutther didn't argue about it. Gwenn and Hudson were a package deal.

"That might be easier anyway. Sebastian's vehicles can pass the barrier without issue."

"How do you know that?" I said.

"I ride his motorcycle now, which I'm sure was the reason he gave it to me in the first place. How about you grab the keys to the Mercedes? Sebastian won't get mad if you drive his car, and that way, we can all ride together."

"I'm not driving his car. No way. If it gets scratched, he can have your head on a platter. Not mine. I'll take Miss Kitty."

He let out a low growl.

"Grumble all you like, but this is on you, buster." I folded my arms and took my obstinate stance, staring him down.

"Just get the keys," he groused. "You can follow the car. And don't think I won't be keeping an eye on you in my rearview mirror."

"Fine." I went to where Sebastian kept his keys in the hall leading to the foyer. I pushed open a narrow cabinet door that mimicked the wood paneling that ran along the area below the staircase. It was a clever way to disguise the location of all the keys. When I returned, I tossed Mutther the keys to the Mercedes. "Be sure to bring it back with a full tank."

"Very funny," he said.

"Oh. I'm serious. Just remember who we're dealing with here."

He gave me a disgruntled glare and stormed off. Gwenn and I bit back laughter that I knew would send Mutther over the edge of reason. I didn't want to push my luck.

Mutther brought the car around, and Gwenn got in the front with Hudson. I started Miss Kitty and followed him as he drove away. I made sure to ride close so that it would annoy him. He rolled down his window and gave me the middle finger salute. I gave him a smug grin and rode even closer. If he slammed on the brakes, I'd be on the Mercedes' roof, but I knew he wouldn't risk any dents in the car. I relaxed just a little. I've been learning to enjoy the small things in life, like being a thorn in Mutther's side every now and then.

CHAPTER 16

RUSE

We made it to Mutther's bar without a single scratch on Sebastian's car. I parked Miss Kitty in her usual spot while Mutther hovered nearby. He practically stepped on my heels as we went inside. It was payback for me tailgating him, but I didn't care. I'd had my fun and would gladly pay the price.

Gwenn ran a hand along the bar top's smooth finish. "This is really something," she said, giving Mutther a look of pure admiration. "It's hard to believe it was blown up not long ago."

He stepped around me. Now that I was indoors, he could stand down from guard duty, which was fine with me.

"I'm glad you like it." He beamed with pride. "The guys worked hard with the restoration."

"They did an awesome job," I said. "I think it's better than before, minus the hotel portal. But honestly, I think it's a good thing not to have to be a gatekeeper. Who knows what riffraff they'd let into the paranormal hotel?" I'd seen a great deal on my visit to the interdimensional retreat for supernatural beings. Some of the people had rather questionable backgrounds. But it's how I met Alex, so it would always have a place in my heart.

"I couldn't agree with your more." He chuckled. "Which are you? Riff or raff?"

"I'm going to let that slide because that is *so* lame."

I could tell he was in his happy place and thrilled to be sharing it with Gwenn. They had good chemistry, although I might have to give him a nudge to do something about it. He wasn't the dating type of guy, which always amazed me. He could have had his pick of any of the single women in Sleepy Hollow but was content to keep to himself.

He gave Gwenn a tour of the bar and the new apartment while I tagged along, biding my time.

"I thought we could cook up some burgers for dinner," he said.

"I could go for a loaded quarter-pounder." I dug into his refrigerator for the package of meat. "Are you chief chef this evening? If not, I can manage. Besides frozen pizza, I can whip up a mean burger."

He took the meat from me and unwrapped it. "Nah. I have it. You ladies can relax for the night."

I was not thrilled that he expected us to hang out here for the evening. I glanced over at Gwenn and prayed the lift in my brow and the wide-eyed expression I gave her would clue her in to come to my aid. She gave a slight nod and moved closer to Mutther. I couldn't help noticing that keeping him occupied and focused on her didn't seem like it would be an unpleasant task. I suppressed a grin at how quickly the pair had come to enjoy each other's company. She began helping him make the colossal patties and tossing them on a griddle. In no time, the aroma practically had me drooling. I wasn't about to leave on an empty stomach, and when the burgers were finally served, I ended up enjoying each mouthful.

"Pretty good," I said, finishing off my last bite.

"Thanks. The days of cardboard-tasting microwave meals are in my past. I'm a new modern man."

"Sure you are," I said, licking my fingers. "But I give credit where it's due, and these are yummy."

"They are truly delicious," Gwenn said. She broke off a piece of hers and placed it on the floor for Hudson.

He meowed and gobbled it in mere seconds.

This gave me an idea of how to escape from Mutther's watchful eye. I collected the plates and brought out coffee for everyone, filling Gwenn's mug and giving her a discreet nudge with my foot.

"Gwenn," I said. "Why don't I take Hudson outside to do his business while Mutther regales you with his latest cooking lesson?"

"Oh! I would love that." She turned toward him expectantly. "Please, you must share what you've been learning. I'm afraid my skills aren't the best, and I've often thought of taking classes myself. It's all online, right?" She put her elbow on the table and cupped her chin in her hand in rapt attention.

Mutther started to get up when I went to the door with Hudson.

"No fuss. I've got this," I said. I did my best to hide the thrill of excitement at coming up with the perfect excuse to go outside. I took a breath to keep my heartbeat level.

To my relief, he sat back down and began a diatribe of the benefits of olive oil.

Hudson and I left the apartment and headed to the back entrance. "Sorry, buddy. I hope you can hold it a while longer." I gave him a pat on the head. "I have an appointment. You understand, right?"

He meowed once and rolled onto his back for me to rub his belly. I accepted his bargain for skipping his outside time.

"Be a good kitty and wait until I clear out before you go back upstairs."

I opened the door and ran smack into Nick.

"Janda, whoa, where you off to?"

Thankfully, Hudson saved me by sauntering past our feet. I rubbed my nose, which had collided firmly with Nick's chest in my rush to escape.

"Cat duty," I said. "If you know what I mean."

We watched Hudson poking around the dumpster. He slowly worked his way toward a patch of dirt just beyond the edge of the building.

"Oh, gotcha," Nick said. "Where's Mutther?" He'd dismissed Hudson's activities and started inside, then stopped.

"Upstairs. Go on ahead. This could take a while."

Hudson was obligingly sniffing and discarding several likely spots to relieve himself. I swear this cat knew exactly what he was doing. God bless him.

Nick still hesitated.

"Before you go in, can you give me an update on the search?" I acted like I hadn't noticed his indecision about leaving me outside alone.

Nick propped open the door with his arm and had one foot on the ground and the other inside. "There were a few locations up by the old quarry where someone has been digging. There's no saying what the digging was from, though. Other than that, not much to tell. We're calling a halt to get some rest. Everyone has been busting butt with little or no sleep. I came to check in with Mutther and crash here for a while."

I nodded. "Okay. Thanks." I glanced over at Hudson, who was still surveying the land for just the right spot. "Seriously, go on up. Mutther made some awesome burgers, and Gwenn is there. I won't be long."

"Burgers? Sounds good." He went inside and then stuck his head out from behind the door. "Be quick."

I pointed to Hudson. "Not up to me how long this takes."

He gave the cat a fleeting glance and went into the bar and shut the door.

I heaved a sigh of relief. Hudson immediately finished his bathroom needs and pattered over to me.

"Thanks." I opened the door far enough for him to slip inside. "Remember, give me a good lead."

He purred and went off in the direction of the bar's kitchen.

I prayed he didn't get into anything that would create a lot of noise to draw attention too soon. I shut the door, glanced up at the tiny window I knew went to Mutther's bathroom, and sprinted to Miss Kitty. I didn't dare start her up here. I began the laborious task of pushing her down the street until I could get her engine revving safely. The similarities to how I'd first entered this street when I was hunting Alex for the bounty on his head did not escape me. This time, though, I was being discreet so I could find a way to save my panther shifter. I'd give anything to bring him safely back from the Underworld.

Daylight was fast receding. I started Miss Kitty and rolled the throttle grip toward me a little more, careful not to pop a wheelie but enough to pick up speed. I took the curves as fast as I dared, heading toward Sleepy Hollow

Forest. Gwenn would let slip that I wanted to return to the area around Hulda's cottage ruins to draw my guards in this direction. I made a quick stop on the side of the road to leave tire tracks for anyone following me. When I felt confident enough about my ruse, I veered off to a side road and made my way into town.

Sunset loomed. My heart beat faster. I avoided going down the street in front of the historical society and opted to stop near the aqueduct trail. I couldn't risk Miss Kitty's engine noise giving away my location. Not that I anticipated any interference, but I had to be cautious. I hid my Harley by trash cans between two homes running along the trail. I picked my way carefully along the tree-lined path and found a spot by a shrub that had been scorched by the flames and still smelled of burnt wood. The area was clear of the gawkers that had been present during the fire. I knelt beside the shrub and waited.

I prayed Gwenn would be able to find some way to meet me. She didn't even have transportation. Mutther had brought her to Sebastian's and left her car parked down the street. I risked taking a peek to look for it. It was gone. I only knew which car was hers because it caught my attention on my first visit. The license plate said HUDSON.

After I discovered her cat's name, it was clear who owned the car. Someone could have moved it for her to keep it safe after the fire. There was no way for me to know for sure. My nerves were as tight as a guitar string. If only I could play the guitar. I took a deep breath. Once this was over, I should learn to play. I could serenade my man. It was a silly idea. I didn't have a musical bone in my body, but thinking about it helped me relax.

The horizon glowed orange. I wouldn't be able to wait

much longer. But Gwenn had assured me it would be fine. She would be here. I had to believe in her.

A rustle of fallen leaves crunching beneath someone's feet had me frozen to the spot. Then a faint meow reached me, followed by a loud purr.

"Gwenn?" I whispered.

Hudson scampered to my side and rubbed his sleek body against me. I stroked his fur. Gwenn crouched beside me.

"Sorry," she whispered. "It took longer than I thought to make my getaway. Once the guys realized what you'd done, the place was buzzing with activity. I'll tell you about it later."

"This is Sebastian's fault," I said. I did my best to keep my temper in check and my voice low. "He treats me like I'm incapable of taking care of myself. Hell, I've been mostly on my own since I was a little kid."

"Yeah. I gather he thinks of you as his own daughter. A vampire's daughter. You won't be getting much of anything past him."

I let what she said sink in and realized she was right. "Crap. We have to get moving. Once they tell Sebastian, he will find me pretty damn fast."

She gave me a puzzled look.

"He marked me. I have to work hard to keep my emotions under control, or he might sense me. It's annoying, but so far, I've dealt with it."

"Oh," she said, drawing out the word slowly. "Then you better hurry. Where do we go from here?"

I pointed down the trail that led toward the river. "We follow this until we get in sight of the river. After that, we wait."

"How will I know when Hulda appears? Will I be able to communicate with her?"

"I hadn't thought about that." I shrugged. "I can't say for sure. She said it was good for you to go with me, so we'll just have to wing it. Sorry."

"Then that's what we will do. Lead the way." She didn't have her pet travel bag to put Hudson in and had to scoop him into her arms. She positioned herself directly behind me.

I stayed hunched over to keep as hidden as possible while we wound our way down the trail. The smell of the river loomed in front of us. We paused now and then to listen for anyone approaching. The only thing I heard was water splashing.

The waves lapped against rocks protruding from the muddy banks. Fog rolled in and kept us invisible within its folds. Tonight I was grateful for the Hudson River that could sometimes be ruthless to those seeking refuge on its waters. Tonight its natural rhythm worked in our favor.

A soft voice sang out farther down the line of rocks. Gwenn grabbed my arm. I met her gaze. We'd both heard it.

I raised my palm toward her to indicate she should stay put. I then pointed to myself and the direction from which the sound emanated. She nodded her understanding. I braced myself for what would happen next.

CHAPTER 17

GHOST WITCH

Standing within the fog, which grew denser as the moments passed, was a woman wearing a long, billowing skirt and wrapped in a shawl. She knelt on the largest boulder amidst a cluster of rocks that stretched into the river. A wave sloshed high against the rocks, spewing water in an arc just in front of her. She didn't retreat. Instead, she raised her arms wide with her palms up and began rocking from side to side. The fog grew and spread up and down the river as far as I could see.

I stood mesmerized until Hulda appeared next to me and put a finger to her lip. She didn't have to tell me to stay silent. I didn't think I could have said a word even if I'd wanted. I was too consumed with watching the woman, who could only be Agatha.

The foam created by the churning water reached the spot where Hulda and I stood at the water's edge. Of course, my feet were the only ones getting drenched. Hulda and Agatha couldn't get soaked. It explained why Agatha had not stepped back from the arc of water. I'd seen Hulda take on a more solid state where she definitely could be affected by things like splashing waves from the Hudson River's strong current. It dawned on me now the only time I'd seen her in such a condition was in the Underworld.

It seemed spiritual energy behaved differently there than here in the living realm. I took my cue from Hulda and stood statue-like while she moved slowly toward Agatha.

"Sister?" Hulda said.

Agatha spun around and glared at Hulda. "Go away!"

"I've brought someone. She's anxious to meet her great-great-great aunt."

I stepped closer for her to get a better view of me. "Hi," I said.

Agatha let her shawl fall from her shoulders but quickly pulled it around her again. She looked from Hulda to me and back to Hulda. "She's my niece? Is she a witch?"

"Great-great-great niece. I'm a hybrid shifter and a witch," I said. I couldn't swear to the last part, but I didn't think it would hurt to include it.

She was in front of me in an instant. I hardly blinked, and there she was, standing eye-to-eye with me. I stood stock-still as she circled me. She glanced over at Hulda and then took a step back from me. It was more like gliding than stepping. She moved the same way Hulda did, floating just above the ground.

"Shifter *and* witch? That is a rare combination. What kind of shifter are you, child?"

"Lykoi," I said.

"What is a lykoi? I have never heard of such a creature."

"She is one of a kind," Hulda said. "She is both were-cat and wolf."

Agatha tilted her head to one side as if searching for a clue to prove her sister spoke the truth.

I surveyed our surroundings to be sure we weren't

being watched. Other than Gwenn, who remained out of sight, all was clear. I gave Hulda a short nod and took off my clothes. Agatha hadn't vanished. She seemed truly intrigued, just as Hulda had predicted. I let out a breath and closed my eyes, allowing my mind to connect with my inner lykoi. Shifting was quick and easy for me. Within seconds my lykoi was prancing around Agatha and enjoying stretching its limbs.

"Oh, my!" Agatha said. "You're beautiful."

No one had ever called my lykoi beautiful besides Alex, who, in my opinion, was a tad biased. I was finding it hard not to like her, even though I knew she was responsible for what was happening with the pirate ghosts. I leaped onto the boulder she'd vacated and shifted back to my human form. I grinned, unable to help from showing off what my lykoi could do.

Agatha covered her mouth, then slowly lowered her hand to clutch her shawl to her chest. "Magnificent."

"Thanks," I said.

I stepped along the rocks to reach the bank and my clothes. I dressed while Agatha spoke with Hulda. I kept quiet and took my time with my boots to avoid interrupting the two sisters who hadn't spoken for several hundred years.

"I'm sorry," Hulda said to her Agatha. "I thought I was protecting you. I didn't take into consideration what you wanted. For that, I am sorrier than you could ever imagine. I love you."

Agatha's shoulders drooped. "Time has finally shown me that you acted out of love. We cannot change the past. Hearing your genuine apology is all I've wanted for so long. Thank you."

It was strange to see two ghosts attempting to hug.

They reached out toward each other, but Hulda's hand went through Agatha's arm. In the end, they gave up and simply laughed it off.

I stopped pretending to tie my boots and stood up. I took a few steps in their direction and waited for them to acknowledge me. Now that the two sisters were back on speaking terms, I prayed Agatha would remove the curse.

Hudson came trotting over to me. I gave him a little scratch behind his ears. I assumed he couldn't see my ghost family until he turned and walked straight at Agatha. Once in front of her, he sat and stared up at her. Cats really could see ghosts. I'd always thought that was a myth.

"My goodness," Agatha said. "Aren't you a handsome fella?" She bent to stroke him and, oddly enough, succeeded.

"He belongs with my witch friend, Gwenn. I brought her with me and would love for you to meet her." I motioned for Gwenn to show herself.

Gwenn walked slowly to my side and whispered to me. "I don't see them."

"Okay. We can work around this. Just follow Hudson's lead," I said.

"She can't see or hear us," Hulda said. She turned to Agatha. "I'm not at my best right now. Could you possibly pitch in to assist me?"

"Another witch, I see. In that case, I would be delighted." Agatha stretched out her arms, and the fog shifted. It came closer to us. She allowed it to cover us completely.

"Oh! I see them," Gwenn said. "I'm not getting all the details, but it's enough for me to see their basic shape." Excitement filled her voice. She grabbed my arm. "It's amazing."

"It would be even more amazing if you'd let go of me. I like my limbs in one piece and still attached to my body."

Gwenn chuckled. "I got carried away."

"I figured that part out." I shook out my arm to get the circulation going again.

"I don't hear them, though," Gwenn said.

"If we link hands, then Gwenn may be able to communicate with us," Hulda said. "After all, we are witches. Joining hands in a circle should create a pathway for our voices to travel. As long as she is part of that pathway, she should be able to hear us."

"You realize I'm not a very good witch?" I said. "Besides, I saw you trying to hug your sister and failed. How are we going to hold hands?"

"It will work," Agatha said. She reached out her hand for mine. "The main issue is whether or not we can create enough of an energy surge to allow us to physically touch. Which is where you come in, Janda."

"Me? What can I do?"

"Your energy force will be the catalyst we require. Trust me," Agatha said. "Focus on the outcome desired—Gwenn hearing us. All of us will concentrate on the same thing."

I took Gwenn's left hand in my right one and held my other hand out to one side. "They want us to try holding hands."

"Of course," Gwenn said. "If you and I can muster enough energy, we can manipulate it to create a link to them. I've only ever read about this, but I think we can make this happen. Take off your shoes, Janda." She tossed hers off to the side.

I did as she asked and then held her hand again. The earth was moist and squishy between my toes. The air was brisk. It was the kind of coldness that was more than a crisp autumn evening. I sensed magic swirling around us.

Hulda came to my left side. She held her hand over mine but didn't make contact with it. She held out her other hand, and Agatha moved to stand between Hulda and Gwenn. Agatha placed one hand face down over Hulda's and the other over Gwenn's.

Fog rolled thick over us, keeping us hidden from any possible onlookers. I prayed Sebastian wouldn't show up too soon and ruin our moment. Hulda had closed her eyes. Her body took shape more solidly than I'd seen since we were in the Underworld. It lacked complete solidity but was no longer the wavering, fuzzy Hulda from earlier.

"As above, so below," Gwenn said, looking straight in front of her.

She held my hand firmly in hers and repeated the phrase. Hulda opened her eyes and nodded to Agatha. They both followed Gwenn's example by saying the phrase over and over again. Hudson entered our little circle and began rubbing against each of us in turn. He stopped at my feet and put his paws on my toes. A tingle ran through my legs. Hudson then sat next to Gwenn and turned his face to look at her. She smiled but kept on with her chant.

"As above, so below," I finally said. I knew the term referred to the earthly plane in relation to the astral plane. I supposed it was appropriate in our current circumstances. We were attempting to bring the astral plane my ghost family occupied into the living realm of Sleepy Hollow.

"Concentrate Janda," Hulda said. "You can do this. It's all inside you. Find it. Bring it forth."

Her words shook me. Alex had said something along that line. He also said I only had to find the way. My breath hitched, and my pulse quickened. I sensed my lykoi but also something else. My toes warmed as if pulling heat from the ground. I glanced down at them. They didn't look any different. Yet, there *was* a difference.

"Feel it," Agatha said. "This is who you are meant to be. This is our witch blood. Embrace it, Janda."

I swallowed hard. I was a witch. A real witch. I reached for the earth's warmth and accepted its offering. The feeling grew, scaring me a little, but I pushed past my fear until every part of me touched that energy. My body exploded with it. Then it glowed a warm, golden glow as if touched by the sun or something even more intense—the astral plane.

Gwenn inhaled sharply but kept a tight hold on my hand. Hudson purred while staying in his spot by Gwenn. The light traveled from me to Gwenn and onward to Hudson. My instincts took over. I pushed the light further along our connection. It reached Hulda with a crackle of energy.

"Oh!" Hulda said. The light expanded to include her and Agatha before circling back to me.

"Yes!" Agatha's voice was filled with triumph. "You are a true descendant. This is a special day for us all. Your light will save us from our foolish past."

I saw Hulda and Agatha as if they lived again and had their former human bodies. They were beautiful. They held hands and gazed at each other. Their bodies were lit from within by my energy, which seemed to draw their astral forms into this plane. I concentrated on the stream to hold it steady. It was hard, but I was determined to give these two sisters the family reunion they sought.

"I'm honored to meet you both," Gwenn said.

"As are we, you," Agatha and Hulda said simultaneously.

"How long do we stand here like this?" I said. The beginnings of a headache over my right eye made me squint.

"Let us find out," Agatha said. She and Hulda broke the circuit by withdrawing their hands from our circle.

I immediately felt the pressure above my eye lessen. I looked over at Gwenn. "Well?"

She smiled. "I can still see them."

"We won't be able to keep this form. However, I believe Gwenn may still be able to see our astral bodies," Hulda said.

"This is wonderful," Agatha said. Her happiness was infectious.

Hulda gave her sister's arm a gentle squeeze. "Yes, sister, it is. It fills my heart with joy to have you back with me. But now I beg you to keep an open mind about what I'm going to ask of you."

I saw Hulda struggle to find the right words and couldn't help but blurt them out. "We need your help to defeat the pirate ghosts."

Agatha was silent for far too long. I held my breath, waiting for her to respond. I prayed she wouldn't leave.

I met her gaze. "Please. The man I love is trapped in the Underworld, and I believe you can help me get him out by removing the pirate curse."

CHAPTER 18
NOTHING'S SIMPLE

Agatha stood very still. She looked sad. "I am so sorry, dear niece. I can't."

My heart sank. "Why not?"

She came to me and gave me a hug. Her body was cool to the touch. While she appeared solid, it seemed she lacked the warmth of blood flowing through her. I hugged her back.

"I understand all too well how you are feeling, Janda," Agatha said. "What you are asking is out of my control. I am as much a victim of my curse as the pirates I placed it upon. I'm not able to remove it." She turned toward Hulda. "I wish I had not done it. But it is not something I can undo. Forgive me for dragging you into my misery."

Hulda nodded. "We will find another way."

"How?" Gwenn said. "If the person who placed a curse can't break it, then how would another witch be able to do it?"

"There could be a way, but it would be complicated and rather dangerous," Agatha said.

"No!" Hulda said. "It would be too risky. We don't know what would happen to her."

"True. There is no guarantee of success. Yet Janda is the only one who may be able to do it." Agatha held her hands in the air, turning her palms back and forth in front of her before gripping her shawl more tightly around her. "I have no blood. I am a corpse. You, Janda, have our ancestral blood flowing through your veins. We stand a chance of removing the curse with your blood sacrifice."

Okay. That was not what I was expecting. "What kind of blood sacrifice? Do I have to die? It's not on the top of my list, but I'll do it for Alex."

Agatha shook her head. "Posh. You don't have to sacrifice your life. It's hard to say how much blood, though. A cut across your palm should do it. At most, both palms."

Relieved I wouldn't have to kill myself to get the necessary blood, I pounced on the plan. "Let's do it. Now. I'm ready. I don't have a knife, but a sharp stick or rock might work." I began searching the ground for something sharp.

"You made a blood curse?" Gwenn said, staring directly at Agatha. "That's dark magic. That's scary, dark magic."

"Who cares?" I said. "If it frees Alex, then I don't give a crap how dark and scary it is."

"I did," Agatha said. "I regret it. I do. You see the problem, Gwenn? You're a smart witch. Janda will require your skills to aid her."

Gwenn sighed. "I'll do what I can."

"Janda, do stop searching for a sharp implement. This is not where you will perform the sacrificial spell. Preparations must be made. Hulda will help Gwenn make a potion and prepare a protection spell for you. We will meet where the treasure has been buried. If all goes well, your blood will unlock the chest and release us from this terrible burden."

I tossed a jagged rock back to the earth. "The ghosts want an old buried treasure? I expected it to be something more significant than a bunch of loot. Why would the Headless Horseman want treasure?"

Agatha startled. "The Horseman?"

"Yeah. He's controlling the pirates somehow and searching for the treasure." Hudson meowed at me. I got his hint, pulled the map from my pocket, and handed it to Agatha. "Sebastian believes this is the key."

"The Horseman wants Janda dead, Agatha. Now, do you see why she shouldn't do this?" Hulda said.

Agatha clutched the parchment tighter. "Then we best take care he never gets what's inside the chest."

"What's in it?" Gwenn said.

Agatha looked around the area and lowered her voice as she spoke. "There is a piece of brimstone inside the chest, which would be no great matter, except this particular piece originated from the demon's mine. It can be used to mend the mask and give him more power than he can be allowed to have. He will bring destruction down upon everyone if he gets it."

"That's wonderful," I said. "Just what I needed to hear to brighten my day. Honestly, can it get much worse?" I took one look at the witches surrounding me and sighed. "Don't answer that."

"There's also the issue of the coins I put in the chest. It's part of the curse." Agatha bit her lip.

"Go on," I said. "I can't wait to hear this one. What did you do?"

"I'm not proud of what I did. I was hurt and angry. I used the blood curse on the coins, so those are the only ones the pirates can use to pay the Ferryman to cross over into the Underworld. Without those coins, the pirates are doomed to roam the earth as ghosts forever. But my blood linked me to the coins and somehow tethered me here as well."

"Wow," Gwenn said, putting her hand over her chest. "This is terrible."

"No shit," I said. I had a better grasp of my role in this little plan and was not enthused. "First we find the chest, dig it up, and get it open with my blood sacrifice. But then I will have to give the coins to the pirates to undo the curse? Do I have that right?"

Agatha nodded. "That is an accurate assessment. Yes."

"This is quite a pickle you've gotten us into," Hulda said. "But it isn't impossible. Look at us. Four witches, who, by working together, have manipulated the astral plane. Agatha and I stand on solid ground for the first time in centuries. I have hope that Sebastian will see me once more. Janda has a hope to release Alex. These are the things we fight for and will allow us to win."

It was a good speech, even if it was filled with holes. She failed to mention some key players. "There's a human working with the Horseman, and if I'm right, he's looking for the treasure. Even if he can't open it without my blood, he could prevent us from gaining access to it. We have to find it first." I turned toward Agatha. "Can you show us where it was buried?"

She held the map, rotating it on its side. "If you hold it this way, it looks familiar. I believe I could take us to it. It's along the river in the direction of where you have this prison. But it's been so many years that I can only get us to the area I think it should be. I may or may not be able to narrow our search once there. I'm sorry. Civilization has altered the land so much over the years that many land-marks are gone."

Gwenn had been tapping her finger on her chin while Hudson wound his way between her feet. "We know why the Horseman wants the treasure and the pirates, but what's this guy want with it?"

Her eyes grew wide with alarm. "This is bad. Greed makes men do terrible things. If they find out Janda's blood is the only way to open the chest, she'll be in terrible danger."

"Sebastian is hoping the police can shed some light on who the man is," I said, doing my best to ignore Gwenn's doom and gloom. "Greed is a pretty good motivator for most humans. Power, too. As to terrible danger, well, what's new there? Keeping Sebastian from detecting when I'm in serious situation bothers me more than the danger itself. I can't have him getting in my way."

I had a very uneasy feeling we would soon be having a visit from Sebastian. While I didn't often know when he was near me, I could sometimes sense his agitation with me, which almost always ended with him finding me. "I think we've run out of time for tonight. Sebastian will be looking for me soon."

"Let's get back to the historical society," Gwenn said.

"Very well," Agatha said, folding the map. "Tomorrow evening, meet near the quarry by the prison. Look for my fog, and that's where I'll be. I will do what I can to search the area before then."

She handed me the map, which I stuffed into my pocket. She gave Hulda a kiss on the cheek and then vanished. Hulda sighed.

"You've given me the gift of my sister, Janda. I can never

thank you enough." She slowly backed into the fog and disappeared.

"Too bad we can't teleport or something," Gwenn said. "We will have to do it the old-fashioned way on foot." She started off toward the aqueduct trail. Hudson padded along beside her.

I glanced around as the fog dissipated. I felt vulnerable without its cover. The glow in my body faded, but it left behind a heightened sense of awareness. It was as if I could sense things moving beyond my sight. I wasn't sure if it was possible, but it seemed as if I was detecting the fluctuations in the energy of the astral plane.

"Janda, come on," Gwenn said in a hushed tone. She'd reached the entrance to the trail and waited.

"Coming," I said, keeping my voice just as low.

We made our way back up the aqueduct trail to the rear of the historical society. It was well after ten o'clock.

My stomach grumbled. "I'm hungry. Do you think the bagel shop might be open this late?"

"I think it doesn't matter. Let's go. I'm hungry, too."

We walked several blocks to the bagel shop. A dim light illuminated the kitchen, but the sign on the door indicated it was closed.

"Blast. I was looking forward to a bagel and some coffee."

Gwenn chuckled. "Not to fret. Your belly will be satiated soon." She tapped her knuckles on the front window.

An older man wearing an apron was busy wiping tables. He looked at Gwenn and waved. He came to unlock the door and ushered us inside.

"Gwenn, love. What a nice surprise! What can I do for you?" He had a heavy Brooklyn accent.

"I'm so sorry to bother you, George. But we've been

dealing with stuff at the historical society and overlooked stopping to feed ourselves. Do you think I could impose on you for a couple of bagels and some coffee?" She gave him her winning smile.

"Of course. Come. Sit. Keep me company as I work." He went to the kitchen and returned with a tray loaded with bagels and pastries. He placed two mugs of hot, black coffee on the table and then put a saucer of milk on the floor. "Here you go, Hudson. Enjoy!"

"George, this is my friend Janda."

I nodded and mumbled "hello" between mouthfuls of my everything bagel heaped with lox.

"It's good to see people enjoying my bagels." He turned to Gwenn. "This is late for you to be out. Perhaps it's not good after all that went on with the fire. I worry about my best customer."

Hudson pawed at George's leg.

"Yes, Hudson, that includes you, too."

We all laughed. Hudson purred, then went back to his milk.

"I'm fine," Gwenn said. "I'm afraid I'll have a lot of these late nights for the foreseeable future. There's so much to do at the historical society and other places, if you know what I mean."

George put a finger to his lip. "I do know how to keep secrets. Yours are locked away. Trust me." He made a zipping motion across his mouth and returned to the kitchen.

I raised my brows at Gwenn. "Secrets?"

She shrugged. "George and I have a working relationship. He picks up bits of valuable information about certain rare artifacts and passes said bits along to me. Hudson and I investigate and often acquire such objects of interest. That's what brought me to the attention of the Council." She blew on her coffee before taking a generous sip. "I'm a purveyor of unique and magical items, which I either sell to the right person or donate to various museums and library archives. It often becomes my job to catalog what has been procured. Aside from the historical society, I've been setting up the cataloging system for the supernatural vault." She looked over the top of her mug and winked. "I am a librarian for hire, so to speak."

I leaned back in my chair. "You're a fascinating person, Gwenn Sheiretth."

"I know," she said, laughing.

I barely knew her, yet I'd confided my secret plans to her and was sure I could trust her. I had a feeling she had a talent for disarming people and winning them over. It's no wonder she was privy to information others were not.

I raised my mug of coffee. "To tomorrow evening and a long and profitable friendship, wherever it may lead."

We clinked our mugs together conspiratorially just as Sebastian appeared in the doorway.

CHAPTER 19

TRUTH WITH A TWIST

"I trust you two are enjoying your night out?" Sebastian said as he pulled a chair up to the table.

"Most definitely," Gwenn said. "It's good to escape the chaos of the historical society rubble, even if it's only for coffee."

She brought out her disarming smile from her arsenal. I kept busy sipping my coffee and sneaking furtive peeks at Sebastian as he struggled to find an appropriate way to respond to Gwenn's charm. I found it amusing but didn't dare let Sebastian know just how much I enjoyed his discomfort. It was good to see someone other than him as the master of beguilement.

After a few moments, Sebastian returned Gwenn's smile but said nothing.

I broke the stalemate. "What brings you to a bagel shop at this hour? It's not even open to the public.

His upturned lips did a quick downturn as he glared at me. I had a feeling he didn't like being lumped into the public category. More likely, though, it was his general disgruntlement with me getting under his pasty vampiric skin. I ignored his ire and put my mug between my hands, letting the warmth sink into my palms.

"What do you think brings me here, Janda?"

I shrugged. "Unless George has a special vampire concoction, I wouldn't know since you're not the bagel type of person."

"It's true that I do not care for bagels." Disdain colored his tone. "I don't see what all the fuss is about with them. But your idea of a menu item for vampires is worth pursuing at a later time. I'm here for you. More precisely, because of you. I felt a disconnect that alarmed me. I couldn't sense you for a period, and then the connection returned out of nowhere. I find that interesting, don't you?"

I stared into the depths of the shadows within his eyes and did not falter in my response. "Not really. I didn't get that sensation at all. If anything, I am relieved the connection can be undone. I've been after you for months to unmark me."

His long fingers tightened over the table's edge, digging into the wood hard enough to leave an impression. "That isn't how it works. I can't simply remove the mark I placed on you. At least, not easily. Without it, I am blind to your whereabouts. I cannot have that. The Horseman could be attacking you, and I'd be unable to help."

My blood practically boiled at his overbearing manner. I gripped my mug firmly to control my emotions and spoke as calmly as possible. "You see? That's why I want it removed. Not that I don't appreciate the help. I dislike how you always have to know where I am and what I'm doing."

I rose and stalked off to put my mug on the counter for George, who had inexplicably disappeared. I wouldn't be surprised if he was lurking unseen to eavesdrop. I had to give him credit. He was a talented information gatherer.

Hudson brushed up against my leg. I glanced down at him and froze. He held the map in his mouth. I did a quick look in Sebastian's direction. Gwenn was busy keeping his attention. I knelt as if petting Hudson and secreted the map in my back pocket. I gave Hudson a pat on the head and whispered my thanks. He'd retrieved the map, which must have fallen from my jacket. We didn't need Sebastian seeing I'd taken it and interfering with our plans.

I returned to my seat and switched tactics. "Gwenn and I were getting ready to return to your house. Did I miss anything new from the Council? What can we do to help?" I gave him my best charming smile, which didn't hold a candle to Gwenn's.

He seemed a little thrown by the sudden shift from my disgruntlement with him. "There's little news. In fact, so little that I'm calling a meeting this evening to implement a larger sweep of the area with more manpower. I'm calling in the rest of your uncle's pack and several area groups to help ferret out the human involved and tackle the issue of where to find the pirates. I don't hold much hope with the pirates, though. How do you summon and capture ghosts? Impossible."

Gwenn flashed me a look of concern. I was right there with her. "I think that's a great plan. Honestly, I don't know why you haven't called in reinforcements sooner."

Sebastian stiffened. "I do hope you aren't insinuating I haven't done my job."

"Neither of us think that," Gwenn said, cutting in to diffuse the tension.

"Of course not," I said. "It's been frustrating for all of us. I'm sorry. I wasn't implying you weren't doing your job. I was only mentioning what the others have said about getting more people on the ground. That's why I'd like to volunteer Gwenn and myself to do some sleuthing."

Sebastian cast me a narrow-eyed gaze. "What exactly do you have in mind?"

I shifted in my seat, pausing to choose my words carefully. "As I see it, you view me as a weak link, a liability of sorts."

His chest heaved.

"Let me continue. I'm not saying it in a bad way. I get it. I do. You had to come searching for me tonight to make sure I was okay when you should be concentrating your efforts on the manhunt."

Sebastian relaxed into his chair. "Go on."

"What if Gwenn agreed to be my backup? That frees you to do Council business. Gwenn and I could come at this from the paperwork angle. You know, boring research. We might get lucky and uncover more about this guy working with the horseman."

"Hmm," Sebastian said, "that could have merit. I'll think about it."

I bristled but kept from engaging in a verbal battle with the vampire studying me. Hudson jumped onto my lap. I stroked his soft fur. I waited. I wanted an answer now, not tomorrow when it'd be too late.

After what seemed an eternity, Sebastian gave in. "Fine. It isn't ideal, but Gwenn is trustworthy and a talented witch. I know she will watch out for you." He turned to stare at Gwenn.

She nodded. "You can count on me."

"I am," Sebastian said. His tone was sharp.

Gwenn took it in stride and gave him a broad grin. Hudson purred in agreement. I shut my mouth so I wouldn't say anything that would lead him to change his mind.

Sebastian stood and pushed his chair in but didn't leave. He stared down at me for several long seconds. I maintained eye contact and kept petting Hudson in slow, even strokes. I tried really hard to ignore the cat's nails biting into my thighs.

Not responding to Sebastian seemed to irritate him more than if I'd done my usual, which was to say something like, "What? Did you have something more to say?" I thought it but took the silent approach. I let out the breath I'd been holding only after Sebastian strode out without saying anything to me.

"Well done," Gwenn said.

"Not really. If he stood there a moment longer, I think I would have blurted out some sarcastic remark that would have made me feel good for about ten seconds and then launched me into a heated debate with him about his overbearing attitude."

Hudson jumped off my lap, nudged against me, and trotted into the back kitchen.

"What do we do now?" Gwenn said. Gone was the calm she'd previously exuded. She sat angled away from the table with her legs crossed and one foot bouncing up and down. She got up and began shuffling things around on the table. She put her empty dish between us then took several napkins and placed them around the dish.

"We are the dish. The napkins cure the Council's reinforcements. Once the extra manpower arrives, we won't be able to avoid them. You'll be forced to tell them what you know, and the jig is up. Agatha won't cooperate with anyone but those she considers her own. We can't have them scaring her away." She plunked into her chair, defeated.

I'd been doing some quick calculations while Sebastian was here and had a solution I prayed would work. I moved her mug between the dish and a nearby row of napkins. "The mug is our way out."

"I don't get it," she said.

I grinned. "We do exactly what we said we'd do. First, we go to Sebastian's, aka the mug, put the map back on his desk, and gather anything from the lab that might help us when we meet with Hulda and Agatha."

"And?"

"And we call in our own reinforcements. We have time before the rendezvous to connect with Angie. I'd like her take on the human involved. She has access to the police database that could prove useful to us. I would have thought if the prints from the glass shards we gave Shawn pinged their list, Sebastian would have mentioned it. It's also possible they are still running the prints with only a partial to work with. My idea is to follow the paper trail just like I said we would until we are ready to make our next move. Sebastian's is a place no one will bother us. No one can get in without help getting past the protective barrier."

Gwenn lifted a brow. "But we can get out! They think we are safely tucked away, and we have our way past the napkins before anyone is the wiser. Truthful misdirection. We do as promised but with a twist. It'll still be tricky but doable. Nice."

I rose and took a bow. "Thank you. First things first."

I headed to the kitchen. "George!" I called as I approached the doorway. "Can I have a word with you?"

I jumped when he popped around the corner to face me. The man appeared almost out of thin air. If I didn't know better, I'd swear he was a supernatural of some kind with a talent for invisibility.

"What can I do for you?" he said, dusting flour from his apron.

I scanned the kitchen. All the counters were spotless. Why he had on a floured apron when he clearly was not baking was suspicious. "Good try," I said. "I'm not buying it. You can take off your apron disguise and join us for a chat."

He chuckled. "I'm hurt. I thought the apron was a nice touch."

I shook my head and walked back to Gwenn. George followed.

"George here has something to tell us. Don't you, George? Tell Gwenn what a fantastic baker you are."

He shrugged. "I'm a simple man. I do bake. Sometimes. Most of the time, though, I act as a middleman and sell what I acquire elsewhere. This is true of my bagels and my information."

Gwenn started laughing. "You and Janda would make a great team. You both tell the truth with a twist!"

George and I stared at her like she'd lost her marbles. Once she'd gotten control of herself, I took a sugar container from a nearby table and placed it next to the mug.

"This is George," I said.

"Oh, yes. I see where you're going with this," she said.

George did not see. He scratched first his head and then his chin. "I am sweet?"

I pulled out a chair for George. "If you say so. Sit. I have a job for you."

"Not so sweet. Fine. What job am I doing?"

"Only what you've been doing all along. Spying." When he appeared offended, I rephrased it. "Information gathering. That's all. And in return, we will keep your middleman bagel enterprise a secret."

He scowled. "Your job sounds very much like blackmail."

"Nah. Not really. We just need your particular expertise. You seem to know what people are doing and where they will be at any particular time. That's exactly what we need, and your skills make you an asset." I moved the sugar container closer to the mug.

Gwenn's eyes brightened, and she rubbed her hands together.

George looked concerned. "Gwenn seems excited by your plan, but I have yet to hear what my role is in this caper of yours."

I gave the sugar container that represented George a little shove in the direction of the napkins blocking its path. It pushed past them easily.

"We require someone who knows what the Council does and will know where to find security gaps in the perimeter at Sebastian's. We need a getaway guy."

CHAPTER 20
LOVE STORY

Gwenn entered her number into George's phone. "Text me as soon as you find out anything."

George nodded. "I'll call in a few favors and see what the Council has planned."

I opened the door, glanced outside, then turned back to George. "We'll need a clear exit path. Gwenn will text you when but look for us at nightfall tomorrow."

"That's All Hallow's Eve. In Sleepy Hollow." He fidgeted with his apron ties. "I'm not a fan of that day. It's best to stay indoors when the Horseman is around."

Gwenn put a hand on his shoulder. "Don't worry. He's not after you. He's after Janda."

"Well, that makes it *all* better. Doesn't it?" It came out snarkier than I had intended, but my knack for ending up as a target for the bad guys made me defensive.

George shrugged. "Actually, it does."

I shook my head and walked out to the street. George locked up the second Gwenn and Hudson stepped onto the sidewalk. I stood in the middle of the street, looking up and down it.

"What are you doing?" Gwenn said, joining me.

"Something's not right."

"I'll say," a deep voice said. Mutther appeared from the shadows of a building a few doors down from the bagel shop.

"I should have known Sebastian went away too readily." I strode over to Mutther. Now that he was acting as a bodyguard and spy at Sebastian's command, our fun banter had taken a hit. I realized I missed those earlier times. "How long have you been tracking us?"

"I haven't," he said.

Gwenn came over and grinned like a schoolgirl with a crush.

He tugged on the bottom of his shirt, cleared his throat, and then turned his attention to me. "I got here just as Sebastian was leaving."

"So you're not here on his orders?" I scanned his face to see if he was lying. He met my gaze. Either he was telling the truth or was a pretty good liar. "Hmph. If you say so."

"Believe what you want."

Gwenn picked up Hudson to keep him from winding his way around all of our legs.

"You missed an excellent cup of coffee," she said. "I can knock on the door to see if George can give you a to-go cup."

"I'm good," he said. "After staying at Sebastian's, it became apparent if I was going to get a decent cup of coffee, I'd better invest in a machine for my place."

He took a step closer to me and gave me his pissed-off glare.

"What?" I wouldn't back down. My back stiffened. My lykoi pushed for release, sensing a challenge.

"You know what." He did a low warning growl.

I knew he was mad about me leaving his place alone, but I didn't care. "Growl all you want. Everyone has forgotten that I'm also a Sleepy Hollow Hunter and don't need to be coddled. I was taking care of myself long before I met you or Sebastian. I earned my place as a Hunter."

It took a moment, but he relaxed his stance. "You're right. I've seen you in action. You're a force unto your own for sure. That doesn't mean I can stop being who I am."

"Neither can I. So, you be you, and I'll be me. We'll have each other's back." This was a core belief. I knew I would always be able to count on him and he would count on me.

Gwenn grabbed us into a group hug with Hudson sandwiched in the middle.

"You guys are amazing," she said.

Mutther and I peeled her off us.

"I think we should tell him," she said.

"You can't be serious. I'm not telling him squat."

"Does this have anything to do with the exit path I overheard you mention to George?"

"Yes," Gwenn said.

"Oh, my God! Gwenn! Seriously? No."

"Too late," Mutther said. "Whatever it is, I'm part of it now."

I closed my eyes and took several deep breaths. When had my life gotten so out of control? Then I had my answer. This was Alex's fault. Yup. That man had grabbed my heart and ripped me from my solitary existence where I had called all the shots. I'd let him into my life, and once that crack opened, all these other people slipped in behind him. Damn.

I opened my eyes to see them both waiting for my response. "You know I don't do the team-player thing well."

"That's an understatement," he said.

"And you being you means I'll have a tracker on my heels no matter what I say or do, so I guess I'm stuck with you." I paused to look around us. "Wait. Is Nick hanging around, too?" Biker Nick was an outstanding tracker and loyal friend to Mutther.

"Guilty." Nick's voice echoed toward us from a nearby alley.

"Come on out," Mutther said.

"Janda," Nick said, "you're slipping. I thought you'd have found me out sooner." He chuckled.

I sighed.

Hudson jumped from Gwenn's arms and went to sniff Nick. After making a complete circle around the wolf shifter's legs, the Bengal purred loudly and made his way over to Gwenn, who scooped him up.

"Now we have a team," she said.

"Oh, joy." I didn't want to admit it, but having Mutther and Nick helping us would greatly improve our odds.

"What are we doing?" Nick said. He rubbed his hands together, eager for action.

"Don't look so thrilled. It's nothing exciting. You won't be fighting anyone or causing mayhem." I couldn't blame him for itching to do something besides playing babysitter to me.

"You sure can burst a guy's bubble." His excitement dimmed but didn't go out entirely.

"That's me," I said. "But life tends to mess with my plans, so there's always a chance you'll get your wish."

"Now you're talking." He moved back and forth on the balls of his feet and did a few air jabs with his fists as if getting ready for a fight.

Gwenn laughed.

"Don't encourage him," Mutther said. "Come on. We've

stood in the open long enough." He lowered his voice. "We'll go to the bar." Then he glanced around. "Where's Miss Kitty?"

"She's safely tucked away near the historical society. You and Nick can go on ahead. We'll meet you there." I still had to call Angie and wasn't about to do it in front of Mutther.

"We'll drop you off. Our bikes are over there." He indicated the alley where Nick had come from.

Gwen put Hudson down. "Sorry. I left Hudson's travel pack at work. Janda and I will walk there, then she can give me a lift to the bar."

On cue, Hudson let out a plaintiff meow. Gwenn patted his head. "Come along. Time for a ride." She gave Mutther a small wave and tapped the side of her leg for Hudson to follow her to the aqueduct trail.

"See you soon," I said to a very disgruntled Mutther. His exhalation of frustration brushed the back of my neck as I turned away from him. I suppressed a grin and followed Gwenn.

We'd reached the trailhead and started down the path when the two bikers revved their engines as they sped past us.

"Thanks for getting us out of that," I said.

"No problem. I assumed you'd want some alone time before we meet them."

"You assumed right."

I left the trail and crossed the backyard of the historical society, stepping over scorch marks in the grass from the recent fighting. I had so many questions to ask Agatha about how the ghosts used fireballs and why my presence had made them retreat. Her connection to them might be my only shot at understanding how to defeat them.

"Pretty weird," Gwenn said. She bent to brush her fingers over one of the burn marks.

"Yes, it is." I paused to examine the blackened earth but started to feel uneasy standing there. I took the steps to the porch two at a time, suddenly anxious to be inside.

Hudson shot past me to the door, where he sat and meowed. I waited for Gwenn to pull out her key, but she simply came up and turned the knob. The door was unlocked.

"You don't keep it locked?"

She shrugged. "Seeing how badly the place is messed up, I didn't think it would matter."

"You have a point." I followed her inside. Hudson meandered through the first-floor rooms, burrowing beneath piles of papers Gwenn had lined up against one wall as she worked to clear space to begin the monumental task of reorganizing the archives.

"Tsk!" Gwenn shooed him away. "I worked hard on that mess."

Hudson merely looked at her, swished his tail, and moved off to another room, where he could be heard digging into yet another pile.

Gwenn sighed. "I give up."

I pulled out my phone. "I'm going to see if Angie has an update."

"Sounds good. It's time for me to see what Hudson is up to." A second later, a loud crash came from the adjoining room. With a groan, she left to find what mischief her cat had gotten into now.

I stepped over a group of vintage photos and waited for Angie to answer my call.

"Angie here. What's up, Janda?" Her voice was as perky as ever.

"I'm hitting roadblocks in my investigation. Do you have anything for me?"

"Not much. The prints didn't turn up anything useful, so whoever it is doesn't have a profile in any of the databases. Sorry. I wish I could be more helpful."

"Not your fault. I appreciate it. I'm stumped on how to find this guy."

"Yeah. Shawn is frustrated. We've released a news update that should buy you some time with the public, but if something doesn't break soon, I think we could be facing public outcry over the recent deaths. I'm not sure how many accidental deaths we can have in one month. Folks want to feel safe, especially at this time of the year."

"If they only knew the Horseman was real." I chuckled.

"Actually, I'm using the upcoming festivities to divert attention away from what's been happening. You know, playing up the fun aspects of folklore in Sleepy Hollow. Shawn has even volunteered to assist with a costume party in the center of town at dusk. Food, drinks, and games. And lots of pumpkins. You should come."

"It sounds fun, but I already have plans. Good luck with the event."

"Thanks. And if I hear anything, I'll let you know."

Gwenn rushed into the room, waving a piece of paper. "Look what Hudson found!"

"A piece of paper?"

"Not just any piece of paper. He found a love letter."

"I assume you'll explain its relevance sometime before I die of old age."

"It's written to Agatha! From her ghost pirate lover! Well, just pirate lover since he was alive when it was written."

I snatched the paper from her fingers. "What's it say?"

At that moment, Hudson came strutting around the corner, all proud of himself. I wanted to kiss that mischievous feline. I skimmed the page, glancing up at Gwenn every few seconds. She leaned closer, impatient for me to finish reading. I flipped the page over and kept reading, but it ended mid-sentence. "Where's the rest of it? It stops with, *farewell my lovely Agatha. I will——.*" I flipped the page again to be sure I hadn't missed anything. "He will what? What happened all those years ago? He mentions finding love with another but still caring for her. That sucks, but what else was he telling her?"

"That's all Hudson found. Whatever else the guy was saying doesn't matter much. Who cares that he thanked her for helping him hide the treasure when he cheated on her? The scumbag pirate was telling her he was in love with another woman who was having his baby!"

I frowned. "Do you think this is what made Agatha go nuts and curse the pirates?"

"Well, yes! Don't tell me you wouldn't go a little crazy if someone did this to you?" She sputtered in sheer outrage. "I would want to give him a piece of my mind and then some! Seriously. I can't imagine what Agatha was going through when she read this."

"How do we know she did read it? And he never mentioned a baby, so how did she know about the child?" I handed the letter back to Gwenn, who was slowly regaining her composure. Her reaction had me thinking she had experience with being dumped.

"Hmm. We don't, but she found out somehow and killed the other woman."

"After meeting her, I can't see her killing anyone despite being heartbroken. And the other woman didn't die until after she had the guy's baby. I don't know. Something doesn't seem right with the story passed down through the years."

l tried to think of myself in Agatha's place and could feel my lykoi stirring. "Too bad we don't have the last page. The signature would have been useful." I glanced around the room. "Do you think it could still be here?" I began sifting through papers on the off chance I'd get lucky.

Gwenn's jaw dropped. "Good grief. Do you think the intruder was searching for answers just like us?"

"I think he has a vested interest in the ghost pirate legend. He may be after the treasure. It's possible he's a descendant of Agatha's lover or one of the other pirates." It felt right. It made sense as to why he had aligned with the Horseman.

"We have to get it first," Gwenn said.

"We sure as hell do."

CHAPTER 21

LEGENDS

Gwenn and I searched in vain for the last page of the letter.

"I can't do any more of this tonight," I said. "We can try again in the morning. Maybe Sebastian will back off from haunting my steps if he thinks we're here working all day. Besides, it'll give me something to do to keep my mind off what will happen if I fail tomorrow night."

"You're too hard on yourself. None of this is your fault, and no matter what happens, you've brought two sisters together who would never have seen one another again without your help." She placed yet another old photograph in a file box, straightened the growing mountain of bound newspapers, and sighed. "It's a start. But the morning is reserved for potion making."

"You're right. Potions first and then make our excuses to leave. We'll have to go back before we meet Agatha and Hulda so Sebastian thinks I'm safe at home." The thought of pulling it all off stressed me. Failing meant losing Alex.

A clock gave a choked chime from down the narrow

hallway. Gwenn picked it up from where it lay partly on its side and set it down on a drop-leaf table where, it could chime properly.

My phone pinged to announce a text message from Mutther asking if we were on our way.

"He is really getting on my nerves. Telling them may have been a mistake."

Gwenn retrieved the pet travel bag from where she'd left it earlier and began stuffing an unenthusiastic Hudson into it. "I think it's nice he wants to protect you."

I grunted my disgust, but Gwenn simply chuckled and continued wrestling with an uncooperative Hudson. The cat was hissing loudly when I strode out the back door to get Miss Kitty ready. I was almost to the edge of the aqueduct trail when I caught the faint whiff of sulfur that froze me in my tracks. My lykoi sent a warning reverberating deep inside me. I spun around to see a middle-aged man lurking near a tree, glancing at me carefully from behind it.

"Come on out," I said, lending as much authority to my voice as I could muster.

The man took a few steps away from his hiding spot. "I know who you are, traveler. I know we want the same thing."

I made no motion to advance in his direction. This guy had something on his mind, and I wanted to know what he wanted from me.

"Is that so?" He'd called me a traveler. Few knew about my ability to go between worlds. How he knew made me even more curious about him.

"Yes," he said, keeping his voice low. "He wouldn't like me talking to you, but I had to risk it. You have to open the chest and free the pirate ghosts."

"You're the human working with the Horseman?" My

mind raced to think of a way to capture him, but he took a step back toward his cover.

"I'm bound to him. I do his bidding. You can't stop the Horseman, and you can't save your guy. But you *can* release my ancestor from the witch's curse." His voice wavered uneasily, and he kept glancing around as if expecting to be jumped at any moment. But it wasn't me he seemed to be scared of. "I can't stay. I just had to see for myself if the stories were true. I can see they are."

"What are you talking about?" I took half a step in his direction but halted. I didn't dare scare him away when he might be able to shed light on the pirate curse and how to break it. He was also a murderer who had to be brought to justice.

He let out a low rumble of laughter. "Just look at yourself. How can you not know the power you wield? Only you can break the curse. Then my ancestor will be free and I'll get what's rightfully mine."

"What power? What's rightfully yours?" I was stalling, and he knew it.

"Never you mind about what's mine. That's between the Horseman and me. You should worry about yourself." His laughter grew, but he caught himself before it got too loud. "You'll understand soon enough. You may not like it, but destiny never asked us what we wanted in life. Sleepy Hollow has legends and secrets it keeps hidden to this day. Good luck, traveler. You'll need it." He ducked behind the tree.

I ran over, searching all around, only to discover he'd gone. "Hell. How'd he manage that?" I strained my senses to see if he was still there but came up empty.

I placed a hand against the bark and caught sight of

what the man must have already noticed. My skin was glowing—again.

"This is some freaky shit."

"What's freaky?" Gwenn asked, coming up behind me and lugging a very unhappy Hudson.

"Me," I said. I held my hand out in front of her. The light was rapidly fading, but there was enough residual light to cause her to gasp.

"What happened? Why are you glowing?"

"I have no clue. However, I just met our elusive human."

Gwenn stood open-mouthed for a few seconds. "Holy crap!"

I took her arm and guided her toward Miss Kitty. "We can talk about it at the bar. This is way bigger than the two of us can handle. I'm think it's time to disclose everything to Mutther." I couldn't believe I'd just said I needed help.

Once Gwenn had Hudson safely on my Harley, we took off. More than once, I glanced in my side mirror, wondering what might be following us. Nothing would surprise me at this point.

As we rode, Gwenn leaned in and chatted into my ear. "Did your lykoi get anxious when you encountered the man?"

Not wanting to yell back at her, I just nodded.

"Then I have a theory about why you're glowing. I'll explain later."

I was glad when we pulled into the alley by the bar and parked Miss Kitty near the rear entrance. My nerves were rattled, not that I'd admit it to anyone.

"Where've you been?" Mutther stood in the doorway, looking as angry as he sounded. His hand gripped the edge of the door frame with such force the wood creaked.

I ignored his attitude and squeezed past him. I glanced over my shoulder to see he had moved aside to let Gwenn through and was securing the back door. I joined Nick at the bar. He sat with a bottle of beer in his hand and a smirk on his face.

"He's not too happy with you," Nick said.

"Nothing new there," I said. I grabbed a handful of peanuts from a bowl stationed in front of Nick and popped a few in my mouth.

Mutther went behind the bar while Gwenn took a stool next to me. It was obvious there was something going on between them, but I had too much on my plate to be concerned about two grown people skirting their attraction to one another.

"I'm done with you shutting me out," Mutther said. His brown eyes grew so dark they were almost black.

"Fine with me. I have a lot to share." My stomach rumbled so loudly that they all turned toward me with raised brows. "Sorry. I'm hungry. That bagel wasn't enough. Do you have anything besides peanuts?" I stuffed a few more nuts into my mouth.

Mutther proceeded to his upstairs apartment in search of something to satisfy my hunger.

Nick elbowed me. "You need to shift, don't you?" he said. "Your lykoi must sense a fight and wants to hunt."

"Really?" Gwenn said, staring at me as if she was waiting for my lykoi to show itself. "So, that's a real phenomenon? Your inner animal is preparing to fight?"

"I guess." I'd never thought much about it before.

It was Nick's turn to stare at me. "All these years as a shifter, you never connected the dots. Don't you know your own body? Do you know anything about being a shifter?"

That rankled me because, if I had to be honest, I didn't know my own body and how my magic worked. I didn't know a lot of things about myself. I ran off instinct. "I know you piss me off. Does that count?"

Nick burst out laughing.

"What's so funny?" Mutther returned with a steaming tray of meaty pizza.

Pepperoni, sausage, and tiny meatballs mingled with gobs of cheese. The aroma taunted me. "Oh, my God. Pass me a slice." I was salivating so much that I nearly drooled. I didn't care that it was piping hot and scorched my tongue. I folded the sides of the pizza inward to get a larger bite. This was heaven. I scarfed down one slice in record time and reached for a second.

Mutther yanked the tray just as my fingers touched the crust of the next slice, sending a mini-meatball tumbling to the floor.

"Hey!" I leaned across the bar toward him, but he stepped back out of my reach.

"Not another piece until you start talking," he said, holding the pizza above his head with both hands.

"Not fair," I grumbled.

"When has anything in your life been fair?" he said.

I sat back on my stool. He was right. My lykoi would have to be patient for its food. I thought about where to begin and came up short. I glanced at Gwenn for help.

"Maybe start with your ghost-witch family?"

"Yeah. Even that is complicated, but here goes."

I noticed that Mutther had placed the tray at one end of the bar, still well out of my reach, and stood with his arms folded in front of him, waiting. Nick had put down his beer and turned toward me on his stool, as alert as I'd ever seen him. Gwenn gave me an encouraging look that let me know she had my back.

"You all know I can see and speak to my great-great-grandmother. You know she has helped me enter the Underworld to see Alex. Well…" I paused, took a breath, and continued. "She also introduced me to her sister, Agatha, the ghost witch who placed the curse on the pirates."

Nick let out a low whistle.

I met his gaze then looked at Mutther, who seemed equally surprised. "Yep. I have two ghost witches in my life. We plan to see them after nightfall. We have to get through the rest of today and plan our strategy for when we meet up. Crazy stuff, let me tell you." I squirmed in my seat, thinking about what I was about to reveal. "And they have informed me that I'm also a witch. Thankfully, not yet a ghost, just a regular witch."

"That's not actually true," Gwenn said. "You are far from regular. *I'm* a regular witch, albeit one who can communicate with my cat, but still fairly normal. You, on the other hand, have something extra in your blood. You are a traveler. You can go between the world of the living and the dead. Your witch magic is surfacing to the point you now glow when you feel threatened and form a protective barrier around yourself. That light attracts the spirits seeking passage."

I stared at her and mentally counted to three to calm my nerves. Counting to ten was never an option for me. I wasn't that patient.

I narrowed my gaze at Gwenn. "And when were you planning on telling me all this about why I light up? Crap. What's happening to me?"

I was truly rattled by her revelation. I flexed my fingers and turned my hands to stare at my palms. An ever-so-tiny glimmer surfaced on my skin.

Nick gaped at me.

Mutther leaned closer and grabbed my hand. He ran a

finger from the base of my index finger to the opposite edge of my hand. The motion left a faint trail of light that faded in seconds.

He spent a few moments deep in thought.

"How is it that the human working with the Horseman knows more than me?" It wasn't easy being thrust into magic you had zero experience with and still be expected to defeat your worst enemy with it.

Nick almost launched himself at me. "You know who the human is? Who? Where do I find him?"

I held up my hands. "Slow down. I only just met him tonight and—"

Mutther's nostrils flared. "I knew it! I should never have left you alone!"

Gwenn shook her head. "Look at the two of you. Male hormones raging and seeking revenge. Honestly! I don't know how Janda has dealt with you this long."

"Yeah. What she said." I straightened to my full height and squared my shoulders. "If you would back off a minute, then maybe I could continue my story." I glared at them. Mutther and Nick glared daggers back at me.

"Continue," Mutther said with clenching and unclenching his jaw.

"The short version of all this is that I don't know all the details. I can tell you that Agatha can't break the curse and neither can Hulda. They say I'm the only one who can. Which is also what this human told me." I turned to Gwenn. "That's the part you missed earlier."

"No worries. Did he say anything else?"

"He said he came to see if the stories were true. When I asked him what he meant, he laughed at me for not understanding what he was talking about." I gave Gwenn an imploring look. "But I still don't know, which makes me feel pretty stupid."

Mutther and Gwenn exchanged looks.

This wasn't the first time I'd seen them giving one another a knowing gaze.

"I'm not so stupid as to not see you're hiding something from me. What's going on?"

CHAPTER 22

KNIGHT IN SHINING ARMOR

"It's not mine to tell," Gwenn said.

"The man I met claimed there are legends that remain secrets in Sleepy Hollow. Do you have any idea what he's talking about?"

I met Mutther's gaze. His entire body tensed. I'd hit a nerve for sure.

"Mutther?"

"I'm not hiding any Sleepy Hollow secrets. But in all fairness, since you're being open about your family and the revelation that you're part witch, I'll confess I have my own family drama."

I sat on my barstool and gave Nick a sideways glance.

"Don't look at me," Nick said. "We don't talk about family much—mine or his."

I turned my attention back to Mutther. "What kind of drama? Basic family stuff or shifter stuff?"

"A bit of both," Gwenn said. "At least that's how I would define it."

"Gwenn's right. Let's start with my family name." He

cleared his throat. "It's not Utther with a double T. It's Uther, as in Pendragon."

"What? You royalty or something?" Nick said through a mouthful of peanuts.

"The royal part is pretty watered down by now, but the curse part keeps going strong."

"No kidding?" I was impressed. No matter how diluted the gene pool. Mutther was implying something very important that made his appearance the night the historical society went up in flames make sense. "You're a dragon shifter. I didn't imagine your gray skin. I knew something was going on with you."

"Holy smokes!" Nick said. He rose from his seat, leaned across the bar, and grabbed Mutther by the arm to examine it. "I don't see any dragon scales."

"He's able to call on his dragon to emerge," Gwenn said. "That's why he could enter the burning building and not get hurt. And that's how he saved me." She beamed at Mutther.

"That's way cool," I said. "But how is it a family curse?"

Nick's face grew solemn. "Hybrids with two dominant entities have to choose which path to follow. You haven't chosen yet, have you?"

"Exactly," Mutther said. "That's also why I haven't joined a pack. I don't know how to figure this out."

"Why do you have to pick one side of yourself? I don't. I'm both wolf and a werecat. Why can't you be both?" I was truly perplexed by the belief a person had to be just one thing.

"It's not that simple," Mutther said. "Your wolf and cat have melded, taking the dominant features of each to create a new form. Your lykoi is unique. I don't think I can do what you've done. My family is from a long line of kings. My dragon wants to be dominant while my wolf wants to also claim that role."

"And if the wolf wins out, you'd have to move away or fight to become a leader." My heart sank. I understood now that Mutther's heritage made him extremely powerful. He was a natural alpha and wouldn't be able to yield beneath any pack leader. He'd have to fight Nick or my uncle.

"Now, do you see why I've kept this to myself?" Mutther's shoulders slumped.

A thought occurred to me, and while I knew the answer, I had to ask. "Alex knows, doesn't he?"

He nodded. "I made a vow to him that I'd keep you safe. I'm bound by that vow. If I intentionally break it, my dragon will fade away, but not before it takes my wolf with it."

"What if you were released from the vow?" I was not happy with Alex, no matter how good his intentions were at the time. I searched for a way out of the dilemma and found none.

"It would have to come from Alex or someone he gives that authority to in his stead." Mutther paced behind the bar before stopping in front of me. "If Alex never returns, I'm afraid you're stuck with me for more years than either of us will care to count."

"No way! That is not going to happen." I stood up and slammed a hand onto my stool. "I refuse to have a knight in shining armor following me wherever I go."

Nick chuckled. "More like a pet dragon."

I whipped around. "Dragon?"

"Yeah," Nick said. "His dragon is bound to you."

"But if he shifts into a full dragon, then his wolf will

fade." My heart sank. "Is that why only your arms and face had dragon scales when I saw you carrying Gwenn out of the fire? You stopped yourself from shifting completely."

"Yes," Mutther said. He came from behind the bar and touched Gwenn's shoulder. "It's also why I can't get involved in a relationship. Until Alex releases me, I'm stuck in a kind of shifter limbo."

"It would suck to lose your wolf, but your dragon would dominate, and you could go on with your life as a dragon shifter. Right?" I was still confused by the tug-of-war that raged within his body.

"Ah, I thought you'd get to that part," Mutther said. "That's where the curse comes into play. If I shift into a full dragon, even while retaining my wolf as a beta, I may never be able to shift back into my human form."

Gwenn brushed a tear from her cheek.

"That would force the packs to hunt you down and destroy you," Nick said. His voice was low and full of anguish. It was evident that he'd kill Mutther to protect his pack. It might tear him apart to do it, but do it he would.

"Believe me," Mutther said, "I'm trying my best not to have that happen. Alex didn't understand the ramifications of his request, but once it was out there, I had no other options than to accept it and the consequences if something went wrong."

Hudson trotted down the hall toward Gwenn. He'd been let out of his travel bag and had been investigating Mutther's apartment upstairs. When he got close, he made a detour and jumped onto the stool next to me. He meowed several times. I looked over to Gwenn for a translation.

"Oh. It seems Hudson has been listening in and believes that Janda could reach Alex and get him to designate her as his oath bearer, which means she could, in turn, release Mutther from his vow. It would solve one problem. Unfortunately, not the issue of becoming a crazed dragon." She reached over and ran her hand down Hudson's back. "You're just full of ideas today. You lovely cat."

I wouldn't describe Hudson as lovely, but he did seem to be coming up aces today. Mutther's predicament was one more reason to save Alex. If I freed him, I wouldn't have to be his proxy. He could revoke the vow.

Gwenn placed a reassuring hand on my arm. "Don't worry. Hudson says you can do this."

She patted my arm before going back to stroking her cat.

I gave Hudson a quick scratch behind his ear. "Thanks for believing in me, but I don't know how to cross into the Underworld anymore. Which brings us back to my family and our plan of action to bring Alex home."

Gwenn took the lead on the whole plan thing. "Janda and I will be meeting with Hulda and Agatha near Sing-Sing to unearth the treasure and hopefully break the curse."

"Sing-Sing? An active prison? Guarded by not just humans but supernaturals? You make it sound easy," Nick said. "Until it isn't easy anymore. What then?"

"We haven't gotten that far," I said.

Gwenn smiled broadly at Nick. "That's why we're letting you in on our plan. We need backup."

"My idea of having their help was for them to run interference with the Council, not be our backup."

"That too," she said. "But we aren't any closer to understanding what will happen if you're successful in breaking the pirate's curse. That's when things could get a little out of hand."

"We may not get that far if we can't stay off Sebastian's radar," I said.

Mutther settled onto a stool near Gwenn. "For argument sake, let's say the Council and Sebastian are preoccupied with matters other than Janda. I'm more concerned with whatever you're planning with Hulda. I can't let you go alone."

I sighed. "Fine. We'll figure out how to make this work. But there's also the crazy human who apparently is bound to the Horseman, or so he says."

Gwenn's eyes grew bigger. "He's bound to the Horseman?"

My stomach still rumbled in protest of that missing second slice of pizza, but I ignored it. I shared my take on the human.

"The man is middle-aged and has nothing remotely intimidating about him besides hanging out with the Horseman. In fact, he seemed afraid to be found talking to me. How he could have murdered people is beyond me. But like others before him, it would seem the idiot gave his allegiance to the Horseman."

"The twit," Nick said.

"Agreed," I said. "He did say I have to succeed in breaking the curse for his pirate ancestor to be set free and for him to get some kind of reward he feels is rightfully his. And while that may sound like he's on our side, I wouldn't look to him for support. He has to do whatever the Horseman commands."

"They never learn," Mutther said. "Nothing good comes from taking the Horseman's side."

"Yeah, there's that for sure." I was brainstorming as I filled them in on what we knew. "As I see it, this guy wants his ancestor's spirit freed and wants what he feels belongs to him. The Council wants the Horseman and the human and the treasure. Then there's us. I, for one, need to break the curse to free Aunt Agatha, who is as much a victim of the curse as the pirates. I also need to get the brimstone before the Horseman." I glanced around our little group. "Do we know of anyone else who wants the treasure?"

"Brimstone?" Mutther's face turned ashen. "There's brimstone in that treasure chest?"

"Yes," I said. "Agatha claims it's a piece forged from the demon's mines."

"The Horseman can't get it first," Mutther said, his voice tight. "If he does, we're all doomed."

"I gathered it was bad, Mutther. No need to go all doomsday on us," I said. "Besides, the Horseman will have to go through me to get to it. The brimstone is mine."

"That seals the deal," Nick said. "You're in a tight spot with a low probability of success. You need us." He slapped his thigh. "You have your backup. What now?"

I glanced at Mutther. "And you?"

"Even if I wasn't bound to protect you, I'd help. The Horseman has managed to elude capture for too long, and if he gets that brimstone, Sleepy Hollow will become a ghost town—literally," he said.

"I don't intend to let that happen," I said. I met Gwenn's gaze and knew we would each do our utmost to defeat the Horseman.

"There's one more thing," Gwenn said. "You should know that if Agatha senses any interference she'll disappear. We can't find the treasure without her help, so we're doing what we can to circumvent Sebastian and the other Council members."

"Sebastian has become obsessed with tracking my

every move," I said. "It's infuriating. That blasted mark of his has become a real problem."

"Then get rid of it," Mutther said.

"I can't believe you just said that. Only Sebastian can remove it, and he's claiming it can't be done. Where does that leave me?" My annoyance escalated, and I realized I was taking it out on those closest to me. "Sorry. It's not your fault."

"Sebastian's lying to you," Nick said. "Marks can be removed, but it takes a good witch to do it." His gaze drifted to Gwenn.

"Oh. Wow," Gwenn said. "Well, I can't say I've ever attempted such a complex spell before, but I think it can be done."

My hopes rocketed. "Let's do it."

Mutther cut in. "I suggest you wait until you're in Sebastian's house, or he will come searching for you the second he realizes it's severed. Doing it there will give him the sense that you're still within the safety of the protective spells around his home."

"True," Gwenn said. "You have a fair point and one we best heed."

I huffed my disgruntlement. "Fine. But the sooner the link is gone, the better."

"I understand," she said. "We'll also be working on protection spells, in particular a potion that should help hide her presence. Her witch powers are emerging at an alarming rate. She has yet to understand her witch side, and we don't have time to wait for her to grasp that part of her heritage."

"It's definitely a lot to absorb," I said.

She smiled. "It would be for anyone. Also, while I think

it's pretty awesome that she can call upon a glowing shield, that same light is attracting the ghost pirates. They see her as a conduit to the Underworld and will attempt to cross the divide through her, even if she can't control her portal. Ghosts entering the pathway Janda provides could create instability that might suck Janda into the Underworld forever."

"Wait, wait, wait. I'm a portal to the Underworld? Ghosts can travel through me?"

"In theory, yes," she said. "That's what I'm saying. It answers why the pirate ghosts reached out for you during the battle and why they didn't attack you. Testing my theory is tricky."

"How's she supposed to test it?" Nick said.

Gwenn clasped her hands in front of her and inhaled as if drawing courage. Her words came out in a torrent. "She will have to open the chest with a blood sacrifice, remove the brimstone, release the pirates from the torment of their curse by giving them coins to pay the Ferryman, and open her senses to draw upon the strength of her natural surroundings so her ability as a traveler can create a pathway that Agatha, and possibly the pirates, can use to crossover." She released a loud exhale and met everyone's gazes.

Nick and Mutther just stared at her in complete silence. It seemed they struggled to take it all in, just like me. It didn't sound like a test to me. It sounded like a sink or swim situation. I was at a loss for words. After all, what was there to say? I looked around at our motley group who'd sworn to help one another, even when they had no idea how to do that, and was grateful. Emotions were still a learning curve for me, and I think for Mutther and Nick, too, so I kept those feelings to myself.

Instead, I nodded and did my best to sound confident. "Right. That sounds doable. Maybe."

"Okay," Mutther said.

"I'm with you," Nick said.

My stomach rumbled. I should have insisted on that second slice of pizza. If this insane plan flopped, I might never get to have any for the rest of eternity, and I loved pizza.

CHAPTER 23

THE GATES OF THE UNDERWORLD

Midnight had passed by the time Gwenn and I reached Sebastian's house. But with Mutther and Nick in tow, I figured I'd get a pass on coming in so late. Living under someone else's roof had many rules and inconveniences that irritated me. I thought more and more lately that I had to find my own place, but being close to Hulda was important to me, so I was reluctant to leave. Besides, despite Sebastian's old-school ways, he had grown on me, and I cared very much for him.

I looked up at the house and saw the lantern light in our designated war room flickering through a gap in the drapes. I assumed my presence with the others allowed them to pass through the protective boundary unimpeded, but I couldn't be sure if it was Sebastian or me who let them through the barrier. He pulled aside the window covering to give us a cursory glance before letting the fabric fall back into place.

I wondered how he was doing. The strain of the attacks had been eating away at his patience and made it difficult to gather the sustenance he required. The dead of night was his realm, a time when he was invigorated and lusting for his natural food—blood. With me back in his house, perhaps he'd venture out to take care of himself and not worry about me. I did enough worrying for us both. Not that he had to know that particular point.

I was stressing that Mutther, Nick, Gwenn, and I only had the barest of plans for our meeting with Hulda and Agatha. The guys would take a position far enough away so as not to frighten Agatha but close enough to lend a hand if trouble ensued. They'd also have to work around their obligations to the Council.

Gwenn had yet to hear from George concerning any intel on the Council's activities that could interfere with what we were about to do. She trusted George to dig deep and relay any information that Sebastian and the other higher members of the Council might be withholding.

I placed my future and that of Alex's in the hands of what I now thought of as my inner circle. Sebastian was excluded from the circle, which was not easy when he had a built-in radar for my stress levels. The entire upcoming event seemed like a choreographed dance of avoidance and secrecy.

Sebastian glowered at me as soon as we got inside and my foot crossed the war-room threshold. I ignored the icy glare and proceeded to my favorite chair near the fire. My ass didn't have time to settle into the cushion before he started on me.

"You're late," Sebastian said. His tone seemed more weary than angry. "I suppose dragging the others with you makes you think it's fine to come in at this hour."

I looked at him over my shoulder. "You aren't really going down that road. Are you?"

Sebastian stood by one of the walls of books with a

thick volume in his hand. "Humph." He returned to the tome and flipped a few pages.

"Nick and I made sure they were safe," Mutther said. "Just like you asked."

Sebastian gave another grunt but didn't look up from his book.

I narrowed my gaze at Mutther. He smirked, knowing I couldn't retaliate. From the corner of my eye, I caught Gwenn suppressing a laugh. She'd taken a spot on the loveseat and draped a nearby quilt over her lap. Hudson jumped up and kneaded the quilt several times until he curled into a ball and dozed off. I yawned. Fatigue spread through my body, and I knew it wouldn't be long before sleep overtook me. Sleeping in a chair did not appeal to me.

"As much fun as this has been, I'm going to bed since there doesn't appear to be any pressing news from the Council."

Sebastian ignored my comment. A glance at the mantel clock made it clear why I struggled to stay awake. It chimed a soft dong three times.

"Sebastian," Mutther said, "are you going out?"

"No. I don't think it's wise to leave Janda alone, even if Gwenn is with her."

Gwenn had fallen asleep with one hand on Hudson's back.

I couldn't stop yawning. "I'm fine. Go. Do your thing. We don't need a hungry vampire getting all grumpy for lack of eating."

Nick, who had nodded off in the chair opposite mine, let out a giant snore. It amazed me that Gwenn and Nick had zonked out within the five minutes since we got here. I had sleep envy.

"I'm not tired," Mutther said. "You go hunting. I might

as well hang here for the night." He pointed at Nick. "It appears he won't be going anyplace, so it's not a problem for me to stand guard while you take care of your needs."

Sebastian paused his reading, closed the book, and put it back in its spot on the bookshelf. "Fine. I won't be long. Call me if anything out of the ordinary happens."

Mutther nodded toward the group of us sprawled near the fireplace. "A wolf, a lykoi, and a witch are sleeping in a vampire's house. It doesn't get much more out of the ordinary than that, my friend."

Sebastian nodded. A faint smile spread over his austere face. "Very true."

"Let me point out that I am not yet asleep and shouldn't be lumped into said category. But I'm going to bed, so say what you will." I headed out the door and climbed the stairs to my room.

Mutther and Sebastian spoke in a murmur in the main entrance below me. I caught a snippet of their conversation and froze in my tracks.

"With my life," Mutther said.

A chill ran down my spine at his words. "Please don't let it come to that," I whispered into the darkened hallway. Words held value. Such declarations shouldn't be said out loud lest they came true. I glanced down the stairs at the men and shivered. I'd be damned if I'd be responsible for either of them getting hurt.

With the weight of responsibility heavy on my mind, I went to my room and shut the door. A moment later, I heard Sebastian leave, and Mutther's footfall indicated he was headed into the war room.

I pulled off my boots and let them drop to the floor with a thunk. I took my clothes off, tossed them in the dirty clothes pile, and rummaged in my dresser for the one shirt I refused to wash. I found the white button-down shirt that belonged to Alex and put it on. I buttoned the first few buttons just as the coolness of the air hit my skin and caused my nipples to stiffen. I sighed, wishing Alex's touch had caressed me instead of the air in a frigid room.

"I miss you, my love," I said then climbed into bed and drew the quilt over me.

I reviewed the details of the past day, and as they became a swirl of revelations and emotions, I fell asleep. Cold swept over me, forcing me to near wakefulness. I reached for the quilt to snuggle deeper into it but couldn't find it. My hand touched smooth stone instead.

My eyes flew open. My muscles tightened. My mouth opened in an empty gasp.

"Holy shit." I managed to sputter the words in total disbelief. I placed my hand flat against a cave wall. My lykoi shifted uneasily just below the surface of my skin, ready to fight. I inched barefoot through the darkness and let my instincts carry me forward. A waft of sulfur hit my nose. I paused. An orange glow loomed in the distance. Hot air intensified the closer I moved toward the fiery light. This could not be good.

I stepped out from the tunnel and into a large chamber with several pits that tossed lava into the air. The eruptions sizzled and fell to the ground. Streams of hot liquid meandered around the edges of the pits. An archway as wide as the chamber lay on the other side of the blazing hot holes. I walked toward it, careful to avoid burning my toes.

I stood in the archway's center and gawked at what lay ahead. A throne as black as night took up the middle of an obsidian dais. On that throne sat a demon. He was beautiful. His skin was burnt umber, long strands of dark hair tumbling over his broad shoulders. His chest was bare. He wore black leather pants that clung to him and showed every ripple of muscle. His beauty took my breath away, yet he was still a demon. His eyes blazed orange, and two red horns jutted from his head, completing the dramatic visage of a being who must be royalty in the Underworld.

"You came," he said, his voice deep and sultry. "Good."

"Is it?" I said, keeping my distance. I hadn't meant to come here, yet he made it sound like I honored him with my presence.

He laughed. "I've been dying to meet you, Janda Gray. You are even more intriguing than the rumors of you that have made their way to my ears."

"It seems that you have me at a disadvantage." I took a step closer. "You know me, but I don't know you." My lykoi was clawing for release. I held it in check. There was nothing my lykoi or I could do to defend against the evil that sat before me.

He rose from his throne and descended the steps. The sulfur that clung to him turned from pungent to sweet as he drew nearer. He stopped a foot in front of me, but I held my position. He brushed the white strands of hair back from my face.

"You may call me Jasper."

I didn't miss the hidden meaning of his statement. "What do others call you?"

He stepped back and let out a hearty laugh. "You are clever, Janda Gray. Very clever. But I'm not the type to reveal too much too soon. I prefer to develop a relationship before divulging my other names."

"A relationship? With me? What kind of relationship?" My nerves were tingling. My skin grew slick with sweat from the heat billowing out of the lava pits behind me.

"Business, purely business. For now," he said. A glint of yellow sparkled in the orange irises of his eyes.

I swallowed the lump forming in my throat. "I don't do business with demons."

"You're a bounty hunter. I require such service and pay well for it."

I smiled as politely as I could. "Thanks, but no, thanks." I turned to go in the direction I'd come, uncertain how I'd be able to get home but determined to leave. I'd transported myself here somehow, so there had to be a way to reverse my actions

A wave of heat kissed my backside. Angering a demon isn't smart, but I wagered he wouldn't kill me. At least not yet. If he did, then it could well be my ticket to Alex. I no longer feared death. I just wasn't a fan of pain.

"You're eager to leave before I've told you what I'll pay you." Confidence filled his voice.

He might be accustomed to getting what he wanted, but he hadn't met me. That was exactly the attitude that had me digging in my obstinate heels, and I dug them in deep right now.

I pivoted to face him. "I must not have made myself clear. I choose my jobs, and I don't choose yours."

His lips thinned then curved into a wide smile. "I can give you Alexander Holden."

CHAPTER 24

DEAL WITH THE DEVIL

Whatever contract the demon proposed, I'd take it. Damn him. He was probably already damned, so cursing him in my mind was pointless. I did it anyway.

"I know what you're thinking," he said.

"I doubt that."

I'd never heard of a mind-reading demon, but what did I know? Even if he could read my mind, let him. I had nothing to hide. That annoying yellow glint appeared again in his eyes. I strode toward him and stopped far enough away so I wouldn't have to strain my neck to look up at him. The guy was huge.

"I'm not the devil," he said, his tone casual. "That's my father. As a prince of darkness, I rank high among his many demons." His eyes were glazed over, his tone dark. "However, even as a favored son, I must answer for my mistakes."

He was right. I had briefly considered that he was the devil but just as quickly tossed that idea away. Not having parents growing up, I had no experience pissing off a powerful father. I managed more than a few times to make

Uncle Damon mad, but I didn't think the demon was talking about the same level of parental anger that I'd been exposed to during my childhood

"I don't know what you did to make your father mad at you, and I don't care. Getting in the middle of family issues isn't part of my job, so get on with whatever it is you have to propose about Alex. I'm not saying I'll take the contract, only that I'll listen. And if by chance, you can turn Alex over to me unharmed, then I might be interested in whatever it is you want me to do. Got it?"

His dark mood visibly lifted. "I would expect nothing less."

He waved his hand in a circle, and a portal window appeared against the wall opposite me. I sucked in my breath. The scene before me was of Alex steering a gondola-style boat across a turbulent river. The boat swayed as it bounced precariously over the many waves in its path.

"Can he see us? Hear us?" My voice cracked with emotion as Alex landed the boat safely to shore, unaware of us watching him. "Alex!" I shouted to him, rushing over to the portal window.

"It's one-way," Jasper said. "I create these to keep track of my workers. Alex aids the Ferryman and thus aids me. He performs a necessary service, and I'm reluctant to allow him to leave." He turned away from the portal window, which caused it to disappear. The rocky cavern wall became solid once more.

I faced him with heat unrelated to the lava pits coursing through me. "What do you want me to do?"

"Nothing too difficult. I want the brimstone mask pieces you procure," he said.

He reached over and tugged on my brimstone necklace that I always wore to help me reach Alex in the Underworld.

"You are beyond the need for the likes of this. It's from my mines but lacks the power I infused in the Horseman's mask." He let it slide through his fingers. "You may keep it as a token."

The necklace fell back against my skin. I narrowed my gaze at Jasper, the son of Satan. "What's the catch?"

"Catch?" he said, giving all the appearances of being offended.

"Yeah. You know. Loopholes that get me in trouble. Or killed. That sort of thing."

I watched his jaw muscles tighten. This was not a contract to enter into lightly. Deals with the satanic kind could land you in eternal punishment or worse.

A faint wisp of smoke came from his nostrils. His skin turned a shade darker. "Very well. If it's the truth you want, so be it. But be warned. You may not want to hear it."

"I'll take my chances. Go ahead. Give it a shot." I caught a movement in the shadows and repositioned my body to defend against any attack.

Jasper noticed.

"Come out," he commanded.

A small man-like creature scurried to kneel at Jasper's feet. He was part lizard with gray scales for skin but had the proportions of a man. His facial features were also that of a man. He was bald. He didn't seem to have any body hair and had a stub for a tail, which made me think his predominant genes were that of a lizard.

"What does his Highness wish from Wart?" The lizard man gazed up at Jasper.

"You will aid Janda however she deems fit. I want back what is mine. Do you understand?" He spoke in a deep, commanding voice.

"You're right. I don't like it. I don't want his help," I

said. I moved closer to the kneeling creature and addressed him. "No offense, Wart."

"Do not worry about offending me, Miss Janda," Wart replied. "I live to serve my master."

Jasper let out a long sigh. "Get up, man. Have some dignity. Janda does not believe she needs your help, but there may come a time when that will change." The demon prince met my gaze and held it for several minutes. "Wart will be discreet. However, he will lend his assistance if such a time arrives."

I pursed my lips and flattened my hands against my thighs. That was when I became acutely aware of my attire. I was still in Alex's half-buttoned shirt. No wonder the demon kept giving me salacious glances. I hastened to adjust the garment. I finished buttoning it and gave it a slight tug to cover more of my lady parts. Jasper smirked at my awkwardness. Damn him again.

"Let me get this straight. I procure the piece of brimstone that's in the chest, and then you release Alex. Correct?" I glared at him and waited for his answer.

"Not just the one in the chest. I need both pieces, including the one you previously had in your possession and gave away."

His annoyance was evident in how he clenched and unclenched his fists and how his ramrod-straight arms were so taut that his biceps twitched.

He remained civil, so I attempted to do the same. "As you pointed out, I no longer have that piece of the mask. I couldn't begin to tell you where to find it."

"Oh, but you will find it. You took it to the dredges of the Underworld, and you will get it back."

It was my turn to be angry. I could sense the rise in heat within my body and let it surface. My skin gave off a tinge of light. "In case your spies," I said, glancing at Wart when I spoke, "didn't tell you. I can no longer cross the veil into the Underworld. I've tried. I'd love to regain that ability."

"Yes," Jasper said, his voice smug. "I'm sure you would. But you never lost the ability to cross. You just need the proper focus and motivation. And…direction."

With that, he waved his hand once more, and the portal window came into view. Alex turned as if he knew I was watching, but after a moment he went back to work. He was rowing the gondola on his return trip across the river.

Jasper's tone became impatient. "Until now, you've relied on your dream state to carry you across, which is how you came here when I called upon you. What you lack is the confidence to make the journey while you're awake."

I pointed at Alex, my voice rising. "Don't you think I would have done that by now if I knew how? Alex is what's important. He's the only reason I will work for you. I'll retrieve the piece from the treasure chest, but the other one is out of my reach! What don't you understand?"

"You try my patience. I'm telling you that you can do it. Wart will assist you and act as a guide. You will do it now."

"Now?"

"Yes. Now." Jasper closed the portal window and motioned for Wart to get up.

I pulled myself together and kicked my brain into motion. "Wait. Why do you need me to get the piece in the Underworld? This is your domain. Not mine."

He quirked a brow. "Finally. You're starting to think like a bounty hunter." He strode to his throne and relaxed into it. "My father is punishing me. I cannot go outside a certain boundary. Thus, Wart has been my eyes and ears and has told me about you."

I stepped closer to the dais. "You're grounded?" I stifled a laugh.

"If you must put it that way, fine. Yes. I have been restricted to these rooms until the entire mask is back in my possession."

I thought for a few minutes about the mask pieces and how long they'd been separated. "It's been hundreds of years," I said, glancing around the cavernous room. "Are you telling me that you've been here that long?"

Jasper's teeth ground loud enough for me to hear it from where I stood. He worked his jaw several times and took a deep breath. I found myself feeling sorry for him. I couldn't believe that I felt bad for a demon. *A demon.* Who'd have thought it?

"Don't give me your pity," he said. "Time is nothing here. I have an infinite amount of it. But I'm ready for a change in scenery. And that won't happen until I hand over the entire mask to my father."

I let everything sink in. Then I got worried. Really worried. "Hold up. If I agree to your contract, does that mean I'm also making a deal with your father?"

Jasper rubbed the back of his neck. "Questions. Always questions from you."

"I'm not so naive to think this is straightforward, so yeah, I have questions."

"The answer is no, mostly." He hopped off his throne and stood on the bottom step of his dais. "The contract and any consequences of its failure are strictly mine. However, since this directly involves my father, I cannot guarantee that you wouldn't get caught up in his wrath if we don't give him what he wants."

"Collateral damage," I said.

"Yes," he said, staring down at me. "Think of it as a subcontract job. It's just one you can't screw up."

"Fabulous." I wiped the sweat from my arm. "Unlike you, I don't have unlimited time to fix this mess."

Jasper moved to the center of the room. "Then I suggest you get started."

Wart came to my side and reached his hand out to me. I hesitated but took it. A wave of current washed over me, and we were no longer in the cave. We were standing at the edge of a river. It was the same river I'd seen Alex rowing on earlier. "We're in the Underworld?"

"Yes, mistress," Wart said.

I surveyed my surroundings, peering deep into the darkness. "Is he watching us?"

Wart shrugged. "Most certainly."

"Great. A voyeur. My day is now complete."

Wart chuckled. "Not to worry. He sees but does not hear. He only sees when he has a connection. That is me. Sometimes it is one of his other servants, but mostly me."

I began to understand more about how Jasper controlled his world. His confinement hampered his powerful reach. He couldn't see me unless Wart was nearby. I tucked that interesting bit of knowledge away for now.

The sound of the river rushing past us was like one of those ambient noise machines. It soothed me and made it easier to think. I let go of Wart's hand. "Okay. Now what?"

"What does your heart tell you?" he said, straightening to his full height of about four feet.

"My heart says to seek out Alex, who obviously isn't at the river anymore. I know where he lives, but finding my way won't be easy."

There was nothing around us except the flowing river,

mud, dark skies, and barren trees. The town could have been ten feet away, and I had no way of detecting it.

"Let your heart guide you. You think too hard. You block your own way forward."

"Wise words, Wart." I closed my eyes and took a deep breath. I didn't feel a thing. I took another breath and another. I was about to give up when a small flicker behind my eyelids caught my attention. I opened my eyes to see a path illuminated, stretching from the tips of my bare toes to the line of trees to my left. "Oh! Do you see that?" I said.

"Wart does not, but Wart trusts that Miss Janda knows the way." He grinned.

I liked this odd little creature who was part human and part lizard and seemed incredibly loyal to his demon prince.

I smiled at my companion and took his hand in mine. "This way, Wart."

CHAPTER 25

PAYMENT

As we pushed through the woods, branches and shrubs scratched my legs, but I didn't care. The light guided us to the edge of town. The pull toward Alex grew in intensity. I paused to allow it to point me in the right direction.

Wart tugged on my shirt. "Quick," he said. "We hide."

I didn't question him. I followed. We took cover behind a dumpster. Not the most pleasant of hiding spots, but it worked. A band of unnaturals gathered at the corner where we'd been standing. I glanced down at Wart and nodded my thanks. I'd been so intent on finding Alex that I'd forgotten about the dangers lurking in the Underworld.

It seemed to take forever for them to disperse. Their presence was another reminder of what would happen if the Horseman mended his mask. Unnaturals would be at his beck and call and rise to the realm of the living as his devoted servants.

Tonight was All Hallows Eve, which meant the Horseman would be desperate to break the veil and gather followers. My gut churned at the image the sight of them provoked.

The smell of the trash didn't help the sensation of wanting to hurl my last meal onto the ground. I forced myself to rummage through the bins and pulled out a piece of a large plastic bag. It was black, which was vital, and once tied around me, it made a decent garment to hide the white shirt.

"Good idea," Wart said. He took some rotten fruit, smashed it in his hands, and then rubbed it over his body.

"Why are you doing that?" I wasn't a fan of the stench that shrouded him.

"Disguise," he said.

"As what? Trash?"

He grinned. "Yes. Camouflages my sweetness."

He was serious. But I found nothing sweet about him, and if there had been something, it was obliterated by the nastiness of rot. I motioned for him to follow me as I headed toward Alex's building. We clung to the shadows, and between my trash bag attire and his stink, we didn't garner a glance from a single soul.

"Go inside." I kept my voice low, afraid I'd attract attention.

We ascended the stairs to Alex's room, passing several people slouched against the wall or slumped in a heap on one of the steps. I touched the doorknob and paused to speak to Wart. "I know Jasper can see you and will know where to find Alex. This won't be a safe place for him anymore, so if there is anything I should know before we enter, please tell me."

Wart twisted his hands together and stared at the floor.

"What should I know?" I repeated with more force.

Wart let out a whimper. "My master will not be happy."

"I'm the one you're with right now, and I won't be happy if you withhold information, so take your pick. Him or me?"

"There is always payment that must be made for removing items from the Underworld. Either you or your Alex must pay to take the brimstone out." He pressed his body against the wall and shut his eyes.

"And there's the fine print that the royal demon pain in my ass kept from me." I sighed at the sight of Wart. "Good grief. Stop cowering. I'm not going to hurt you."

I knocked twice on the door, then waited a few seconds before turning the knob. The door opened. I stepped inside. Light filtered into the space from a small neon sign on the building opposite this one. My eyes adjusted to the dimness only to discover the room was bare save the mattress I had once made love to Alex on. My heart ached. Alex was gone. Wart came up behind me.

"It's empty," he said.

I gritted my teeth and forced myself to let go of the tension in my body. Unfortunately, I couldn't take a breath without coughing. Wart and I stunk.

"I don't get it. I was pulled here. Why?"

"If your Alex was here recently, then he would have left an energy trail. You're a hunter. You followed the trail."

"Okay," I huffed. "But the trail ends here. Wouldn't I find another one to follow him out of here?"

"You would unless it was covered up."

"He's concealing his tracks?"

Wart glanced around the room. "He is stealthy, this man of yours. He has secrets to keep."

"That's an understatement." I sank onto the musty old mattress. Then I jumped up. "Maude's! I'll go to Maude's place." I grabbed Wart by the arm and pulled him along after me. "Come on. I have some business to do with a certain black marketer. But this time, you won't be going with me."

"Wart must go. His prince said to go with you."

"Jasper said you could stay nearby if I required help, which I don't." I didn't have a watch, and we hadn't passed any kind of clock on our way here. It occurred to me there weren't clocks in the Underworld. Yet, my gut told me I was running out of time for this mission. "Wart, I have to leave soon, with or without the brimstone."

"All will be fine. You will see." He shuffled out into the hall and down the stairs, weaving past prone bodies.

I didn't share his confidence in my ability to find the brimstone. I'd been tracking Alex, not the brimstone. I'd been following my heart. I couldn't let my feelings sway me and keep me from my goal. I had to find the brimstone I'd given Maude and get out.

We reached the street and kept our heads down. I led the way in the direction of Maude's but stopped several blocks away. Giving the prince this much information was still dangerous. I couldn't lead him to the heart of the Underworld black market.

I pulled Wart to the side of a building and bent over to be on eye level. "You have to stay out of sight. I'll be back as soon as I can. No matter what happens with the item of interest, we leave when I return. Okay?"

"I agree to leave. But I will go with you now."

He took hold of a fistful of my plastic garment. I tried to pry his fingers loose, but he had a tight grip.

"Wart. Stop. I can't take you."

"You're seeing old woman Maude. My prince knows of Maude. There's no danger to her if I go with you. I have met with old woman Maude many times."

I about had a stroke. "Are you serious? You've known about Maude all this time? And you've made deals with her?" Now it made sense how Jasper was privy to what I'd done with the brimstone.

Wart shrugged. "Of course. I make many agreements with her for my prince."

"If you are on such good terms with Maude, how come I'm the one stuck doing Jasper's dirty work? Why aren't you getting it?"

"Wart cannot touch magical objects. It is painful to touch such things. It's how my prince bound me to him."

"That's horrible," I said. "He's a monster."

"Not horrible. Smart," Wart said. "Whoever possesses items of magic the prince created could use them against him. That is why his father is punishing him. Prince Jasper must learn a lesson."

"Interesting," I said. "Okay, then. Let's go see Maude."

We walked in silence the rest of the way there. I knocked on the door and waited for the ragged little woman who screened all visitors to answer. We stood there for several minutes. I tapped my hand against my leg in a staccato of irritation. I glanced down at Wart, who shrugged. I rapped on the door again. This time, I could hear the sound of approaching feet. The door opened a crack and then wider to reveal Alex.

My knees almost buckled. Alex grabbed me and pulled me to him. Wart slipped past us into the hall.

I kissed Alex. He returned the kiss tenfold. Somehow between gasping for breath and embracing one another, Alex shut and locked the door. He was a man of many talents.

"Hey." Maude's deep voice filled the small entryway. "I hate to interrupt this happy reunion, but we have to take care of business." Her nose wrinkled as she drew nearer. "You stink, Janda."

I laughed. "Nice to see you again, too."

She got a whiff of Wart, who stood off to one side. "God Almighty! What have the two of you been doing?"

"Blending in," Wart said proudly.

Maude shook her head. "A little too much if you ask me. Well, come on then." She motioned for everyone to follow her.

Heads turned as we strode through the bar area to the back room. I wasn't sure if our presence or our stench caught everyone's attention. I would be glad to get home and wash before meeting my ghost-witch family tonight. My stomach twisted at the idea of all the preparations still to do and how little time was left.

Once inside Maude's office, I began tearing off the trash bag. Alex helped, which heightened my desire for him. By the growing bulge in his pants, he seemed to be thinking like me. Heat rushed into my face. Alex finished removing the bag and let out a low whistle. I was wearing his shirt, which had several rips and smudges of dirt on it.

Maude coughed. "I'd say the two of you need to get a room, but we don't have time. You'll have to get a grip and save it for later."

Alex smirked. He planted a kiss on my forehead. "Until later."

"This is when I despise my job." I sighed. "Okay, Maude. I'll tell you why I'm here."

Wart pulled up a stool and sat by Maude's desk. She heaved her body into her chair. Alex wouldn't let me go, so the two of us stood glued to one another in front of her.

"I'll cut to the chase," I said. "I need the piece of brimstone I gave to you for safekeeping."

She raised her brows and looked at Alex. "He has it."

Alex let his hand slide off my shoulder as I turned toward him.

"You have it?"

He winced. "Yeah. Sorry. Maude felt it best to get it out of town, and since I have access to a boat ..."

"Oh, my God! You didn't!" I started pacing. "This is not good." I paused and grabbed his arm. "You have to get it back. Like now!"

He gripped me by my shoulders to get me to settle down.

My body thrummed with tension. "I'm serious. I have to have it right away!"

"Slow down," he said. "It's fine. The brimstone is safe."

Wart let out a whimper.

I broke free from Alex and knelt by Wart. "I'll get it. I promise. But I'm running out of time."

"Are you in trouble?" Maude said, pushing back from her desk and attempting to get to her feet.

"We're all in trouble," I said. I let out a groan that Wart echoed. "If I get the pieces of brimstone back to the demon prince, then Alex can get out of here and the Horseman will be defeated." I had a tinge of doubt in my voice that Alex didn't miss.

"What happens if you don't get the brimstone?" he said.

I froze. "I don't exactly know. But it won't be good and will most likely be painful."

"So," Maude said, coming to stand behind Wart, "you made a deal with the demon and will have a price to pay if you don't come through. Am I right?"

"That about sums it up." Then it dawned on me how utterly stupid I'd been. I never found out what would happen if I failed to deliver the brimstone. A shred of fear ran through me, not for what would happen to me but for what might happen to those I cared about. I glanced at Wart. "Your prince left out some details. You said payment had to be made to take things from the Underworld, but no one said what the price is for failure. Tell me about the payment?"

You could have sucked Wart up with a straw for how he seemed to melt with fear. He wrung his hands and hunched his shoulders.

"Someone will have to stay behind in the Underworld to serve him," he squeaked.

"Alex?" My heart faltered. "Jasper said he was reluctant to let him go. He doesn't want me to succeed, does he?"

"He does," Wart said. "But only to recover the brimstone in the chest. The one here, he could convince Alex to get for him."

I burned with anger as I approached Wart. "Why did he send me here?" Then I got it. "I'm Alex's motivation. Aren't I? My being here is how the demon gets Alex to cooperate. Because now you've kept me from my other mission. I'm late, aren't I?"

Wart hunched even lower and let out a tiny yip.

I faced Alex, barely able to look him in the eye. "I'm sorry. I botched this up big time."

"You're worth far more than me to the demon," Alex said. "Janda, you must get out of here."

I forced myself to let go of Alex and nodded my agreement. "I'll make this right. I promise."

CHAPTER 26

BLAZING A TRAIL

It took far too long to develop a feasible plan of action. I hated that Alex's fate was tied to my success in outsmarting the Horseman and now the demon. We shoved Wart out of Maude's bar so he couldn't report our plans to the demon prince. We'd managed to coax out of him that the demon could only see Alex on the river and could only see me if Wart was close by.

Alex agreed to bring the brimstone piece back from the opposite side of the river and place it near where Wart and I had appeared when we traveled over from the demon's confines. We would get the piece to the demon, but only if I could get the one out of the pirate's chest first, and then we'd secure Alex's return and my safety from the demon. I had to rush back to Sebastian's and hope I wasn't too late to carry out the night's furtive activities regarding my ghost family.

"This sucks," I said.

I kissed Alex and reluctantly stepped away from him as he stood inside the doorway to the bar. Sadness creased the corners of his eyes, and I felt myself waver in our plan.

"You've got this," he said, then closed the door.

Wart sidled up to me and reached for my hand. "We leave?"

I took his hand in mine, realizing he was as much a pawn in this dangerous game as the rest of us. "Yes. We leave, but first, I'm taking you back to Jasper."

He sighed in defeat.

Since I could only leave the Underworld wearing what I had on when I entered it, I borrowed a dark cape from Maude and pulled it close around me. It was better than the trash bag. With the hood covering my face, we hurried to the river. The way back was easier and faster since Alex gave me directions that allowed us to stick to the edge of the road and not deal with the woods. We stopped once to hide behind a boulder as a band of marauders stomped drunkenly past us.

At the river, I turned toward Wart for guidance. "What do I do? My power is unstable when I attempt to cross the veil."

"It's the prince who has been blocking your entry to the Underworld. You brought us here, not me, and you can get us back. The prince knows this but let you think it was the curse."

Even though I was steaming mad to learn Jasper was responsible for severing my communications with Alex, I gave a short laugh. "So I'm Dorothy on her quest through Oz."

Wart's face scrunched up. "You are Janda."

"Never mind. It was a joke, but it doesn't matter."

"This I do not understand, but we must hurry." He rushed to the river and bent over it until a dark reflection rippled on the surface. "Okay. It is time. But you must give the cape to the river for me to go with you."

I started to question him but thought better of it. I handed him the cape Maude had given me. Wart proceeded to roll it into a ball and set it afloat on the river. I wanted to object, but the cape was already drifting away. Suddenly, it dipped under the water and bobbed back up again. A second later, it disappeared entirely under the surface and didn't return.

Wart grinned. "The offering has been accepted. Now we leave."

He took hold of my hand and beamed up at me. I gathered my inner witch and sank my bare feet into the muddy shore. My lykoi sent a wave of power to meet the energy I soaked up from the earth. There was a pushback of darkness, but knowing the source helped me overcome it. I let my mind choose where to go from here. And my instincts led the way.

A confusion of noise greeted us. We'd popped up on the perimeter of Angie's town festival.

"Janda!" Gwenn shouted.

I'd hardly caught my breath when she barreled toward me and yanked me into a hug. Mutther and Nick jogged over to us.

"Where the hell have you been?" Mutther said. "Do you have any idea how hard it's been to cover for you after Gwenn discovered you missing?"

"Way to blow up the plans," Nick said.

He tipped his head to see around me. "Who's that?"

Wart pressed himself against my backside.

"This is my companion, Wart," I said. "He's been helping me reach Alex."

Angie caught sight of the group and hurried over. "It's good to see you." She touched the torn shirt and wrinkled her nose. "But maybe you should wear the costume I have for you."

She produced a dark cloak similar to the one Maude had given me.

"Thanks. I had to leave my other cape in the Underworld."

"You made it to the Underworld?" Gwenn squeezed my hand. "This is huge!"

"Not as huge as me messing everything up. How did you guys get past Sebastian?" I thought about my connection with him and realized I hadn't felt it the entire time I was gone or now.

"He's furious," Gwenn said.

"He sure is," Nick said. "He's been riding Mutther about not doing his duty."

"I'm so sorry," I said, frowning at Mutther.

"I can handle it," he said. "I think it's more the part that his mark on you isn't working anymore. He went nuts when you weren't in his house and he couldn't feel you."

I glanced down at Wart, who seemed relieved not to have been sent back to the demon. "There's a good explanation, but we don't have time for the full story. It's vital we meet Hulda and Agatha."

Gwenn seemed to get the seriousness of the situation. "We can go through it on the way to Sing-Sing. And, just so you know, I told Sebastian that I'd made a potion to help protect you. He liked the idea for the most part."

"Right up until she told him it was probably the reason he couldn't feel his connection with you anymore," Mutther said.

"It wasn't a pretty sight," Nick chimed in.

Angie's eyes grew large, and her brows shut up practically to her hairline. "Oh. I would have loved to have been there to see it."

Gwenn laughed. "Just be glad you weren't there." She had been stealing glances at Wart and finally addressed him. "Why do I have the sensation that I should be careful around you?"

Wart stepped out from behind me. "Because you should. Janda has been kind to me. More than I deserve. The demon prince can see what she's doing if I'm by her side. He can see whatever goes on around her."

Mutther's jaw muscles flexed. "Janda! You brought the demon's servant?"

I squared my shoulders. "I've inadvertently made a deal with the demon to get Alex back. The problem is, I was sloppy and left a loophole for him to trip me up. But I'm here to make it right. Wart's part as a spy for the demon won't matter. The demon can watch all he wants but he can't stop us."

Gwenn nodded. "That's good enough for me." She pulled a tiny glass vial from her pocket. "I didn't lie to Sebastian. I went ahead and made a potion for you. Hulda helped. Take one gulp and pour the rest on your hair."

"Okay. That's a little weird, but whatever." I did as directed. The potion started sweet but had a sour aftertaste that made me pucker my lips and wince.

Gwenn took the empty bottle and tucked it in her pocket. "Also, if Sebastian asks, you took the potion in the wee hours of the morning while he was out hunting."

Angie laughed. "Now that we know you're back safely, I'm going to help a certain police investigator with public relations. I'll do all I can to add to the cover story the others concocted to buy you some slack from Sebastian."

Now I was really puzzled. "What's my cover?"

The others seemed a bit nervous at the question.

Hudson appeared from a nearby bush, holding a dead mouse. He dropped it at Wart's feet and sat on my bare toes.

"Thank you," Wart said. He ate the mouse.

"Yuck!" Angie said.

"Hudson is giving an offering. That's sweet." Gwenn beamed at the feline and patted his head before returning to the question of the cover story. "Well, Janda, your cover is that you were coming to help Angie with the festival. Specifically, you're going to help with a reenactment of the Headless Horseman's ride through town."

"You didn't actually tell Sebastian that, did you?" I could see him now, having a coronary, if that was even possible for a dead man walking.

"Sure, I did," she said. "In case you missed it, you were gone. I mean, really gone! You didn't astral project. You flip-ping disappeared!"

"Sorry," I said. "I don't know how that happened. I thought I was astral projecting to Alex, but the demon manipulated me to get me to him instead. He's been using my connection to the curse to get my attention. But I'm gaining control over traveling so I don't end up in unex-pected places."

"So you did intend to come here?" Gwenn said.

"Not at first. I aimed to return to Sebastian's but taking Wart with me would have been bad. Midway through my traveling, I redirected us to come here. Damn. I'm going to catch hell when Sebastian sees me."

"Better you than us," Nick said.

"Never mind about Sebastian. The big news is that Janda's powers are evolving," Gwenn said, her voice rising with excitement. "This is important. Really, really important."

Shawn came up to our group dressed as the Horseman and leading a gentle black mare. "We're on in five."

"What am I supposed to do?"

"Sebastian arrived, so we have to make this look good," Shawn said.

I glared at Angie. "And I suppose you told Shawn?"

"Told me what?"

"That Janda is not a good actress," she said, smirking.

Shawn pointed to a spot at the end of the road near the woods. "Don't fuss about your lack of acting skills, Janda. Just stand over there and wait for me to go blazing past. Jump aside, and you're done. The Headless Horseman escapes and rides another day."

"I suppose I can manage that," I said, giving Angie a sideways glance.

"Good luck," she said. She followed Shawn to their designated starting point.

"The rest of us will be scattered around the perimeter, ready to take off once Shawn draws everyone's attention," Mutther said.

"What about Wart? I can't take him with me or Sebastian will know I'm up to something."

"He can go with me," Gwenn said. "With all the folks in costumes, Wart won't stand out, and Hudson can help keep an eye on him."

Hudson got off my toes and repositioned himself to face Wart. It seemed the cat was taking his job seriously.

"Okay," I said. "An impromptu plan B it is."

"George! You made it," Gwenn said. She grinned at the bagel store owner as he meandered through the crowd to greet us. "Any news?"

"Plenty," he said, lowering his voice. "My source let me know the Council has changed their plans."

"I knew this stuff with Sebastian's link to Janda would spook him," Nick said. "What changed?"

"Nothing for the two of you, which, as I hear it, is to keep tabs on Janda," George said. "The basic strategy of bringing in reinforcements and scouring the area for the human and the pirate ghosts remains the same. What's new is that Sebastian will lead them to the hollows where he fought the Horseman, and from there, they will converge on the river area near the prison."

"Blast it! That means I have one shot at finding the treasure before Sebastian can interfere." My anxiety about failing peaked.

"Janda! You're up," Angie said, shouting over the crowd.

"Wart, you stay with Gwenn. I'll meet you later." I pulled the cloak over my head and prepared for the role I was to play. The crowd took up spots along the roped-off road down the center of town. I strode to my position over the bridge and opposite the church gates, which stood open and ready for my exit into the labyrinth of tombstones. Sebastian spotted me and gave me a fierce glare. I smiled and waved.

Angie spoke through a microphone to announce the dreaded return of the Headless Horseman. "Everyone, hold onto your heads!"

Shawn appeared dressed to resemble the Horseman. He carried a flaming pumpkin in one hand and galloped down the road with it raised above his head. I caught sight of Gwenn. Her lips moved in unison with her hands. The next moment a trail of fire blazed a safe distance behind the horse, causing onlookers to clap in delight. I was so mesmerized I almost forgot to jump off to the side as

Shawn approached. As I leaped out of the way, he tossed the fiery pumpkin into the air and rode off beneath a burst of fireworks that shot out from the pumpkin as it exploded overhead. The crowd went wild.

I gazed at the spectacle for a second before tossing off my cloak and lunging for the safety of the open gates. I shifted into my lykoi and used the tombstones to cover me as I raced deeper into the cemetery. Hope spurred me forward. I would save Alex.

CHAPTER 27

TREASURE

My lykoi exalted in the rush of air as I ran. Several miles stood between me and my destination. I kept to the stream and then up into the hills. The color of the fall leaves was lost in the darkness, but I let the smell of autumn give me another surge of energy. My witch side grew as I learned to draw upon my natural surroundings. I crested another hill and paused to scan the highway that I prepared to cross. I assumed Gwenn's potion would protect me from serious injury if I got hit by a car, but I didn't want to test that theory.

Two cars zipped past. Once their rear lights faded, I jumped to the pavement and kept going. I ran and ran, my breath finding an easy rhythm. I followed the old aqueduct system to the river and kept to the shoreline the rest of the way. The towers of Sing-Sing grew closer. I slowed as I approached them and waited for directions from Agatha. My ears pricked up. I crouched beside a log and waited. I wished the others would hurry.

"I'm telling you she'll be here." Gwenn's voice drifted through the air.

I rose from my hiding spot and pawed at the ground.

"See?" she said. "There she is."

I shifted back just as the others came into view.

Gwenn held a bundle out to me. "I took the liberty of taking some clothes from your room before I left for the festival. I stashed them in one of the booths. You know, just in case."

"Thanks." I hurriedly dressed in my usual black pants and a dark top. I pulled on some socks and my boots, then removed them.

"What's wrong?" Gwenn said.

"I think I prefer the feel of the earth."

"Agreed. Maybe I should take my shoes off, too." She tossed our footwear into a heap by the log I'd vacated.

Hudson appeared with Wart. The two seemed to be fine together.

"How's that going?" I said.

Gwenn shrugged. "Hudson says it's all good."

"I hope he's right." The cat was not an ordinary creature. He'd pointed me in the right direction more than once, so I had to trust him now.

"We're going to drop back and survey our surroundings. If luck holds out, Sebastian won't show up for a while," Mutther said. "We'll stay in the woods so we don't scare Agatha away."

"It's not like we'd even know if we did," Nick said. "I don't know about Mutther, but I can't see ghosts."

Gwenn scooped up Hudson. "Nick, you can be a funny guy sometimes."

"I wasn't being funny. It's true."

"It doesn't matter," Mutther said. "Come on. Let Gwenn and Janda do their thing." He glanced at Gwenn, sighed, and dropped back into the shadows of the woods.

Gwenn stroked Hudson's fur. "I'm counting on you to keep our guest in line."

She put Hudson onto a large rock. He jumped off it and nudged Wart toward the woods but away from Mutther and Nick.

I fidgeted as my adrenaline plateaued into a steady stream of alertness.

"It'll be okay," Gwenn said. "You're not too late. They'll come."

"If anything happens to me," I said, "I want you to know I'm grateful for all your help. And by the way, that fireworks display was awesome."

She grinned. "Thanks."

I tossed a pebble into the water and watched the ripples fan outward. "I've been thinking about the human with the Horseman. I know when I started the hunt for him, it was to seek justice for the deaths he caused, but after seeing how the demon works, I'm not sure what justice means anymore."

"Shades of gray," Gwenn said. "It becomes pretty murky when you begin to see things from a different perspective. Maybe that's how it was for Agatha and Hulda. They each had their version of the events that tore them apart. Both were mainly true. Neither was wrong in their core belief. Yet their truths clashed until you came along."

I shrugged. "Maybe."

"There is no maybe about it." The whispery voice of Agatha was like a petal floating unhurriedly on the wind. It was soft and calm and brought a sense of imminent peace. A moment later, she materialized beside me. "You've done well, niece."

Hulda's form took shape a little slower than usual. I still worried about her. Something had been off with her for months. But her lips curved into a smile that touched my heart.

"You've been busy," she said. "You've discovered how to travel in your full form. Impressive."

Agatha's eyes grew wide. "That *is* something."

"Yeah. Not to pop your bubble, but I've managed to put us in quite a predicament."

"I heard," Hulda said. She drifted nearer. "Do not let it sway you from your goal. What we do this night affects many souls."

I couldn't have felt any more burdened than if I'd been carrying around a load of bricks. Only my blood sacrifice could lift the curse and save the souls of the damned. But would it be enough to bring Alex back?

Agatha scanned the area. "It's changed so much."

"You must try, sister. We're here to assist," Hulda said. She reached for Gwenn's hand and stared at the low-hanging moon. "It's witch hour. Form a circle. Our combined energies should help Agatha."

I took my place in our circle of three, which was more of a triangle, but it was the connection that was important. Agatha stood in the center. We closed our eyes and asked for directions from Mother Earth. Heat traveled beneath my feet. I opened my eyes. Agatha was swathed in light.

"Yes," she said. "I feel it now."

We put our hands down and watched as Agatha wandered along the river's edge, periodically dipping her toes into the water. Then she paused and began walking backward. She changed direction a few times but continued her backward journey. It led her into the woods. We followed her.

"What if she trips?" I whispered. "Oh. Right. She's a ghost. Never mind."

I shook my head in an attempt to clear the muddled feeling I'd had since my return from the Underworld. Travel in my full form seemed to have a few unexpected side effects. I tilted my head toward the moonbeams that found their way between branches and felt the fog in my brain begin to clear.

Agatha stopped by a group of three ancient trees in a small clearing close to the once-active quarry. It was amazing the trees hadn't been uprooted by now.

"Here. The energy stops here," she said.

"Okay. Do I dig?" I said. Why hadn't I thought to bring a shovel?

"Excellent," Hulda said. "Tell us where to direct the energy, sister."

"If I remember correctly, I'd say six paces in front of the cluster of trees." She stood an inch or two above the ground, floating in a circle that increased in diameter several times before she halted. "This is the target area. Shall we begin?"

"Begin what?" I said. Even though my fog-battered brain was doing better, I didn't understand what she was saying.

"We create an energy vortex that acts as a digging drill," Gwenn said. "Am I right?" She peered over at Agatha and Hulda.

Their eyes brightened, and so did their entire bodies.

"Yes. Isn't it thrilling?" Agatha said. "Soon, we will have the answers we seek."

I took my cues from the others and made a swirling motion with my arms. I didn't feel a thing. "What am I supposed to be doing here? I feel like an idiot flapping my arms around."

"You can sit this one out," Hulda said.

I did as she suggested. I sat down and watched. It didn't take long before the soil cracked and bulged within the designated area. A small mound of dirt grew into a large pile. They dug a hole and stopped. Then dug another hole and stopped, and another and another. Gwenn wiped the sweat from her brow. I stood, surveying the pock-marked earth.

"Are we in the right spot?" I said.

Agatha's brows knit in concentration. She moved to yet another spot and repeated the spell with Gwenn and Hulda helping. I heard a thunk and froze.

Gwenn's eyes grew wide with anticipation.

"Did you find it?" I hurried to where they gathered at the edge of the newest hole. The top of a brown chest poked through the dirt.

"That has to be it," Gwenn said. "A little further, and we can bring it to the surface."

"Hurry," I said. Dirt flew in all directions as the vortex spell continued. I dodged a clump of soil in my haste to get nearer. The chest was fully exposed for the first time in centuries. We stared in awe.

"This is amazing," I said.

"Yes, it is." A man walked among the holes toward the treasure chest. "I knew you could do it."

I turned to see the human who'd been working with the Horseman. I positioned myself between him and Gwenn. "We meet again. Where's your master?"

"I'm not sure. I suppose he'll come along shortly," he said.

He made no motion to attack, so I did the same. "What's your name?"

"Erick," he said. "Never knew my real last name."

I remained as calm as I could, even though a part of me

wanted to rip him to shreds. "Well, Erick. We're at an impasse. You know I can't give the Horseman the brimstone."

"Understood," he said. "If my pirate ancestor is set free and I get my fair share of the bounty, then you can have the brimstone for all the good it will do you. The Horseman will fight you for it, and that is none of my concern."

"You killed those innocent people," Gwenn said.

She moved to stand beside me as she spoke. I was pretty sure he couldn't see Hulda or Agatha and that he assumed we were alone.

"It served a purpose. I had no choice," he said.

"There's always a choice," I said. "You didn't have to kill them."

"What purpose could such cruelty serve?" Gwenn said, her tone dark.

"It's true that we gathered little useable information from any of them, but in the end, their deaths got Janda to act. She'd spent months hiding. The Horseman grew impatient as All Hallow's Eve approached."

My breath caught as the realization that I was the reason those people had died hit me like a kick in the gut.

"Don't pin the blame on Janda," Gwenn said. "You did the Horseman's bidding for your own selfish reasons. Greed and revenge. But you're mistaken about a few things." She walked toward the man. "Your ancestor, the woman who gave birth to the pirate's child, was not murdered by any poison from Agatha. She died from complications during childbirth. Agatha attempted to help her, not kill her."

I heard a sniffle behind me and realized it had come from Agatha. She was speaking to Gwenn, telling the story of two women who'd been jilted by the same man. Both had believed his words of love, and both had paid a heavy price.

"Even if what you say is true, it changes nothing." He jabbed a finger at the treasure chest. "What's in there is rightfully mine!" He lunged for it.

Grayish-white light erupted around us. The man halted in his tracks. One-by-one, the pirate ghosts appeared.

"Now you did it," the man said, smirking. "The Horseman is coming for the brimstone."

Hudson darted to Gwenn's feet. Wart pushed his way through some shrubbery and stood next to me. I glanced down at him, and he nodded. I sighed. This was not going to end well.

"I think you'll find that the demon prince has something to say about who should have the brimstone." I glanced at Gwenn and my ghost-witch family. "And so do I."

CHAPTER 28

COINS FOR THE FERRYMAN

I vaulted over the hole separating me from Erick and slammed into him. We both tumbled to the ground in a twisting of arms and legs as he fought to free himself from my grip. The pirate ghosts closed in but did nothing more than watch the struggle.

I pinned Erick to the ground. "Stop squirming, you imbecile."

"It's mine," he said.

"Yeah. Sure it is," Gwenn said. She pulled his hands together and cast a binding spell. "That should hold you."

Agatha drifted forward, circumventing the ring of pirate ghosts. One of the pirates cast his gaze downward, avoiding Agatha's gaze as she went by them. He glanced up, caught me glaring at him, and looked at the ground once more. He was as much to blame for the events surrounding the curse as the human who'd struck a bargain with the Horseman. I wasn't sure I wanted to save that pirate's worthless soul, but no one deserved the fate they'd been dealt.

"How do I do the sacrifice?" I said, growing anxious

under the stares of the pirate ghosts who moved restlessly in their little group.

Gwenn tried to open the chest with no success. "I sense a magical seal. Is that correct?"

"Yes," Agatha said. "Only my blood or that of my descendants can open it." She sighed. "I'm sorry. I did not think of what might happen centuries later."

"So, it's up to you, Janda. Only your blood can open the chest," Gwenn said, straightening from where she crouched beside the treasure chest.

Erick looked at Gwenn. "Are you saying I can't open it, even though my pirate ancestor took part in the original event?"

Gwenn glared at Erick. "That's right, genius. It all comes down to Janda."

He scowled at the pirate ghost who must have been his ancestor. "Reggie, you're worthless!"

Erick had given me the name of Agatha's ex-lover. I glanced at Agatha and realized she'd never told us his name. She'd cut him from her existence because he hurt her with his betrayal.

Reggie glared at Erick.

"Do you see all ghosts?" I said. "Or is it only your ancestor you see?"

"I see him and the rest of the crew. Ever since I was a kid, he kept urging me to find the treasure. He's the one who introduced me to the Horseman. I believed in him. But no more." Erick tried in vain to break free. "I earned that treasure. Do you hear me?"

"I hear you," I said.

Erick confirmed he couldn't see Hulda or Agatha, which I was counting on. I didn't want him directing his rage against them when I wasn't sure if he could hurt them somehow. After all, spending a lifetime listening to ghosts meant he had some supernatural ability, even if it was limited to communicating with a select few apparitions.

Gwenn produced a small knife. "Here. This should do it."

I took the pocketknife and pulled out the blade. I held my hand above the chest and glanced at the ghosts surrounding us. Hulda held Agatha's hand. The pirates drew closer in anticipation of the release they sought. I drew the blade across my palm and let my blood drip onto the chest's curved top. I stepped back and waited.

"I smell blood," Mutther said, rushing toward us from the sheltering trees.

"It's just Janda's blood sacrifice," Gwenn said. She grabbed his arm to slow him down.

"The pirate ghosts are here?" Nick said. "What the hell?"

Gwenn attempted to reduce the tension building. "We've got this. Give Janda space to work."

Mutther and Nick grumbled but stood off to one side where they could keep an eye on everyone, especially the ghosts.

"I'm sorry," Reggie said. "Agatha. I've always loved you. Please forgive me."

"She's here?" Erick said, twisting his body to search the area. "Where?"

"Never you mind," Gwenn said. "This is none of your concern."

Wart also had scanned the area when the pirate ghost mentioned Agatha's name. I thought he'd be able to see all ghosts, but he seemed to be as perplexed as Erick.

Agatha faced her ex-lover. "You don't know what love

truly is, and while you don't deserve forgiveness, I'm giving it to you. Rest in peace if you can."

"Thank you," he said.

"We're obviously missing part of this conversation," Nick said. "I only hear the pirate. But I don't think I need to hear the rest of it either."

"Yeah, sorry, guys. Hulda and Agatha are here, but none of you can see or hear them. The ghost pirates are visible to you, but who knows why?"

Erick laughed. "It's because the pirates threw their lot in with the Horseman. You see the Horseman, so you see them when the Horseman is near."

"Hmm," Gwenn said. "Interesting."

She didn't get a chance to say more. Our attention was drawn to the chest, which started emitting a low hum. Then it began vibrating. Next, the entire chest flew several feet into the air and landed with a crash that splintered the wood.

"Damn," Mutther said.

I glanced at the others. No one moved. I stepped closer to the broken chest. The instant I opened the lid, an immense glow shot upward. I jumped back.

"Is that good or bad?" I said.

Agatha moved nearer to Hulda and away from the chest. "I'd say the magical seal has been broken. You should be safe now."

"*Should* be safe?" I said.

She shrugged. "There's no guarantee."

I looked from Hulda to Gwenn. "How long does the protective potion last?"

"It's not like we've had a chance to test it before, so I don't know," Gwenn said. "Sorry."

"That's encouraging." I took a tentative step forward.

"Here goes nothing." I leaned in close enough to peek over the edge of the open chest. "Holy crap!" Throwing caution aside, I bent down and thrust my hand into its contents. I withdrew a fistful of jewels and gold coins.

Nick let out a whistle.

Erick flailed around in an attempt to get close. Mutther interceded and yanked the man up by his shirt collar.

"It's mine," Erick whined. He tried to kick Mutther.

"Not smart," Mutther said, depositing Erick in a heap at the base of one of the ancient trees. "You aren't going anywhere near that treasure." He planted himself as a guard over Erick.

"Thanks," I said. I knelt beside the mass of loot and began emptying it onto the ground.

Reggie came forward. "Please. We only want the coins needed to pay the Ferryman."

"Will any coin work?" I said, holding up a handful.

He shook his head. "Our ship's masthead broke during a storm. Some coins came free from the base of the mast. A few of us took the coins and put them in a small linen sack. Those are the ones meant to pay our way through the Underworld. The sack was placed inside the chest for safe-keeping until the ship could be repaired."

"I told you he's worthless," Erick said. "Every ship has its own payment for the Ferryman. These dopes removed it to put it back once the ship was repaired. Well, that didn't happen. They were discovered and arrested. Then they were hanged for their crimes. They didn't have payment for the Ferryman. But the brimstone was also in the chest, so they aligned themselves with the Horseman and had me working for years to find it."

I dug deeper into the chest, tossing aside jewelry and goblets encrusted with large gems. My fingers felt rough fabric. I withdrew a small sack. The pirates let out a chorus of cheers as I tossed it to Reggie.

"I hope you find the peace you seek."

While they opened the sack and distributed the coins, I went back to my search for the brimstone. A small black leather box caught my eye. I lifted it and opened the lid. "This is it!"

Wart dashed forward. "Hurry! The Horseman knows you found it and will be here soon."

I heard a horse whinny and turned to find a ball of flame soaring at me. Wart jumped in front of me. It hit him square in the chest. He dropped to the earth.

"No!" I knelt next to Wart and put my hand on his chest. He wasn't breathing.

I rose to face the Horseman. Rage erupted within me. I wanted to send the Horseman straight to hell.

Mutther left Erick and stormed forward. His skin took on the texture of dragon scales.

"Don't!" I tried to stop him from becoming my shield, but he'd already begun to shift.

The pirates ran deeper into the woods but were hauled back by an invisible tether.

Nick took up a position at Mutther's backside. He faced off with the pirate ghosts who reluctantly came toward us to fight.

From the corner of my eye, I saw Uncle Damon and some of my pack members join the fray, followed by the rest of the search party that trickled into the clearing. The smell of burnt flesh filled the air. The Horseman sent volley after volley of flames in my direction. Mutther roared in frustration and completed his inevitable shift into a dragon.

"Oh, no," Gwenn said.

We all scurried to get out of Mutther's way as his tail

whipped around to cut down several ghosts. The ghosts regrouped but didn't stop.

"Why aren't the pirates leaving?" Gwenn said.

"They can't," Agatha said. She brought Hulda over to us. "As long as the brimstone is here, they remain bound to the Horseman."

"Aw, hell," I said. I lifted Wart's body from where he'd fallen and placed it next to Erick.

"I don't want that near me," Erick said.

"You better hope you don't die anytime soon, or you'll be pretty unhappy to meet the demon. And let me tell you, he won't take pity on you." I took more joy in telling him this bit of news than I should have, but I couldn't help it.

The fighting went on with no apparent winners. Sebastian joined Mutther to fight the Horseman.

"It's All Hallow's Eve," Hulda said, yelling over the sounds of battle. "He's at his strongest. I'm not sure he can be defeated."

It was no longer about saving Alex. I had all these people—my friends and family—to save first. I glanced at poor Wart and wondered if the demon could still see us.

"Sorry, Wart, but if you're really dead, then this shouldn't hurt a bit." I bent over the small lizard man and spread out his hands. I placed the leather box against his chest and folded his hands over it.

"Janda," Agatha said, "if you send the brimstone back with Wart, then you may not be able to save Alex. You will lose your main bargaining chip unless you take the brimstone yourself."

"I know."

She was right. I couldn't stay here and get the brimstone to the demon. I wasn't even sure I could travel there, but I had to try.

The pirate ghosts sensed what I was about to do and pulled back. They still fought, but not quite as hard.

The Headless Horseman, on the other hand, fought more fiercely. He spewed great plumes of smoke that drifted across the clearing and made it difficult to see the edges of the nearby quarry. The shifters had to retreat closer to the woods to avoid falling into the deep pit.

Mutther drew dangerously close to the quarry's edge. Gwenn stifled a scream by shoving her fist in her mouth. Nick had been hit and lay motionless. Sebastian and Uncle Damon picked Nick up and dragged him to us. He was bleeding but alive.

"Keep him safe," Uncle Damon said. He went right back to fighting without waiting for a response.

The strong aroma of gardenias enveloped us.

Sebastian froze on the spot. "Is she here?"

I nodded.

He inhaled the sweet scent, smiled, and rejoined the others.

"I can't hold off any longer," I said.

Gwenn hugged me. Hudson scampered over with a single coin in his mouth. He dropped it at my feet. It was one of the pirate coins. I looked over to where Reggie stood half-heartedly fighting some of the pack. He lifted his hand and saluted me. I mouthed my thanks and shoved the coin into my pocket.

"Good luck," Hulda said. "I'm proud of you, my grand-daughter."

I focused on my destination, which was a bit sketchy since I only knew the end point and not the route there. I held Wart in my arms and allowed my witch energy to surface. The lava pits came into view. Beyond it lay the throne room, but I didn't risk going any nearer. I heard the fighting behind me while feeling the heat from the lava in front of me. It was weird to be in two places at once. I stood at a threshold between worlds, or I *was* the threshold. That was an intriguing theory, which I knew at once was correct. Somehow I had become a portal to the spirit realm, or in this case, to the demon's lair.

CHAPTER 29

PRICE PAID

"Well, look who's here," Jasper said. He leaned against the archway of his throne room. "How's the hunt for my brimstone going?"

"You know how it's going," I said. "The Headless Horseman is fighting the shifters. People are getting hurt. The pirate ghosts are fighting when all they want is to rest in peace. But you saw all this through Wart's connection, so you know what's taking place."

I laid Wart on the hard earth where he wouldn't get splashed by spewing lava. I felt the coin in my pocket that the pirate gave me and thought of tucking it inside Wart's shabby garment but decided against it. Wart was already willingly bound to the demon. The coin would be of no use to him. Instead, I removed my brimstone necklace and put it around Wart's neck.

Jasper's face fell. "He's dead?"

"He took a direct hit from the Headless Horseman."

"I'll eviscerate that headless beast!" Jasper's horns turned a shade redder, and his fingers elongated to dagger-sharp weapons.

"You'll have to wait your turn. There are quite a few of us who want to defeat the Horseman."

The demon prince burst out laughing.

"I don't see what's so funny," I said.

"You mortals are clueless. The defeat of the Horseman means nothing unless he pays for his betrayal." His eyes flashed a reddish-orange. "I promise you he will pay."

I was sure he would keep that promise if given a chance, but someone had to capture the Horseman first.

Jasper walked through his lava field, unconcerned with the burning liquid oozing from the pits. He reached Wart and paused, pointing to the black leather box in Wart's deathly grasp. "What's this?"

"The first half of my payment. I guess you missed that part when you were watching us fight."

"The brimstone?" He picked up the box and opened it, fingering the piece of the Horseman's mask. "Nicely done. He can't control or call forth anyone from the Underworld without it. Thanks to you, I have time to devise a proper punishment for the would-be usurper. I look forward the second half of your payment." He scooped Wart in his arms and headed back to his obsidian throne.

I exhaled a deep breath. I was bone tired, but rest was not in my near future. I left the lava pits and took a giant step through the veil of the spirit realm and back to where I'd left Gwenn and my ghost-witch family.

A mammoth screech pierced my ears. The Headless Horseman reared back on his steed. Flames shot in every direction as he tossed fireballs at everyone. Livid didn't begin to describe his anger. Where his skull would have been, there were flames that roughly took the shape of a human head. Within that shape, a white fire burned inside his soulless eye sockets. It went from white to orange to red and finally to black as if the fire within had turned to dark ash. But within seconds, the flame ignited again as he sought me out.

A shiver ran along my arms. I stared at him. "You lost, " I said, placing my hands on my hips. Immense satisfaction filled me. I looked down to see my hands glowing. I was beginning to enjoy my witch magic.

He howled in pure rage, tossed a ball of fire at me, and fled when he missed. A trail of flames licked the ground where the horse's hooves hammered into the earth.

I wanted nothing more than to collapse against the nearest tree trunk. Instead, I made my way to the center of the clearing. Agatha and Hulda joined me.

"The pirates have their coins but not a path to follow," I said.

"Then you must give them that path. Alex might be able to come the other way," Hulda said.

The pirates had dropped their weapons the moment the brimstone was taken away. They gathered together and waited for me to help them. The shifters ignored the pirates and began triaging the wounded. Uncle Damon nodded to me and went to help his pack. The ground was littered with injured shifters, both wolves and werecats. Some lay in their naked human form while others remained in their animal shape.

Mutther had not shed his dragon body. He backed away from everyone, putting as much space as possible between him and the rest of us. Gwenn walked to Mutther with confidence in each stride. As soon as she touched him, he calmed down. He curled his tail inward and lay on the ground beside her. His dragon was massive. He dwarfed the younger trees but seemed equal in proportion to the ancient ones that stood guard over the treasure. It was as if he'd been born from the same magic that made up those trees. Undaunted by Mutther's size, Gwenn continued to stroke his leathery skin and spoke in a soothing tone.

"Will he be able to revert to his human self?" I looked at Hulda for an answer.

"These things can be tricky," she said. "I don't believe his family history has to dictate the outcome. Gwenn seems to be a positive influence on his dragon, so there's hope."

I looked at Sebastian, who wandered among the fallen. I turned to Hulda. "Is there anything I can do for the two of you to see each other again?"

Agatha touched Hulda's shoulder. "Let her try, sister. It can't hurt."

Hulda hesitated. "Please, try," she said.

I waved at Sebastian, who was speaking with Uncle Damon. "Can you come here for a minute?"

He left Uncle Damon's side and met me in the center of the clearing.

"That was quite a show you put on with the reenactment," he said. "I think Angie will be most useful to the Council."

"She has many assets and is loyal," I said.

He huffed. "Loyal to you."

"What can I say? I have good friends." I glanced at Gwenn and Mutther then back to him. I exhaled and hoped I was doing the right thing. Even without our link, I sensed his tension. "I'd like you to be part of my inner circle." Once I said it, I was surprised by how much I wanted to include him.

He raised his brows. "You have an inner circle?"

I squared my shoulders. "Yes. Yes, I do." I took hold of Hulda's hand, who took Agatha's, and then I reached for Sebastian's hand. "Are you ready?"

He seemed perplexed but placed his paper-white hand in my glowing one. I closed my eyes and let my feet welcome the magic coming from the earth. I didn't require any chants this time. I knew it would work. I opened my eyes and felt the thrum of magic race through me.

Sebastian gasped. "Dear God! Agatha! Hulda!" He fell to his knees, his shoulders shaking with silent sobs.

Hulda knelt beside him and tried to put her hand on his cheek. When that didn't work, she drenched him in her floral scent. He met her tender gaze.

"I've missed you," he said. "Can you forgive a foolish vampire?"

I pushed my magic outward until it reached Hulda. She snapped her head in my direction and put a hand to her chest, gasping for air. Her physical body took shape.

I continued to push the magic into her. "I don't know how long I can hold it."

Hulda pulled Sebastian to her. They kissed until Agatha interrupted with a cough.

Hulda flushed. "Sorry, sister. I'm a bit overcome at the moment."

"I see that," Agatha said. "I'm happy for you both."

The couple rose, still holding onto each other.

"I apologize for my manners," Sebastian said.

I burst out laughing. "Seriously? Are you going to get all old-fashioned? You're holding the love of your life. Who cares about conventions?"

Agatha smiled. "She's right. Don't let what others think change what you do. Haven't we all learned that the hard way?"

Hulda leaned into Sebastian's side. "There's so much I would redo if I could."

"We all would like a do-over sometimes," I said. "That's

not how life works." A sharp twinge made me wince. I placed a fist against my stomach. The magic was trying to recede. "I can't hold it." Panic filled my voice. "I'm sorry."

Hulda planted a kiss on my cheek. "You've given us a precious gift. It's time you go after your man."

They held on as long as they could, but the magic boomeranged back into me with a staggering jolt. Hulda transitioned into a translucent apparition that hovered a few inches off the ground.

I glanced at Sebastian. "Can you still see her?"

His smiled. "Yes."

I breathed a sigh of relief. "Good."

The pirate ghosts grew unsettled. I couldn't keep them from their rest any longer. I opened my magic and allowed it to envelope me in a brilliant mist. Sebastian stepped back, all the while keeping his gaze locked on Hulda.

"I love you," he said.

"I love you," she replied. "Forever."

"I don't know what I'm doing," I said. "I can open a path for them to follow but can't guarantee the journey."

Agatha drew close to her ex-lover. They spoke in a whisper, but their words of apology and love drifted across the clearing.

I held out the coin he'd given me. "Here. Take it. The Ferryman always gets paid."

"Keep it," he said. "It matters not where I go. I've made my peace with Agatha and that's all that matters."

My body jerked as a new wave of power passed through me. I swear I lit up like a Christmas tree. Everyone stopped to watch. Uncle Damon took a few steps toward me but halted when I held up my hand. I concentrated on harnessing the magic, drawing it into me one strand at a time. I put both my hands together and began spreading them apart to reveal a ball of light that grew in diameter until it was as large as the opening to the Lincoln Tunnel. The pirates lined up and stepped forward into the light. They disappeared in its glow. Only Reggie remained. Agatha's gaze settled on me, and I knew she'd found what she'd been looking for all these years. She took her lover's hand, and they walked into the light together.

Alex did not appear.

I let the magic drop. It formed a narrow path in front of me. I looked over my shoulder at Sebastian and the others who had gathered around me. "I have to find Alex before the sun rises."

Hulda floated to my side. "I'm coming with you."

"I have a feeling if you come, it will be a one-way trip." Fear gripped me at the idea of losing her. "You should stay here."

She glanced at Sebastian. "It's my time."

"I understand." He made a flourish with his hands and took a deep bow. "Until we meet again, my charming lady. My Hulda."

She stepped onto the path next to me. The light began fading as we walked forward. I turned to look behind me and saw darkness. They were gone.

CHAPTER 30
THE SMALL PRINT

"Don't look back." Hulda's voice wavered as she spoke.

"Too late." My attention faltered, but I kept to the illuminated trail that appeared like a blanket of fireflies laid out before us.

Hulda put one translucent hand out in front of her. "You must focus on where we're going."

My heart quickened when the path faded into oblivion. Now I also had my hand outstretched, groping in the darkness for anything familiar and straining my eyes to detect any obstacles. Our progress slowed. We were enclosed in rock. Not a good place to get stuck if our traveler witch powers failed us. We took a step, then another. Orange-red light flickered a short distance away. We turned a corner, and the heat of lava pits smacked us in the face. I groaned. Ahead lay the obsidian throne room.

Hulda stopped short. "You weren't focusing, were you?"

I winced at her scolding tone. "Sorry." I let my hand fall to my side and braced myself for what was coming. How had I messed this up?

"What a pleasant surprise!" Jasper boomed. The demon prince stood framed within the entryway to his inner sanctuary. His bare chest gleamed with the reflection of the lava's glow.

"Yeah. I'm a bit surprised myself." I gave Hulda an apologetic half-smile.

She shook her head and moved to stand behind my left shoulder. I had no idea if Jasper could see her or not. But I didn't have to wait long for an answer.

"It's marvelous that you brought your great-great-grandmother with you." He clasped his hands in front of his chest as if he'd been given an unexpected gift. "I'm thrilled you came, Hulda."

She moved to where he could see her better. "Sadly, I cannot say the same."

Jasper laughed.

I glanced around at all the lava pits spewing fiery liquid into the air. The space reeked of sulfur. I plastered a smile on my face and addressed the demon whose contract with me was still outstanding. "We took the scenic route on our way into town. I see nothing has changed since my last visit, so we'll leave you to clean up your lava field. "

Jasper sobered, and his eyes darkened. "What? Leaving so soon? I wouldn't hear of it. Come. Follow me."

He walked off at a brisk pace, knowing we had no other choice but to comply. Hulda hesitated for a few moments, casting her gaze around the cavernous domain as if searching for traps. After a moment, we entered his throne room to find him lounging on the steps to his dais like a GQ magazine model. We were entertainment for him. A reprieve from his isolation. I backtracked through my thoughts from when we first stepped onto the lighted path and wondered what I had been thinking that we ended up here, instead of in town.

"Your facial muscles give you away, Janda. You've pieced it together, but your poker face is crap. I know what you're thinking, and you're right." Jasper sat up, staring at a spot against the back wall.

I followed the demon prince's gaze and froze. My worst fear had come true. Alex stood against the wall, his coat almost blending into the black rock. He did not look happy. We arrived at the demon's home because Alex was here and not in the Underworld town.

I faced Jasper, who grinned with satisfaction, and I unleashed my anger. "You can't have him!" My lykoi started surfacing, and I'd gladly let it rip the smug grin off Jasper's malevolent face.

Hulda grabbed for me, but her hand slid through my arm as she continued to lose control of her form. But she managed to sting me with an electrifying zap.

I blinked and bit back a curse. Her ghostly slap was enough to save me from a monumental mistake. You didn't fight a demon on his turf. I tamped down my rage.

Jasper strode toward the back of the room. "Alex requested an audience shortly after your last visit, Janda. He came to offer himself as a trade. If he serves me, your contract ends and you are free." He shrugged. "I don't believe he thought you could obtain the Horseman's mask pieces." He pushed his hand into a hollow spot within the stone wall not far from where Alex stood with clenched fists. Jasper withdrew his hand to display a section of the brimstone mask.

Alex's gaze snapped to mine and back to the demon.

Jasper held up the brimstone for Alex to get a good look at it. "Janda fulfilled half of her contract right before you arrived. All she has left is to retrieve the remaining section from wherever she hid it in the Underworld."

I tilted my head a fraction toward Hulda. She understood my discreet gesture and edged closer to Alex. I knew he could see her in the Underworld, and if my hunch was correct, the demon's home was within those boundaries.

Alex's gaze shifted toward Hulda. I sighed with relief. But instead of allowing her to draw nearer, he moved away from her. Hulda stopped her advance. I'd hoped to be able to create a distraction that would allow her to guide him out of the demon's throne room and to the safety of the tunnel. That plan crashed and burned before it could be implemented. I had no option, except to trust that Alex had a plan.

He continued his progression around the side of the room. "You have that wrong. I have complete faith in Janda's abilities. I requested to see you because I'm aware of your loss. I thought to make a deal in that regard."

Jasper's eyes widened. "Pray tell continue. What loss would that be?"

"Your brimstone smith. The lizard man who died. Word has circulated about his demise."

My breath caught at the knowledge Alex revealed. Wart had been the one who forged the mask, not the demon like I'd thought.

"He wasn't just my smith. He was a loyal companion. I foolishly sent him with Janda and now he's gone!"

He glared at me before he threw the brimstone against the wall. It shot back and flew across the cavern floor, stopping just short of where Hulda stood.

The demon prince strode to his throne and sat rigidly upon it, staring down at Alex. "You have nothing to offer me that I can't find elsewhere." His long fingers curved over the arms of the obsidian throne. "Janda, on the other hand, is a traveler who can create portals. She's worth ten of you. So no, I'm not in the mood to negotiate with you."

Alex kept his gaze on the demon prince but managed to reach me. He took my hand in his. My tense muscles relaxed a fraction at his touch. Alex had been right about Jasper wanting me. He had used Alex to manipulate me. If I wasn't careful, I'd become the next demon's assassin. I'd be a pawn to use at his discretion.

I shoved my contempt for Jasper deep inside and focused on getting us all out of this mess. "You misjudge me. I always fulfill my contracts. But you may have missed my fine print."

Jasper leaned forward. "We have a verbal agreement. There's no fine print in a verbal agreement."

"That's where you're wrong. We have a written agreement. You accepted it when you accepted Wart back into your realm." I couldn't help the smirk spreading over my face.

The demon prince rose to tower above us on his dais. "What did you do?" Venom filled his words.

"I took the opportunity to add a written clause. Whoever accepts the brimstone necklace agrees to take it as final payment and forfeits all rights previously agreed upon." I pointed to the necklace I'd placed on Warts neck, which now hung from one arm of the obsidian throne. "It's a little insurance policy I created months ago. I didn't have a purpose for it at the time, but my instinct urged me to take precautionary measures. You can never be too careful in my line of work. I sealed the clause with a drop of my blood. I can assure you it is binding."

Wisps of smoke rose from Jasper's palms. I gripped Alex tighter while a very angry Jasper examined the necklace. I'd written in a tiny scrawl all along the binding that held the brimstone in place.

Jasper closed his hand over the brimstone, snuffing out the smoke. "I'll honor your deal. But don't forget that you have a deadline to meet. If my calculations are correct, you have no more than an hour to fulfill the contract." He waved one hand in dismissal. "Go. All of you. Let us see how good of a bounty hunter you truly are, Janda Gray."

CHAPTER 31

THE FERRYMAN

We didn't wait for Jasper to change his mind. I set a fast pace as I guided Alex through the lava field and into the tunnel. When we were a few hundred feet inside the tunnel's murky depths, I flung my arms around Alex's neck. "I've missed you."

"Likewise, love." His words came out in a ragged breath.

I kissed him, parting my lips to savor the taste of him. I pulled away only because we were running out of time. "We're both getting out of here. Got that?"

He gave a short laugh. "Yes, love. I've got it. We go back to the Underworld town, and from there, I can lead us to where I hid the brimstone. It's in a rocky area near the river."

"Good. Now, if I can take us to the town, we might have a chance." I groaned. The faintest of light outlined a tunnel section that split off in three directions. "I don't know which direction to go."

"Might I suggest not thinking?" Hulda spoke in a barely audible whisper. "And might I suggest we don't dally?

There are things down here that would be all too happy to detain us, even me."

I stared down each path, probing them with my earth magic. I sent tendrils of power into each of them. Two gave off a nasty vibe that confirmed Hulda's suspicions of evil entities. We weren't going down either of those. The third felt cold but not as dangerous as the other two.

"This one."

I counted the seconds in my head as we walked. Time ticked by. Sixty seconds, then another sixty, and another. I second-guessed my choice of tunnels.

Alex grabbed my arm. "There. Up ahead."

"Thank God."

We jogged until we emerged in a wooded section that ran between the town and the river. The trees had no foliage. I wondered if they had ever had any. Vegetation in the Underworld was sparse and dark. The terrain was made up mostly of rocks, some dark, like in the demon's caves.

Hulda headed in the direction of the town. "Before we retrieve the brimstone, I must see Maude."

I stood in front of her so she would stop. "Why go to Maude? We can grab the brimstone and take it to the prince. He has to honor his agreement. Once he has the brimstone, we get to go home."

The edges of Hulda's body grew fuzzy. "Not for me, which is why I must speak with Maude. I don't know how much time I have left."

I couldn't have heard what I thought I heard. I forced myself to ask what I already knew deep down. "Are you crossing over?"

She nodded. "I made my peace with Sebastian. We said our goodbyes. As for you, I'm ever so grateful to have met you." She glanced back at Alex. "But you have someone to watch out for you now. I've taught you what I could, and you still have my journals. Gwenn can help you control your magic."

"Well, well, well. Look what the cat dragged in." The sound of Maude cackling filled the air. She wasn't alone. Reggie walked beside her on the trail. He had substance to his form in the Underworld that he lacked in the living realm.

Alex greeted her with a hug. She smacked his back repeatedly, still laughing.

"Leave me some air to breathe with, Maude." Alex let out a cough and pulled free from her embrace.

"Yeah, sorry. I'm just glad to see you're all still alive." Her gaze shifted toward Hulda. "You being the exception to the alive part."

Hulda bowed her head in greeting. "It's good to see you."

"Likewise." Maude's features turned all business now that the initial greetings were over. "Did I hear right that you wished to speak with me?"

"Yes. I have a business proposition that involves Reggie."

"That so?" Maude put her hands on her substantial waist. "I'm listening."

Hulda addressed Reggie. "Where's Agatha?"

He stared at the ground before meeting Hulda's gaze. "She passed on shortly after we arrived. I cannot move on until I have atoned for my sins."

I pulled his coin from my pocket. "Here. It's yours. You can move on by paying the Ferryman."

He shook his head and pushed my hand away. "No. Keep it. Use it for yourself."

Hulda sighed. "It pleases me to know that my sister has

completed her transition and that you could share a few moments together." She glanced over at Alex and then Maude. "I know Alex has provided a great service to you as an underground ferryman, but his place is with Janda in the living realm. The demon is trying to use Alex as a pawn to control Janda. He must not have a traveler under his control."

Reggie removed his hat and smoothed back his hair. "I understand where this is going, and I agree."

"Excellent!" Maude slapped the side of her thigh. "Hulda, you're a smart woman."

"Thank you. So, it is agreed?"

Maude turned to the pirate. "Are you sure, Reggie? This is a mighty big decision."

Reggie nodded. Maude let out another hearty laugh.

"What's agreed?" I turned toward Hulda. "Is he taking Alex's place?"

"He sure is." Maude reached for Alex's long coat. "Give it over, lad. There's a new ferryman in town."

Alex did as she said and handed her his coat. He met the pirate's gaze.

"Thank you, Reggie. And while I get what Hulda's trying to do, I'm not able to go back with Janda. She can't take people out of the Underworld."

I gasped and whipped around to face Alex. "Maybe I can." I held the coin out to him. "Pay the river, and I can take you back."

"Looks like smart thinking runs in the family." Maude helped Reggie, who was now the new underground ferryman, put on the coat. She faced Alex with a grave expression on her face. "The offering to the river must be done in secret, or the demon prince will find out and call upon his creatures of the dark to come after you."

My skin prickled. "I have to deliver the brimstone before Alex does his offering, or the contract will keep us both here."

Hulda placed her hand on my shoulder, where it wavered in and out of sight. "I'll take the brimstone to the demon. As soon as I do, you can depart. Stay out of any areas where he can see you, or he'll try to stop you."

"I can't let you do that for me. I'm the one who was tasked with bringing him the brimstone. I agreed to the contract." My voice rose as my fear of losing my loved ones hit hard.

"The contract says you are the one to retrieve the brimstone. Get it and give it to me. I'll carry it to him to fulfill the contract. You'll be far enough away to make your escape."

I glanced around at the ragtag group. Each of them nodded their agreement. "How will I know the demon won't keep Hulda? No. I have to be the one to give it to him."

Alex gripped my shoulders, forcing me to look only at him.

"Let Hulda do this. You don't have to do everything on your own. Those days are behind you. Let us share the burden."

I sighed. "But I have to know she's safe." I pulled away from Alex and faced my great-great-grandmother. "I love you. I love what you're trying to do for me. I do. But I don't want to live my life wondering what happened to you."

Hulda's gaze softened. "If I return to show you I'm fine, will that be sufficient?"

I bit my lip. "Yes."

"Then we must hurry." Hulda stared hard at Alex. "Run with the speed of your panther and bring Janda the brimstone."

Alex didn't hesitate. He raced away from the group and bounded into the woods.

Maude leaned against a large boulder. "Now we wait."

I paced along the path for what seemed like hours, even though it had been mere minutes since Alex left.

Maude forced me to stop. "You're driving me crazy, girl."

"Sorry."

An animal as dark as the deepest shadows darted across the path. Maude jumped, startled by the movement.

"Alex!" I ran to the sleek panther standing in front of Maude.

She pressed her hands over her chest. "Lordy, man. You scared me to death."

The panther dropped the brimstone mask piece on the ground. I picked it up and stood in amazement at the man I loved. His panther was as stunning as ever, but in the Underworld, his eyes had a green cast and wisps of green vapor floated around him as he transformed.

"My, aren't you something?" Maude had a mischievous grin on her face. She eyed Alex's naked body.

He smirked. "Thank you." He turned toward the trees. "I'll be right back."

Maude's eyes widened with delight. "Oh. Take your time going."

I couldn't help but laugh. "Maude. Do you have designs on my man?"

"Honey, if I were a few decades younger, I'd make you earn your place with that man." She sighed. "You are one lucky woman."

"Yes, I am."

Alex returned wearing the clothes he'd abandoned in

the woods when he shifted. "Janda has more than earned her place as my mate. I'm lucky she chose me."

"If I don't give the demon prince that brimstone, no one will be lucky." Hulda put out her hand.

I placed the section of the brimstone mask in her palm. "Be careful."

She closed her fingers over the demon's prize and backed away. "I shan't be long." Then she strode off in the direction of the tunnel entrance.

Maude leaned against the boulder once more. "And we wait again."

Alex finished buttoning his shirt. "I passed some unnaturals on the way back. I'm guessing Janda's presence is calling to them. It's not safe to stay here. We better get into position near the river."

"Blast!" Maude shoved off from the boulder. "It looks like our new ferryman's about to learn the ropes."

We picked our way through the woods, avoiding the main pathways and staying hidden as much as possible. Alex halted several times and made us backtrack to throw off anyone or anything that might be following us.

"Never go directly to the underground station." He whispered to Reggie. "Always be mindful of traps." He pointed to a bent branch with a rope barely visible in the scraggly brush. Beneath the rope, buried in a thin layer of dirt, lay a large net. One false step and the trap would be sprung, catching anyone passing over the net.

I held up a hand for silence. We took cover and held our breath to avoid discovery. Hulda came staggering into view. I ran forward and caught her as she faltered. "What happened? Are you hurt? Jasper's dead if he harmed you."

Hulda shook her head. "Don't be silly. What can he do

to the likes of me? No. I'm holding off the passing. I had to see you, but staying here is growing harder."

We gathered around to hear what happened with the demon.

"The contract is fulfilled, but don't think he won't try to keep you here. He will come for Janda as soon as he proves to his father that he has the brimstone mask pieces." Hulda's form flickered. "He's sent out an order to all the unnaturals. There's a bounty on Alex and Janda's heads. Stay away from the river for now. Don't go into town, either."

"But he said we could go free." The heat of anger flared within me.

Maude hissed under her breath. "That's the problem with a contract made with a demon. He freed you from your obligation. You're free to leave, but only if you can."

Alex slammed a fist into a nearby tree. "I shouldn't have let you bargain for me."

Hulda's form wavered uncontrollably. "Janda is your mate, Alex." Her voice faltered. "Protect her."

He straightened his stance. "I promise."

"We protect each other. That's what mates do." I gripped Hulda's hand as best as I could, considering her body had taken the consistency of putty. "That's what families do."

She smiled and brushed the white strands of hair from my face. "Goodbye, my granddaughter. I love you."

I sensed the portal open and knew my skin glowed in response. I was the key to the portal. I summoned the gateway and brought Hulda into its light. She hugged me, and then I let her go. She became one with the light and disappeared from view.

CHAPTER 32

THE RIVER

Maude gaped in awe. "That's the most beautiful thing I've ever seen."

The glow of my skin dimmed. "Unfortunately, I'm a beacon in a dark realm. It's not safe to be near me."

"Janda's right. Take Reggie and head to the safety of your tavern. I know of a place where Janda and I can hole up until we can get to the underground launch site." He hugged Maude and nodded to Reggie. "Go. We'll be fine."

She hugged him back. "Safe journey."

As soon as they were out of sight, I faced Alex. "You know we may never make it out of here, right?"

He gazed into my eyes and ran his finger along my cheek, sending shivers over my skin while simultaneously causing a wave of heat to stir in my nether region.

Alex grinned, knowing the effect he'd created. "After everything we've been through, you still doubt yourself. You're a traveler. You can leave right now and should. I'm the one holding you back."

"We stick together, so take me to this safe spot." I kissed him but pulled back when he attempted to deepen the kiss.

"You're so stubborn." He took my hand in his. "Follow me, then."

We went deeper into the woods, winding our way past blackened trees that at some point had been caught up in a forest fire. We climbed over a group of soot-covered boulders scarred with deep slashes. "A war?" I whispered.

He placed a finger over his lips and nodded. If this was his idea of somewhere safe, then he had to have lost his mind after spending the last year in the Underworld. Death blanketed this area. I could only imagine the kind of wars that took place in the Underworld.

Alex dipped low between two boulders so big Miss Kitty would have been lost between them. What I wouldn't give for my Harley right about now. I'd ride right out of this forsaken land. Alex's hand popped into view. He motioned for me to follow. I stayed low and practically rolled over the rock formation. The trouble was that I didn't stop on the other side. I dropped into a deep crevice. The landing was going to suck. I drew in a breath and prepared for the impact. Alex caught me, and we tumbled onto the earthen floor in a tangle of limbs.

I rubbed my elbow where the zing of pain shot up my arm. "Damn. A little warning would have been nice. Are you okay?"

He lay on his back, staring up at the opening above. "I'll survive. But you're a lykoi. Aren't you supposed to land on your feet?"

I shrugged. "I'm half wolf, too. Maybe that cancels out the whole landing-on-my-feet thing." I sat up and brushed the dirt off my shirt. One sleeve had torn during the fall. I'd be running out of clothes at this rate. At least it was my own shirt this time. I was grateful Gwenn had had the fore-thought to grab a change of clothes for me. My eyes adjusted to the low lighting. "Wow. What is this place?"

Alex stood, wiped dirt from his face, and climbed a metal ladder bolted to the rock wall. "It's my safe house." He reached the top rung and slid a panel over the opening. "This should keep us hidden for a while." He backed down the ladder and hopped off the bottom rung. He pulled a lantern from a hook and lit it. He handed it to me while he lit a second one. "What do you think?"

I slowly turned in a circle, holding the lamp in front of me. The space was slightly larger than my room at Sebastian's. One corner held a thick mattress topped with a couple of patchwork quilts. Next to it was a small night-stand. The opposite side of the room had a bookshelf that contained a smattering of books. Just off the center of the room was a small wooden table and two chairs. I tilted my head, listening for the source of trickling water, and found it in the farthest corner of the room. A washstand stood next to a tiny waterfall flowing from a gap at the top of the ceiling. Water gathered in a pool at the base of the little falls. I sank my hand into its depths. Cool water slid through my fingers.

"You did all this?"

"I design safe houses, remember? Gathering items was tricky, but I managed."

"Wart said you were covering your tracks. Nicely done, Mr. Holden." I dipped my finger back into the water and traced a wet line down the hollow of his neck and over his right pec. I unbuttoned his shirt and continued tracing. His shiver pleased me. "How long do we stay here?"

"Do you have something in mind?" His mouth twisted into a sly grin.

I laughed. "Don't I always?"

He held my hand against his chest. "I love you."

"And I love you. My life has been empty without you. I've loved you across the realms of the living and the dead, and I refuse to lose you again."

Alex picked me up and carried me to his bed. He pulled at my shirt buttons until they popped, and the fabric fell away from my body. He tore at the edges of my pants until they met the same fate as my shirt. He removed his shirt and tossed it aside. I reached up and helped him with his pants. He slipped out of them and joined me on the bed. I was slick with heat and longing. We both wanted to take our time and savor every touch.

I tried to be patient, but the moment his mouth covered my nipple and he began planting kiss after kiss across my body, I caved. We were not going to go slow. I arched into him, and in a single turn of my body, I lay on top of him. I slid onto his hardness and sank into oblivion.

Our lovemaking intensified into quick, deep thrusts that had us both gasping. Our tongues explored one another, eliciting moans of ecstasy. He flipped me over, reversing our positions, and entered me with the desire of a panther seeking a union with his chosen mate. It was a claiming on both our parts. He took me to the very edge and paused, gazing down at me.

"I want you now and always. I want you as my lover, my mate, my wife. Tell me you feel the same."

I had no words to describe all that he meant to me. My body burned with the need for him. I ached to be his in every way. To be his mate and his wife. I never thought about children until now, but I longed to be the mother of his children and create a family with him. But those words would be spoken later because I could hardly talk for how much I wanted him.

I gasped two breathless words and hoped it would suffice. "I do."

We rode the climax together in a way that meant much more than it had ever done before. We laid in each other's arms, and I drifted off to sleep.

"Janda, love. It's time to go."

I opened my eyes and struggled to get my brain firing. "Go?"

He laughed. "We're in the Underworld. We're trying to escape. We have unnaturals hunting us. There's an obsessive demon prince who wants to control you. Anything ring a bell?"

I groaned. "Yes. Dammit." I crawled out of bed and held up the useless shirt I'd arrived in. "Umm. We have a more pressing problem. I have nothing to wear."

"Right." He rummaged around a box and produced a shirt. It was a green and brown plaid flannel. "Since this is mine and what's mine is yours, here you go."

I caught the shirt he tossed to me and put it on. "This wouldn't happen to come with a pair of leggings?"

He raised one brow. "Do I look like a leggings kind of guy?"

I grinned. "I bet you'd rock in leggings. Robin Hood would have nothing on you."

"Keep dreaming, Maid Marian." He dug around the box and pulled out a pair of pajama bottoms. "Sorry. There's nothing here that will fit you. These will have to do."

I put them on and secured them with the drawstring. "I look like I'm wearing a potato sack." I tried rolling them up, but there was too much fabric.

Alex brought over a knife and knelt in front of me. He cut the extra fabric until it was above my knees.

"That should do it." He stood back to observe his handiwork.

I looked down at the former pajama bottoms that hung loosely around my thighs. "Boxer shorts. How delightful?"

He shrugged. "It's that or nothing. Take your pick."

"Desperate times, I suppose. Fine. I'll take it." I headed for the ladder. "But when we get home, I'm going shopping."

He chuckled. "While I would love the view of your rear climbing the ladder, we aren't going that way."

I had one foot on the bottom rung and looked back at him over my shoulder. "How else are we getting out of this love nest?"

"It's been a wonderful love nest, to be sure. While I'll never forget it, I'd rather have you in a plush bed with a window to gaze out upon the stars as we lay there exhausted with pleasure."

I left the ladder and sauntered to him as sexily as my plaid shirt and boxers would allow. I stood on my tiptoes and kissed him. "That sounds wonderful."

"If we keep doing this, we won't get out of here." He kissed the top of my forehead. "We're using the back door."

"Oh." I glanced around the room. "I don't see a door."

"Safe room designer here. You're not supposed to see a door."

He crossed the room to where the water fell in rivulets down the wall. He stuck both hands behind the waterfall and pushed. A door, camouflaged as rock, opened inward.

"Very cool." I followed him inside.

We stood in a narrow tunnel. Natural light filtered down in tiny rays from strategically placed rocks above us.

"You did that?"

"Nature did most of it. I helped it along." He kept his voice low. "This will take us close to the river where the underground launch point is located. We go quietly from here on out. Once we're there, I'll bring out the boat that can take us across the river. After that, it's up to you."

"We just have to avoid Jasper's army of unnaturals and any other spooky things that go bump in the night." I tensed thinking about it.

"That's why we're going in daylight. They prefer the dark." He led the way down the tunnel.

I caught the part about unnaturals *preferring* darkness, which meant they would hunt during the day if forced into it. Jasper would command them to track us night and day. The smell of burnt wood drifted down from above. We were passing through the forest fire area.

I was still thinking about Jasper and his army when Alex stopped at a small tunnel leading upward. We climbed the underground hill and emerged next to some heavy brush. The sound of water rushing by meant we were close to the river. He motioned for me to stay. It took all my willpower to keep from following him, but this was what he'd done as the underground ferryman, so I waited.

Alex returned and led me over to a small boat. "This is where it can get tricky. The river has a mind of its own. Sometimes it lets me glide smoothly over it. Other times, it tries to capsize me."

I got in the boat. Alex pushed us from shore and hopped in. He grabbed the oars and began paddling. We'd made it a few feet from the shoreline when an unnatural spotted us. He called to the others. They rushed to the water's edge. A few waded in. One lunged for the boat and grabbed the back of it. We rocked from side to side. Alex beat the unnatural's fingers with the oar. It let go and slipped under the surface. The river swallowed the unnatural. Waves churned, hitting the side of the boat and splashing over the edge.

"You best hold on. The river is not happy." Alex rowed, but the waves kept pushing us back toward land.

"Did you think you could escape by crossing the river?" Jasper stood on the shoreline. "You'll drown. Come back."

"No thanks. I'll take my chances on the water." I glanced at Alex. Sweat beaded on his forehead with the effort to keep us from drifting back toward the demon prince.

Jasper sent unnaturals into the water. They either sank beneath the surface or were tossed onto the muddy embankment.

He bellowed in frustration. "I'm free to roam my lands. For that, I'm grateful. I always stick to my bargain, Janda. Hear me out."

"Really? You could have fooled me. How is this letting us go?" I shouted over the sound of the raging water. "I fulfilled my end, but you haven't."

"I did let Alex go. You're both free. I never said I wouldn't try to convince you to stay with me. Alex can go. It's you I want by my side."

"That's not happening." Alex growled as he fought the waves.

Panic filled my chest when Alex lost one of the oars. He used the remaining one, switching from one side of the boat to the other.

I looked back at the demon prince, who stood grinning with his hands on his hips.

"No thanks. I have other plans."

Then I remembered the coin the pirate had given me. I'd

put it in the new shirt pocket when we left Alex's safe house. I withdrew it and held it out. We were past secrecy in our endeavor to escape. Jasper had already sent his minions after us. It didn't matter now if he saw me making an offering to the river.

Smoke billowed from Jasper's hands as he looked on.

I refused to be distracted. "River. Take my offering. Grant us safe passage."

I threw the coin into the air. It turned over several times before plunging into the water. The waves slapped the side of the boat with renewed force. We rocked violently back and forth.

Then half the river grew calm. The half closest to Jasper raged. A current lifted us and thrust us forward. We glided as if on glass, stopping on the river's muddy shore.

Alex jumped out and helped me from the boat.

I knelt at the river's edge. "Thank you." I placed my hand into the water in greeting and felt it return the gesture.

Jasper picked up one of the unnaturals and threw it into the river.

Alex sat on the ground to rest. "He can't cross. The river is the boundary to his domain. We're no longer in the demon's lands."

I glanced at Alex. I had nothing left to offer the river so it would let me take Alex from the Underworld. We'd been lucky to get away from Jasper. I paced up and down the riverbank, trying to find a solution. Jasper walked the shoreline on the opposite side of the river, unable to follow us. I stopped wearing a path in the mud and looked at the man I loved more than my own life.

Alex glanced up. "It's okay. I'm safe here. You can visit me. I'll make a new love nest."

Tears ran down my cheeks. I didn't cry, but I was gushing with tears now. I stood with my bare feet in a pool of river water.

I glanced at my disheveled reflection, then crouched down. "I have nothing left to offer you. But I thank you for what you've done to bring us this far."

I sniffled while more tears gathered in my eyes and etched a path down the tip of my nose to fall into the river. I didn't expect to see my tears floating on the surface, but they did. They swirled in a tiny whirlpool and vanished. Without realizing it, I'd made an offering to the river, and the river accepted it.

Alex came to me and held me in his arms.

"Please don't cry. I'll be fine. Truly."

I stifled another sob and gazed into my mate's eyes. Determination rose up within me. I called forth the magic of my ancestors. When my skin glowed, Alex gasped. The portal opened, and we stepped through, leaving the demon prince fuming on the other shore.

CHAPTER 33

HOME

"Holy crap! It's snowing." I held out my hand. Snowflakes fell around us, glistening in the moonlight. I shivered. "How is this possible? It wasn't snowing when I left."

Alex brushed snow from his hair. "You aren't dressed for the weather, and since that appears to be the prison, we're too far from my house for you to get to it without freezing." He took off his clothes. "I'm shifting. I suggest you do the same."

We ditched our clothes and let our animal side enjoy the winter weather. We ran for miles. The freezing air nipped at me. Though I didn't have the thick fur of Alex's panther, my lykoi still rejoiced in the romp through the snow. We raced into Sleepy Hollow, sticking to the alley-ways as much as possible. My lykoi could blend in but not Alex's panther.

The roads were clear but slushy. We passed the bagel shop, and the aroma of George's bagels made my stomach rumble. The town light posts were adorned with winter decorations. The Halloween ones were gone.

Alex's panther set a fast pace. My lykoi matched it with ease. I nudged him in the direction of Mutther's new bar then took the lead. I approached from the rear of the building, skirting the tree line and heading to the alley dumpster. I shifted back to my human form and waited for Alex to do the same.

"Won't this be a little awkward showing up at Mutther's doorstep naked? We should have gone to my place first." Alex sifted through the dumpster for anything to use for clothing. He pulled out a black trash bag and wrapped it around his waist. He grabbed another one and held it out.

"Nope. Been there, done that. Not doing it again."

I opened the back door to Mutther's bar and walked in like I did this every day. It was a shifter bar, for crying out loud. We'd seen each other's naked asses more times than I could count. I made it halfway down the back hall when Gwenn squealed.

"It's Janda!" She ran down the hall with her hands waving in the air and pulled me to her. "I can't believe this!"

"I can't either. I also can't breathe." I pried her off me. "You wouldn't have a spare outfit lying around? My girls are getting cold." I pointed to my bare breasts.

"Here. Take this." She took off a long, fluffy sweater.

I put it on and sighed at the warmth. "Thanks."

I scanned the bar for Mutther but didn't see him. My heart sank. He'd been in dragon form when I'd last seen him. Now that Alex was here, he could release Mutther from his vow. I was afraid we were too late.

Nick got up from his usual spot at the bar. "Damn. It's good to see you." He pulled me into a bone-crushing hug.

"Maybe now Sebastian will get over his dark mood. He's been impossible ever since you left."

Alex came up from behind me, tucking in the ends of his trash bag. All the shifters in the bar cheered and whooped like their favorite team had won the Super Bowl. Alex received their slaps on the back with grace and returned their greetings. The bar was pure chaos. Some of the shifters pulled out their phones to take pictures of Alex. I grinned. Served him right for wearing a trash bag. All he had to do was go naked, and they'd think nothing of it. Social media would be buzzing.

Gwenn wiped tears from her eyes. "We were so worried when you didn't come back."

"But I am back," I said. "What's the big deal?"

Gwenn frowned. "You were gone for over two months."

Alex heard and came over. "What month is it?"

"It's January. Janda left on Halloween."

I put my hand on the wall to steady myself. "How did I lose time?"

She shrugged. "There are stories of those who cross the veil and return in a different time. It's like going into the land of fairies. They try to detain you, and you lose time."

Alex pulled me to him. "But you got us out. That's what matters."

I nodded. "Yeah. It's good to be home." I glanced around the corner to see if Mutther was in the kitchen. I didn't get why he hadn't appeared when everyone was shouting. "Where's Mutther? Is he okay?"

"I'm fine." Mutther's deep voice echoed down the stairs from his apartment.

He got to the bottom step, when Hudson trotted ahead of him into the hallway.

For the second time, tears pooled in my eyes. "I thought I'd lost you." I reached him and buried my face in his chest.

He wrapped his arms around me. I hugged him tighter.

"You can't get rid of me that easily," he said. "I was the one worried that I'd lost you. I failed to protect you."

I pulled back to stare up at him. "You risked staying in dragon form when you saved me from the Headless Horseman. I couldn't have asked for a better protector."

Alex extended his hand toward Mutther. "Thanks for upholding your promise. She's a tough one to keep from harm's way. I'm back and release you from your vow, my friend. I'll never be able to repay you."

Mutther shook Alex's hand. "It's my duty as a Pendragon and my honor as your friend."

Nick coughed. "That's all well and good. I hope you're both done with the mushy stuff. How about you wrangle up some clothes for Alex and some grub for the rest of us?"

"I have some clothes here." Gwenn had slipped up to the apartment and returned with clothes for Alex. She handed him one of Mutther's flannel shirts and a pair of jeans.

"Thank you." He took the items and turned to leave, but halted when the front door burst open, and Sebastian strode across the room.

"Don't ever do that to me again! Do you hear me, Janda Gray? I got a call a moment ago that you finally showed up. I sent messages to Damon and Silas before I left. The two of you will get an earful from them shortly." He glared at Alex but softened his tone in an instant. He grabbed him into a hug. "It's good to have you back."

"What? You're not glad to have *me* back?" I stood with my arms across my chest.

Sebastian released Alex, who grinned at me and headed to the bathroom to cleanup.

"That goes without saying." Sebastian took a step closer and stopped in his tracks. His eyes widened.

"Why are you looking at me like that?"

He composed himself and proceeded to give me a gentle hug. His hand grazed my cheek.

"You're the great-great-granddaughter of my true love. I will always want you in my life. Hulda would be so happy to know that you're pregnant."

I froze.

Everyone in the bar stopped what they'd been doing. The bathroom door banged against the wall. A half-dressed Alex stared at Sebastian. "She's pregnant?"

Gwenn squealed for the third time that night. "This is so exciting!"

Alex walked slowly toward me, stopping in front of me and bending on one knee. He met my stunned gaze.

"Janda, love. We pledged ourselves to one another at the safe house. And while I don't pretend to understand how time here passed differently than time there, I know that I love you. Will you marry me tonight?"

His words registered somewhere in my brain. I gazed into his eyes and found everything I'd ever wanted. "Yes."

Gwenn swept me off to Mutther's apartment to find something more suitable for me to wear.

"Your clothes are in Mutther's closet?" I stared at her as she searched through her wardrobe.

She blushed. "It's a new thing. We're happy. Hudson approves. So, how could I say no?"

"You're good for him," I said. "You tamed his dragon."

"I wouldn't go so far as to say it's tamed." Her blush deepened.

There was a knock at the door. I opened it to find Sebastian holding a large box.

He entered and shut the door behind him. "A long time ago, I purchased this dress for Hulda. She never had the chance to wear it. I'd like you to have it."

I lifted the lid on the box to see a beautiful wedding dress inside. "I'd be happy to wear it." I kissed Sebastian's cheek. "I know it's traditional for the bride to be given away by her father, but my father's dead. I have Uncle Damon, and I have you. I'd love it if both of you would do me the favor of taking that role."

"It would be my pleasure. I'll let Damon know." He kissed the top of my head and opened the door.

I stopped him before he could leave. "Did you just mark me again?"

He smiled and left the apartment. The dead man walking could be heard laughing all the way down the steps.

"I can't believe he did that."

Gwenn laughed. "I can."

I huffed but took Hulda's dress from the box. It was a simple Victorian-era bridal gown in pale ivory, with fine lace on the bodice and pearl buttons on the long sleeves. It was the most elegant thing I'd ever seen.

Gwenn helped me into the dress that my great-great-grandmother should have worn. She grabbed her phone to take a few pictures. "Hulda would have been so happy to see you on your wedding day."

"I wish she could have been here." I smoothed the fabric around my waist. "Do I look pregnant?"

Gwenn smiled. "You look radiant. And you'll have to get used to how the guys will behave around you. Sebastian's mark is only the beginning. Your uncle, Silas, Nick,

Mutther, and not to mention Alex, will be protective of you."

"That's what I get for falling in love with my bounty hunter target."

Hudson pattered into the room and rubbed against me. I bent to pet him and found a ribbon tied around his neck. Attached to the ribbon was a wedding band.

"Oh, how cute!" Gwenn scratched Hudson behind his ear. "He's the ring bearer."

"Alex. How did he even have time to get a ring? That man's going to spoil me." I grinned. "Part of me just might let him."

Gwenn and I both laughed. She helped me down the steps, where Uncle Damon and Sebastian waited. Together, they walked me down the makeshift aisle in the center of the bar to Alex, who teared up at our approach. He'd changed into a flattering black tuxedo. He was stunning.

The room was filled with shifters who came to share in the event. Mutther performed the ceremony. It was short but lovely. The party afterward was long—just the way shifter weddings should be. Alex and I slipped away to a car he had waiting for us. We drove out of town and away from the direction of Alex's house.

"Where're we going?"

"You'll see. It's something I started working on before we got caught in the bar explosion and I landed in the Underworld."

We turned onto a private road and drove for half a mile before he pulled up to a log home in the center of a clearing. It was my dream home. I gathered up the folds of my gown and stepped out onto the gravel driveway. The path leading to the house had been cleared of snow. A plume of smoke rose from the chimney to welcome us.

Alex swept me into his arms and carried me inside. He didn't put me down until we reached the master bedroom. He was more careful with Hulda's gown than he'd been with the clothes I'd been wearing when he took me to his bed in the safe house. We made love more slowly this time. Afterward, I curled into the crook of his arm. He pressed a button on a remote, and the shade covering the skylight above our bed retracted.

I gazed up at the stars. "It's amazing. All of it." My skin glowed with my witch magic while my lykoi thrummed with contentment.

He pulled me closer and placed his hand over my belly. "You're what's amazing. You're my shining star, and I love you."

Alex fell asleep, snoring and purring in turns—the man and the panther content in our new home. I slipped out of bed, pulled a throw blanket around me, and stepped out onto the porch to enjoy the beauty of my surroundings. I glanced at the starry sky, thinking of my ghost-witch family and all that they had taught me about embracing who I was meant to be.

As I stared at one particularly bright star, the baby fluttered in my womb. The reality of becoming a mother hit me. I placed my hands over my belly and became fiercely protective of a child who wasn't even born yet.

I understood why Sebastian had marked me and why Mutther had risked shifting into his dragon to stand between the Horseman and me. The wolves, the werecats, the witches, and the humans, like Angie, all worked together for a single purpose. My skin glowed more brightly than it had ever done before. I shaped that magic into a shield around my baby.

I was no longer a solo bounty hunter. I was a member of

a community. I had a family, both biological and found. I had learned firsthand about evil in the world but had also discovered there were those who would stand together to protect the innocent.

And I would be at the forefront of the defenders as a Sleepy Hollow Hunter.

READ on with Alex (Sleepy Hollow Hunter Book Four) and discover Sleepy Hollow through the eyes of Alex.

https://books2read.com/Alex-SleepyHollowHunter

Author Notes About the Book

Pirate Lover's Curse took several years to complete. For research, I made multiple visits to Sleepy Hollow and spent countless hours in the Old Dutch Cemetery. I went deep into the heart of the Old Croton Aqueduct system and walked the trails in and around the town. The Old Croton Aqueduct was constructed between 1837 and 1842. Parts of it are above ground and parts underground. It was created to supply New York City with clean water.

While the aqueduct wasn't there during the Revolutionary War, pirates did frequent the waters off Long Island and up the Hudson River.

I took copious notes and an abundance of pictures. If you're ever in the area of Sleepy Hollow, I encourage you to do the lantern tours at the cemetery. You won't be disappointed!

Brimstone—book two in the series—had to be cut short when several family members passed away unexpectedly. It was never my intention for the story to end in such a manner. I did what I could to bring closure to the book and to my losses.

Pirate Lover's Curse picks up where Brimstone left off. It introduces a few new characters and sets the stage for a spin-off with Gwenn and her sleuth cat named Hudson. Keep an eye out for their adventures.

As with many of us who experience loss, I found it hard to return to my normal life. I wrote shorter works that were part of numerous anthologies. I didn't give up on the Sleepy Hollow Hunter stories, though.

Then Covid hit. Enough said. We all have our personal accounts of that difficult time. Instead of writing, I ended up sitting each day with my grandson to muddle our way through virtual school. It's not fun keeping a child with sensory issues focused on a screen all day.

Eventually, I made it back to my series. Pirate Lover's Curse is filled with historical facts that were meshed with the images in my imagination. I hope you enjoy the characters in the story as much as I do.

Happy Reading!

ALSO BY SHERI QUEEN

Discover the next book in the Sleepy Hollow Hunter series and other stories by Sheri Queen. Please note, the heat level rises as the Sleepy Hollow Hunter series continues and the characters commit to deeper relationships.

SLEEPY HOLLOW HUNTER SERIES:

Bounty Huntress (Sleepy Hollow Hunter Book One)

Brimstone (Sleepy Hollow Hunter Book Two)

Alex (Sleepy Hollow Hunter Book Four)

THE NIGHT ACADEMY SERIES:

Wolf's Bane (The Night Academy 1)

https://books2read.com/sheriqueen

If you enjoyed this book and want to know about exclusive deals, upcoming reveals, and extra content, join the Sheri Queen community newsletter.

https://sheriqueen.com/pages/subscribe

You'll automatically receive stories when you join!

About the Author

Sheri Queen writes immersive stories of adventure and romance.

Her contemporary fantasy and paranormal women's fiction stories feature snarky bad-ass women, strong female friendships, found family, and sexy romance.

Sheri received her MFA in Writing Popular Fiction from Seton Hill University. She grew up in the Hudson Valley region of New York—an area she loves to depict as a backdrop for her stories—and enjoys traveling to new places where she is constantly discovering inspirations for her writing. She especially loves visiting old graveyards.

https://sheriqueen.com/

facebook.com/sheriqueenauthor

instagram.com/authorsheriqueen

tiktok.com/@sheriqueenauthor

www.ingramcontent.com/pod-product-compliance
Lightning Source LLC
Chambersburg PA
CBHW061019120726
47910CB00006B/2010